TO KINGDOM COME

TO KINGDOM COME

AN ART HISTORY MYSTERY

CLAUDIA RIESS

LEVEL
BEST BOOKS

First published by Level Best Books 2022

Copyright © 2022 by Claudia Riess

This novel is entirely a work of fiction. The names, characters and incidents portrayed in it are the work of the author's imagination. Any resemblance to actual persons, living or dead, events or localities is entirely coincidental.

Claudia Riess asserts the moral right to be identified as the author of this work.

First edition

ISBN: 978-1-68512-110-5

Cover art by Level Best Designs

This book was professionally typeset on Reedsy.
Find out more at reedsy.com

Praise for the Art History Mystery Series

"My favorite sleuthing couple...combines art, travel, mystery and romance in one thriller."—Jean Thrasher

"Riess has a knack of staging her scenes in such perfect tempo that you just don't want to put the book down to see what lies ahead."—T.J. Clemente (Hamptons.com The Bookshelf)

"Feeling I've made a new friend is a testament to the skill of an author... Riess has bestowed upon my imagination a cadre of new friends and I am delighted to make their acquaintance."—Mo (Amazon)

"...as full of fun as it is of intrigue. Fascinating imagery propels the duo's quest for justice in a world where justice can never be taken for granted."—Joan C. Hand (*East of July*)

"The story is fast paced.The action is nonstop.   HGHLY RECOM-MENDED!"—Jim Harris (Pacific NW Writers Association)

"...really made me reflect on life. I cared about the characters in a way that I have not in a really long time."—Maryann Pereira

Prologue

Kingdom of Benin

West Africa

February 21, 1897

The ashes had settled on the ruins, and the bodies removed, for the most part, by those indigenous people whose lives had been spared for that very purpose. It sickened Andrew Barrett to have been a witness to the operation and to have said nothing, never mind to accuse, but to *question*. It would not have diminished the vigor of the onslaught, but it would have formally registered his objection, both to himself and to that ever-elusive—his devout mother preferred *inscrutable*—God.

Gratefully, as a medic in the Royal Army Medical Service, he was not required to fire his rifle. In fact, the rules forbade it unless he considered himself to be under direct attack. And on this occasion, the opposition had been taken by surprise—would he ever forget the woman kneeling by the river?—so that at no time during the preemptive scourge did he feel the need to raise his Lee Metford bolt-action rifle and take aim.

The villages and towns nestled in the jungle en route to the Oba's—King's— compound had been eliminated by rockets launched from tubes; their inhabitants, the Oba's subjects, by rifle-fire and Maxim machine guns. The Oba, along with two of his wives, had managed to escape the walled-in city before the Niger Coast Protectorate and Admiralty forces had gained entrance, and that appeared only to have energized the avenging spirit.

In short order, palaces, homes, temples, courthouses, mausoleums were reduced to burned-out hollow remains.

Andrew walked aimlessly through the debris, his medical bag knocking against his hip, mocking his silence. Surely, a retaliatory strike had been in order, he argued, devil's advocate to his nagging conscience. Earlier in the year, hadn't seven of the nine visiting British diplomats, along with their carriers, been killed by inhabitants of Benin when they'd come to discuss matters of trade with the Oba? Perhaps the British officials should not have entered the royal compound after having been warned that they would be disturbing its resident ancestors on a holy day, but had that oversight warranted their murder? Certainly not!

His conscience would not be stilled. The assault was fresh in his memory, and he could justify neither its magnitude nor its fervor. As a medic, he had been required to serve six years in India. For his entire term he had been stationed in a Bombay hospital, doted on by the nurses for his burdensome good looks. Caring for the injured and sick had been strenuous and demanding, but it had not prepared him for the wanton devaluing of life.

As he was passing the shell of a building, he paused, caught by the ragged remains of its red clay walls brazenly glistening in the sun—as a last hurrah, he thought. He was thrown back in time, reminded of his painstakingly molded sandcastle, destroyed by the indifferent sea.

He was drawn to the space as if it were his sandcastle's courtyard. As if time could be reversed, innocence recovered. Suddenly weary, he looked for a place to sit. Judging from the variety of sharp-edged tools scattered about the upturned and broken table and chairs, this had been an artisan's workshop—yes, a carver's, for there, in the shaded corner, lay an ash-laden ivory tusk, miraculously intact. Surprising that his comrades had missed it in their hunt for marketable objects.

Another survivor of the attack, a wooden stool, stood tilted against what was left of the wall opposite. He righted it and, with a heavy sigh that sounded to him remarkably like his grandfather's, lowered his tall frame onto it, allowing the strap of his medical bag to slip from his shoulder, the bag to drop to the irregularly cracked clay floor. It was untrue, but he felt as if he had not slept in a fortnight. He closed his eyes, if just for a moment, to give in to the fancy.

Feeling himself slipping away, he snapped open his eyes, straightened his spine. As he did so, a shaft of sunlight struck the area near the center of the floor where a crack in the clay had been split as if from a surgeon's incision. He felt compelled to take a closer look.

On his hands and knees, he peered into the fissure. He glimpsed—or thought he glimpsed—some matter that was neither fragmented clay nor earth resting perhaps two feet beneath the surface. He fetched the small torch from his medical bag and aimed its ray into the crevice, intensifying the light provided by the sun. Yes, there was definitely some foreign object embedded in the earth. He gripped the clay ledge and pulled up. A segment of flooring came away easily, breaking off at another, less gaping, crack in its surface. He lay the slab aside and with his pith helmet, proceeded to scoop out the dark earth he'd exposed. He noticed it had become densely packed over time, and he wished he knew how to estimate for just how *long* a time.

As he grew closer to his goal, he switched tools from helmet to bare hands to avoid causing damage to his find. When at last it lay bare, the last clump of dirt gently brushed from its surface, Andrew gazed at it in awe, as much for the means of its discovery as for the discovery itself.

Who had buried this treasure in the earth—and why? His amazement grew as he was lifting it from its grave, only to discover that another of its kind had been resting directly beneath it, cushioned by a layer of earth disturbed by his excavation.

Andrew knew, as if the decision were telegraphed, that these objects must be kept in his safekeeping. He was aware that many of the artifacts confiscated on these grounds were to cover the cost of the British attack—"punitive expedition," as it had been christened. He also knew that a great many more works—altarpieces, carved tusks, sculpted reliefs less unusual than the two that lay before him—had been seized by military personnel and stuffed into their laundry and duffle bags, eventually to be lugged by their carriers back to the ships that would return them, along with their ill-gotten gains, to the shores of England.

He was grateful no one was milling about to see what he was up to. His cohorts were presently gathered under the pitched tent serving as mess hall, downing their noontime field rations of tinned mutton and soup. The next meal would not be doled out until the following morning, and although he'd known he would be starving by then, he hadn't the stomach to eat. Perhaps fasting was his method of protest—or atonement for *not* protesting.

He estimated the objects weighed about thirty pounds each. A load to haul the twenty miles to the vessel that would bear him home, but if he shared the task with one of the carriers, it could be done.

Leaving his find unattended, he went to fetch his laundry bag from the tent where the men bunked down and kept their gear. Though not given to mystical musings, he had an uncanny feeling the fates would see to it that the site would remain undisturbed.

Chapter One

Manhattan

Present Day

S aturday, mid-May, and summer was reminding the city of what was to come in case it had forgotten. Erika Shawn-Wheatley picked up speed on her final spurt as she headed toward the Central Park exit closest to home. How free she felt on her morning runs—today, in shorts and tank top, limbs glistening with sweat. Flying it felt like, the exaltation enhanced by the prospect of landing.

Jogging in place at the corner of 78th Street and Madison Avenue, she was already anticipating her homecoming, the seven-digit code on the door panel bobbing in her head in sync with the nursery rhyme, *hickory-dickory-dock*—her toddler's favorite, made him laugh every time, who knew why. The light changed and she trotted across the street, pulled up to the wrought iron gate, swung it open and kicked it shut in one deft movement, and strode up to the massive oak door.

She punched in the passcode and entered the lobby of the three-story home she had on first sight mistaken for a multi-family residence. The larger-than-life Botero statue standing between the elevator and the couch no longer cowed her, but the nude's plump grandeur remained a symbol of her acquired privilege along with its residual guilt.

Erika looked up and saw Grace Jones, the Wheatleys' ancient but spry housekeeper, standing on the first-floor landing. It was Kate Mendelsohn's day off and Grace was filling in for the twenty-five-year-old blond bombshell of a nanny while she was off somewhere with her boyfriend preparing for her Final Dissertation for her online Master's degree program in math. It was hardly necessary for Grace to sub for Kate, but she adored Lucas as much as she'd adored Harrison when he was Lucas's age, so who could object? Besides, the more eagle eyes on Lucas the better. *Was that a frown just skidded across Grace's features?* "Everything okay?" Erika called up, panicky. She headed for the staircase. "Luc with Harrison?" she asked, bounding up the steps three at a time.

"Yes, he is. I was only wondering what you'd like for dinner tonight, beef bourguignon or shrimp scampi?"

"Our favorite, the beef, of course," Erika replied, buoyant with relief.

The door to Harrison's study was closed. She knocked and swooped in on them without waiting for a response. Harrison was sitting at his desk moving papers around, while Lucas was sitting in his playpen trying to shove a plastic square into his learning toy's resistant hole. Their chocolate Lab, Jake, was sprawled next to the playpen poking his old paw between the slats as if he intended to give the fuzzy-headed creature some guidance.

"How was the run?" Harrison asked, lighting up upon her arrival.

"Great—must be at least eighty degrees out there. Felt good."

"Come over here."

"I'm too sweaty. She patted the dog's head and bent over the playpen to kiss the top of Lucas's. The boy reached up and grabbed what he could of her ponytail. "Later, sweetie," she said, gently prying him loose. She kissed his chubby fingers. "Mommy has to take a shower first." She glanced at Harrison; detected a pout. She sashayed over to the desk and threw her arms around him. "Better?"

"Much." He smiled, playing along but smarting from the shameful twinge of jealousy.

"Now you'll need a shower, too." She ran her fingers through his thick brown hair, adding to the already tousled look. "There," she said, removing the terrycloth band from her head and slipping it onto his.

2

Lucas's view was obstructed by the chair near his playpen. Harrison cupped his hand over Erika's shorts-encased rear and let it cascade down her enticingly damp thigh. "Don't forget, we have a Zoom meeting at eleven."

"I'm not forgetting, are you?" she asked, as his hand retraced its path, its thumb venturing under her shorts.

"Not at all." His thumb swept back and forth like a windshield wiper on low. "We have time for a shower. A long one."

"I'll tell Grace to keep an eye on Luc." She freed herself. "See you in a minute—I'm looking forward to this meeting, you know?" She started for the door; turned back. "Although I'm not quite sure what they've got planned for us."

Chapter Two

"Thank you for joining me, and at such short notice," host Ikemar—"Ike" in the caption—Umar greeted the dozen or so attendees that had made it past the Zoom meeting's encrypted entry and were settling into the mosaic and smiling in varying degrees of close-lipped cordiality. Erika and Harrison, sitting squarely shoulder to shoulder in front of Harrison's desktop computer were located in a slot in the top row. They were the only twosome occupying one niche, and in their off-white buttoned shirts, matching unintentionally, Erika had the wayward thought that they looked like a pair of dancers ready to soft-shoe their way to center stage.

Ikemar, a broad-shouldered Black man who cut an imposing figure despite his limited screen-share, waited for a newcomer appearing due west to settle in. "Glad you could make it, Amilah," he said, the frame around him lighting up again as he addressed the young Black woman, whose full name, "Amilah Adamu," was registered below her image. The woman acknowledged the greeting with a radiant smile that jumped off the screen, compelling Erika to respond in kind.

The host, similarly stricken, smiled broadly. "Not dinnertime for you, I hope!" Putting on his game face, he added, "In that regard, I did try to accommodate all of you as best I could." He shifted in his seat, as if to mark an end to the small talk. "Before we begin, a word about my choice of Gallery View as opposed to Active Speaker. I wanted us to be on equal footing throughout our discussion and, more important, to feel in our hearts equal commitment."

Ikemar spoke with a foreign accent unfamiliar to Erika, but she knew from Harrison's description of his meeting with him that it was Yoruba, the official language of Nigeria, that gave his British pronunciation its warmth. There was an openness to it created by the vowels, their variety at once unexpected and inviting.

Harrison had met Ikemar several months prior at the University of London at a conference titled "The Influence of British Literature on European Art." Ikemar, a visiting professor from the University of Nigeria in Nsukka, had been in the audience when Harrison had delivered his talk on the literary sources of Delacroix's romanticism, namely Shakespeare, Byron, and Scott. Ikemar had approached him afterward and they'd had a lively discussion on the decidedly non-Eurocentric approach Ikemar was bringing to the course he was teaching at U London: "Post-Colonial African History." They'd exchanged cards with the intention of staying in touch. Ikemar had been the first to make contact with an invitation for Harrison as well as his "co-conspirator," Erika, to attend an upcoming Zoom meeting. "I've heard through the grapevine of your sleuthing talents," he'd texted, without divulging exactly how he intended to make use of them.

"Briefly," host Ikemar continued, "the purpose of our meeting is to discuss ways of expediting the return of Africa's heritage. I promise in a moment we'll have a round of introductions and get down to business, but I want to start off with a quote to get the juices flowing." He flashed a genial smile. "Let me apologize beforehand to my colleague Timothy Thorpe. Tim's an associate curator at the British Museum." Mid center row, a pleasant-looking man in a tweed jacket, dark shirt, and wool tie raised a finger to note his presence. "In no way does the quote reflect your philosophy, Tim. It's simply meant, well, to give us pause." He raised a sheet of paper from a desk or table outside his screen frame and began. "'While the Benin Bronzes in the Museum have as varied and colorful an acquisition history as any other—bequests, gifts, purchases, et cetera, featuring many eminent names among their former owners—all ultimately go back to a swift punitive expedition mounted by British forces in 1897, following the massacre of a diplomatic mission to that kingdom in the same year. Although not one of the major military operations of the time, it had a high profile, being seen as a vindication of national honor. In many ways, it was the Falklands Expedition of its day, with emotional farewells to the ships, a rapid and decisive outcome and reception of victorious forces at Windsor by the Queen, to whom objects from Benin were presented.'" Ikemar cleared his throat. "From the Director's Forward, *The Art of Benin* by Nigel Barley, published by The British Museum Press, 2010."

Assistant curator Timothy Thorpe was shifting uncomfortably in his seat. He opened his mouth to speak, thought better of it, then thought again. "You may have noticed the book was reprinted in 2016," he stated evenly, as the frame around his image brightened. "It should have been edited first, at least to eliminate its superior tone, the barely disguised undercurrent of racism. But I was new to the staff and a coward. I kept my mouth shut. I've regretted it ever since."

"Just the sentiment I meant to stir up," Ike said. "Except not for the use of beating ourselves up. We want to put the passion—guilt, if you will—to good use. Besides," he added with a wry grin, "there's plenty of guilt to go around." He paused, possibly to decide which misdeed to single out. "As an example, in 2017 President Emmanuel Macron of France promised to return to the country of Benin twenty-six objects—thrones and statues—out of about 5,000 it had plundered in 1892. Motivation good. Red tape unfortunate. The objects are legally classified as 'inalienable,' so in order to deaccession them, Parliament needs to pass a new law that overturns the old one. Meanwhile, time shuffles on."

The moody-looking man with the scruffy beard in the square to the left of Erika and Harrison's uttered a harrumph.

Duly noted by the host. "Monsieur Pierre Jolet is no way responsible for the delay and is not to take offense. Which brings us to introductions. Pierre works for the worldwide organization of French Institutes and has for some years been serving as Associate Director of its branch in Portugal. The organization's cultural center in Abuja, Nigeria offers courses to curators in the care and preservation of heritage art, restituted and on schedule for restitution. Kudos to Pierre for initiating the program."

Monsieur Jolet accepted the accolade with a begrudging smile.

Robert Labeque, associate curator of the Quai Branly Museum in Paris, was less grumpy than his fellow countryman when introduced next. The red-cheeked pudgy gentleman, whom Erika had cast as Dickens's Mr. Micawber until she heard his honey-toned voice, freely admitted his museum had been dragging its feet when it came to returning its plundered treasures.

Next up on the block was Helena Simpson, a prim-looking fiftyish woman in a pinstripe suit—bottom half inferred—of the Open Society Foundation. "The Open Society Foundation was established by George Soros in 1993," Ike informed those of the group who might be unaware. "It's a billion-dollar international grant-making enterprise with branches in thirty-seven countries. Ms. Simpson hails from its New York City office and serves as Director of Culture and Art."

"Guilty as charged," Ms. Simpson quipped. "Speaking to the purpose of today's gathering, I should mention that in 2019 George—Mr. Soros—con-tributed a fifteen-million-dollar initiative to aid African institutions in their campaign to expedite the return of art and artifacts looted during the colonial era."

"Indeed he did," Ike acknowledged before continuing down his list of attendees which included, among others, the woman with the contagious smile, Amilah Adamu of Benin City, Nigeria, an administrative officer in the Federal Ministry of Information and Culture; Curator Kurt Reinhardt of the Humbolt Forum in Berlin, a museum of non-European art housing over 50,000 artifacts from Africa seized during the colonial era; an officer from the Welt Museum in Vienna; Jody Adams, a researcher from the Metropolitan Museum of Art in New York City.

When he turned his attention to Erika and Harrison, Ike rubbed his hands together tantalizingly, as if he were about to offer up the pair for dessert. "Erika is an editor at *Art News* magazine, and her husband and sleuthing partner is Harrison, an art history professor at New York University's Institute of Fine Arts. In the art world, these two have come up with solutions to crimes that have eluded folks who call themselves experts."

"We've had a lot of *help* from experts!" Erika corrected, Ike waving her off mid-sentence.

"No place for modesty here," Ike chided with a smile of forbearance. "Our motto is 'full steam ahead.' With that in mind, I segue to the person who'll introduce us to the brain-teaser that will put our modest detectives in motion—Mrs. Olivia Chatham." The sixty-something woman in the square to the right of Erika and Harrison's gave a little wave, the plaid cuff of her suit jacket rising to expose the ruffled cuff of her white blouse, as Ike continued without pause. "Olivia is a math professor at the University of London, where I've been teaching a course on African history while on leave from the University of Nigeria. Olivia reached out to me with a fascinating story that put my motivation to reverse the sins of the past into high gear. Go to it, Olivia."

Olivia tucked a lock of her untamed white hair behind an ear. She was sitting in a large high-back green leather chair that dwarfed her and blocked whatever room details lay behind her. "Thank you, Ikemar. Let me begin by saying that I am a sixty-four-year-old math nerd and long-time widow set in her ways. Totally out of my element in this crowd. Nevertheless, I'm here because I have come upon something of interest to all of you—and to me as well, of course, not because I can help you in any way, but because I share with you the same desire to set things right in the world. Be patient as I give you a bit of the backstory." She smoothed her suit cuff into place. "There's a large estate in Hertfordshire County in southern England called Barrett Farms. My great-granduncle, Andrew Barrett—an army medic, it turns out—inherited this estate from his father. And here the misfortunes begin. Andrew married in 1898 and in 1900 his wife died giving birth to their son and was laid to rest at West Norwood, on the family burial grounds. Barrett Farms was to be passed down to Andrew's son, but both father and son perished during the pandemic of 19 18. As far as I can tell, my great-granduncle's will was never executed, and I'm hoping our two *sleuths*"—spoken with a hopeful rise in her voice—"will help us find out why. Meanwhile, the estate was by default passed down to my great-granduncle's only living relative, his brother William, my great-grandfather. Have I lost you yet? I do hope not."

"We're with you; carry on," Ike urged.

Olivia drew a glass of colorless liquid—water? gin?—from outside her frame and took a sip. "Good. I've laid the groundwork, so I needn't burden you with further details of my family tree. Suffice it to say, Barrett Farms eventually was passed down to me. We're approaching the present now"—again, that rise in register—"so bear with me. I only wish to put into context what you will shortly learn is our present-day mystery."

Slight perking up in the gallery. *Mystery?*

"My nuclear family, I should tell you, never lived on the estate. It was far too costly to keep up, and to boot, it went into disrepair when requisitioned by our military during World War II. We—*I* from adulthood on—tried to make ends meet by opening it up to the public, renting it out to wedding parties and the like, but the heating and gardening—my lord, the topiary trees!—and general maintenance finally got the better of me and I sold the place to a rather eager golf course mogul. The closing took place a month ago.

"Before signing the deed, I was able to auction off the furnishings of the estate house. I should like to have kept half the furnishings of the dear old manor, but my modest London flat was hardly up to the task. However, there were several pieces I simply could not part with—the chair I'm sitting in, a lovely grandfather clock, and a large mahogany secretary desk that just about scrapes the ceiling of my little spare room." She took another sip of her drink. "And it was in that desk, in an easy-to-miss compartment in the bottom drawer, that I discovered my great-granduncle's journal along with a number of curious documents. If I were not such a cleanliness freak, I might never have found these precious things—precious for my own personal enlightenment as well as for one on a far broader scale." She studied something below eye level. "I want to read you a passage from Great-granduncle Andrew's journal," she said, her tone suddenly reverent. "It's dated '24 March 1897'—this is a few days after he returned from the British punitive expedition in West Africa. It describes in poetic terms an epiphany illuminating his life's mission. 'In my vision,' he begins, 'the woman I remember washing clothes by the river jumps to her feet and faces me. She

9

holds out her hands like—'"

"Dammit!" A mild curse barely audible, but loud enough to light up the frame around Timothy Thorpe's image. "Sorry mates, bulb blew." The overhead, it must have been, since the weaker source of light behind his computer was still there, softening his features and maybe for a millisecond the audience's attentiveness as well, so that when the black line appeared just above his shirt collar it took another blip in time for brains to sort it out and reject the idea of a shadow cast by his desk lamp. Which would explain the silence before the first scream, coming from somewhere in the Zoom's mosaic, a woman's scream—*mine*, Erika realized. Likewise, a delayed reaction from Tim himself, gazing wide-eyed at the screen as if someone out there was experiencing the horror, not he himself, that is, before the black cord tightened around his neck and the impossible truth contorted his features like a funhouse mirror.

And then the silence turned into the Tower of Babel, witnesses reverting to their native tongues, as gloved hands—surely visible from the start!—tugged on the cord and disappeared behind Tim's neck to knot or entwine or do whatever was planned or improvised to cut off Tim's air, while Tim clawed at his neck in an attempt to free himself, mouth open in a parody of Munch's *The Scream*, except in Tim's version it was a cry for help mimed to the restless viewers filling his computer screen, twinkling with their useless babble like Christmas lights.

"*Où est-il*—where *is* he?" Monsieur Robert Labeque cried, his red cheeks deepening to scarlet, his returning to the group's common tongue a sign that rational interchange was being restored.

"The museum—his office at the British Museum!" Ike yelled back, as if calling from across a football field. "He said they're preparing an exhibit, staying late—I've got their unlisted number—seeing if I can rouse the damn security guards!" All the while fumbling with his cell phone. "They must seal off the exits. Museum doesn't close for another half hour!"

"Bastard, we see you!" Harrison shouted at the nondescript torso, mostly hidden by Tim's body, rigid against the chair-back while his hands flailed like a mad conductor's. How many seconds had passed—ten, fifteen? A lifetime. "Someone over there call 9-1-1—Olivia?"

"I've already put in the call—it's 9-9-9 over here," Olivia advised, her calmness, real or staged, a reminder that order was possible.

"I'm activating the recording option!" Ike bellowed. Shifting focus to his unresponsive phone, he shouted, "Hello? Hello?"

Harrison tapped on Thorpe's name and spotlighted his square. Instantly it filled the screen. He dove for his cell phone. "Erika, take photos!"

His words sounded harsh, except she was thinking the same thing, already digging her cell phone out of her jeans pocket. "You video, I'll take stills—oh God!" Outwardly, Tim had stopped struggling. But what was happening *within*? Her empathy was suddenly gripped by a primal curiosity, as if only by understanding Tim's encounter with death could she prepare for her own.

"Go!" Harrison prompted.

The command cut off her connection to Tim like a dropped call, and she aimed her cell's lens at his motionless figure in the more useful role as witness to a crime. As she prepared for the second shot, she realized that others were following Harrison's and her lead.

On screen the assailant's gloved finger pressed against Tim's neck, feeling for a pulse. Apparently satisfied, he or she swiftly removed the cord from around the victim's neck and made adjustments to the distribution of weight so that the body would not slump forward. Mission accomplished, the individual glided out of Tim's camera range, leaving Tim, in jacket and neatly knotted tie, to stare blankly into space with only an angry red bruise above his shirt collar to suggest what had just happened to him.

"Where are the museum guards, the *police*?" Pierre Jolet railed. "What kind of system have you got there?"

"The guards and the police were called," Ike answered. "It can't have been more than two minutes ago."

"There's nothing to be done then? We sit here gawking at this poor man on display before us? It's grotesque! I'm leaving!"

"Wait! You're a witness. The police will want to question all of us!"

"You have my contact information. Convey it. I'm sorry, but this hits too close to home. If you only knew…" With that, Pierre's square went black.

Just as the overhead light in Tim's office went on.

"Mr. Thorpe?" A man's voice. Speaker unseen. Must be near the door. "Mind if I sweep up, sir?"

The remaining Zoomers stared mutely, as if they were watching a film, therefore powerless to interact with the characters on screen.

"*Sir?*" The man stepped into the framed space and approached. He had on a white long-sleeved polo shirt and denim overalls and was dragging a broom and long-handled dustpan behind him as if he were walking a brace of dogs.

"Get help, man!" Harrison barked, the crack of sound arousing others to react in kind.

"Do you know CPR?" Erika cried.

"Summon the guard!" Helena Simpson demanded.

But the man had arrived at the posed figure just as their shouts rang out, and he responded only to what was before his eyes. He dropped the items he was holding, and the handles clattered as they struck the floor. "Mr. Thorpe, sir!" he urged, in a voice just above a whisper, gingerly tapping at him as if he were a hot iron. Then, as if remembering, his focus switched to the source of the commotion. With knit brow, he regarded the computer as if it were a spaceship manned by aliens. "Who are you?" he fired back at them. "What did you *see?*"

"CPR, do you know CPR?" Erika shot back, disregarding his questions.

"What?—no! What do I do?" He shook his head, shaking away the cobwebs. Without waiting for a reply, he slipped his hands under Tim, lifted him from the chair, and laid him on the floor, both of them falling out of range of the computer eye. "I hold his nose and breathe into his mouth, yes? Did someone call for help? I'm about to start mouth-to-mouth!" After a brief silence, he rose into view. "Nothing," he reported, before returning to the task.

"Chest compressions!" Erika ordered, taking her cue from the movies. "Now!"

"Yes, okay! I'm placing my hands now, one on top of the other, on Mr.

Thorpe's chest."

"Interlock your thumbs! Energetic pumps—twenty of them—then back to rescue breathing. Alternate between the two."

"I will. Starting...*now!*" A grunt of exertion was audible with the first pressure pump and repeated until the chest compression phase was deemed over and the rescue breathing phase resumed.

He was on his third cycle when a group of additional players suddenly burst onto the set. Viewed piecemeal, like a movie camera might have shot their entry: a medical team wheeling an equipment-laden gurney, one at either end; two museum guards and two police officers in distinctive uniforms; and a confused-looking young man in ordinary street clothes and backpack, who looked like he'd taken a wrong turn and been swept into the group.

One of the medical team, a burly, middle-aged man with an air of seasoned confidence, bade the custodian to move aside, emphasizing the order with a forceful tug at some part of the man's anatomy or clothing off camera. Once he was out of the way, the team began working on Tim in perfect sync, attaching equipment to him and hoisting him onto the gurney in a continuous series of motions, the procedure continuing without pause even as they wheeled Tim off to whatever transport vehicle awaited them.

"All but medics, stand where you are!" one of the police officers—by the looks of him, the one with seniority—commanded. "Let's try to keep the scene pristine for our forensics people. All exits have been blocked. No one leaves the premises but the medical team and their charge. The police are sweeping the building. Stay out of their way!"

The museum guards and the young man with the backpack froze in place, as did the custodial worker who'd been relieved of his duties as Good Samaritan.

"You, too, out there," the officer added, addressing the computer screen. "You're not to go anywhere. We'll get to you shortly. Detective's en route—Detective Clive Hogarty—with his evidence team. I see you're aiming your cell phones in our direction. You'll be given instructions on how to transmit all visual and audio records to us. Please do not delete any material or share it with anyone but us. We're not monitoring you, so I'm asking for your cooperation." He turned his head sharply in the direction of the door. "They're here."

In the pause before the newcomers came into view, a question suddenly occurred to Erika: *What was Olivia about to tell us?*

* * *

An hour later, after the Zoom participants had been cross-examined, lectured, and dismissed by Detective Hogarty, the question still lingered, but had not yet been broached. As instructed, Erika and Harrison had immediately begun transmitting to the British authorities their videos and still shots of the horrific event they'd just witnessed. Burning questions had been held at bay.

"Who attacked him and *why?*" spilled from Erika as she finally laid her cell phone on Harrison's desk, behind which they remained sitting side by side. "A personal enemy? Political? Anything to do with the project?"

Harrison placed his cell phone in perfect alignment with hers, as if this would set the world back in order. "No idea. Let's study what we recorded; may give us a clue."

"I think we were meant to see it."

"Really?"

"Why else was Tim's desk lamp left on, his computer lid kept open?"

"I'm guessing it was a rush job. The overhead light was clicked off, remember."

"I do. The overhead would have given us a better look at the guy. Maybe the goal was not to highlight the perpetrator, just the crime."

"Are you saying this person knew Tim was scheduled to be at a Zoom meeting, and possibly even the *nature* of the meeting?"

"Maybe. Or that having an audience was just his stroke of luck." She shrugged. "Or that I'm creating a scenario out of thin air. Which is more like it."

"Absolutely not. I just don't think we have enough information to come to a conclusion."

She gave a half-hearted laugh. "Look at us."

"What? Acting like a couple of detectives?"

She laid her head on his shoulder. "Yes."

"We should let the real ones do their job."

"Who's stopping them?" she asked, straightening up so she could look him in the eye. "No harm in putting in our two cents."

"I worry that your investment will be a lot more. You have that look."

"What look?" she asked, all innocence.

"Not that one. The one immediately before. Of determination."

"What was Olivia about to reveal to us, I wonder," she posed, heading off Harrison's words of caution.

He reacted to her evasion with a headshake of resignation. "Whatever it was, it must have been crucial. During our debriefing with the detective, Ike gave the subject of our meeting a title 'The Barrett Incentive.' Very cloak-and-dagger."

"Yes, I'm surprised Ike wasn't grilled more thoroughly about it. But the authorities can always get back to us. Our contact information was circulated to everyone in sight. Felt like we were on a dating app."

Harrison smiled, amazed, and not for the first time, at how humor had a way of cropping up in the face of tragedy. Whether due to the resilience of the human spirit or a quirk less admirable, he figured without it there's a good chance the species would be wringing its hands from birth to death. "As long as you swiped right for me," he said.

"*Forever*," she stressed, the impossibility of the notion taking her by surprise, as if it weren't already a wound that would never heal. She looked away.

He took her hand. "What's wrong?"

She turned to him, and their eyes met as if for the first time. "I'm selfish. I don't want it to end, and it will."

"Not for a very long time," he said, softening the truth. "Certainly not before lunch."

Perfect answer to pull her from the deep.

* * *

Beeps sounded from each of their cell phones as they were on their second cup of coffee and picking at the remains of their sandwiches, turkey for her, roast beef for him. The devices were sitting alongside each other in the center of the dining room table. When they punched in, they discovered they'd each been sent an email with a cc to Ike. They read the message silently, on their cell phones, before sharing their takes on it.

Hello, Harrison and Erika:

Once again, I am out of my element but feeling compelled to act before I lose either my nerve or the momentum. As I mentioned at our meeting before the unthinkable event, I am in possession of my great-granduncle Andrew Barrett's journal along with contemporaneous documents that I believe are of motivational and substantive importance in the "effort to restore Africa's heritage," as our host, Ikemar Umar aptly put it. I am sure you agree that no individual event, however tragic, should stand in the way of that pursuit. With this in mind, along with my faith in your investigative powers, I would like to send you the journal and documents for your analysis. I will be keeping copies of the material, but I've chosen to send you the originals because you are bound to see things that I might fail to pick up. In truth, the thought of missing a tell-tale inkblot or blurry marginal note would be an incessant worry.

Of course, I would like to be informed of your progress from time to time, and when you are done with your research, I would expect you to return the items to me.

I plan to FedEx the parcel to you tomorrow, that is, if you agree to commit yourselves to this undertaking. Thank you for responding with a yes or no. Either way, I greatly appreciate your consideration.

All best,

Olivia Chatham

Erika read the email twice before looking up. Harrison was waiting for her.

"There's no hint at what we're supposed to be looking for," she said, stating the obvious.

"No, but you admit it's intriguing. Impossible to turn down, in fact."

"Impossible."

His email response to Olivia was concise. Hers, more profusely grateful. A little over the top, she thought belatedly, after hitting *Reply all*.

* * *

"Do you remember hearing what hospital they were taking Tim to?" Harrison asked, changing his mind about clicking off the lamp on his night table. He rolled back onto his side to face Erika. She was lying on her back, eyes wide open, no doubt as keyed up as he was. The clock said it was time for sleep. His brain said who are you kidding?

Erika turned to lie on her side, their faces almost touching. His breath bore the generic smell of toothpaste; beneath it, the scent of his body: unique, compelling. "The authorities said it was legal to continue recording until they were finished with us. You did continue, didn't you?"

"Yes. I'll check out what I've got." He sat up, grabbed his cell phone, always lying at the ready—or in wait—from his night table.

It took some maneuvering to get to the section where the medical and law enforcement teams had made their entrance. Harrison turned up the volume to the cell's max as Erika scrambled to sit beside him at the edge of the bed. He held the cell between them as they listened attentively to the video's background conversation, mostly unintelligible.

"No use," he concluded, exiting the video. "We could try contacting someone local, say Olivia or Ike, who might know how Tim's doing, but it's not even dawn over there. We'd probably wake them up. Anyway, it won't change the outcome."

"How about we call the hospital closest to the British Museum. What can we lose?"

"Smart." He hit the Google icon and typed "hospitals in Bloomsbury near the British Museum," and a map of the area with location markers along with a scroll-down panel of hospital names and contact information instantly appeared on his cell phone screen. There was a cluster of hospitals in the vicinity of the museum, but almost all turned out to be highly specialized in fields ranging from neurology to virology. It looked like their best bet was the University College Hospital on Euston Road. When Harrison punched in a request for directions from the British Museum on Great Russell Street, the answer read: *2 min (.6 mi) via A400.* The fifteen-digit telephone number was listed below the hours of operation (*24*). Harrison fetched a pen and sheet of notepaper from the catch-all drawer of his night table, jotted down the phone number, and exited Google. "Okay." He hit the phone icon. Instead of tapping in the exit code, for use only when calling from a landline, he held down the zero until the plus sign appeared, then typed in the rest of the number. After hearing the first ring, he activated the speakerphone.

Erika jammed closer to him in grim anticipation. The sudden announcement, a question delivered as a statement, sent a shiver down her spine.

"University College Hospital, how can I help you." As if the answer were already set in stone.

Harrison asked to be connected to Patient Information and the receptionist, without comment, obliged.

The second communication was as declarative as the first, only with better cause. "The patient Timothy Thorpe is deceased," the woman flatly stated.

"What was the time of death?" Harrison prodded, hardly knowing why. Maybe to shake her up.

"I'm sorry, sir, I'm not at liberty to disclose any further information."

"All right. Thank you." Cold. Nothing in his voice giving away his agitation as an image of Tim Thorpe, a virtual stranger with a wool tie and words of self-recrimination, came to mind, a phrase from a stage play following close behind: "Attention must be paid."

Erika took Harrison's hand at the end of the call. The line from *Death of a Salesman* was hardly telegraphed, but she did see in his eyes and downturn of his mouth the helpless fury that had elicited it. She recognized his reaction—sudden, revelatory—to the willful taking of a life. She had seen it before.

* * *

Hope had been lost, a senseless death made official, and Harrison was greedy for answers. "Do you think what happened to Tim is related to what was discussed at the Zoom meeting?" They were tucked back under the covers after the hospital call, and the warmth of Erika's body was conflicting with his desire to *know*.

"Why don't we wait until we have a look at what Olivia's sending us, give us more of an overview?" They were facing each other in the almost dark, with a sliver of moonlight reaching them through a crack in the drapes. Harrison was clad in a pair of jockey shorts, she in a sheer nightgown. The immediacy of being was taking precedence over the call for deductive reasoning; for her, at least.

"I want to get a jump on things," he persisted. "Like it or not, we're part of it. We should help however we can."

"Of course." She moved closer, ran her hand down his thigh ever so lightly.

"What did Pierre Jolet mean by that parting remark of his?" he pressed on. "About the event '*hitting home*'? A red herring, you think? To distract us from his squeamishness, or something more to the point?"

"Like what, his *involvement*?" she asked, incredulous.

"Anything is possible." Absently, he stroked her shoulder; might as well have been stroking his chin. "We have to think out of the box."

It suddenly came to her. To keep the questions from flying off in all directions, a definite plan must be set in place. "First thing in the morning, we'll contact Greg," she declared, leaving no room for debate. "We'll ask him to make inquiries and get back to us. We may not be at liberty to share our Zoom records, but nothing's stopping us from sharing our oral account."

Their friend Greg Smith had helped them on previous occasions. As a member of the executive board of Art Loss Register, the largest private database of stolen art, he had connections in all spheres of the art world, including its darkest. The decision to contact Greg was an action, simple and direct, and Harrison's torturous questions became instantly subordinate to it. "Let's do that," he said, aware he was putting his concern on hold, but

19

that it may not be a sign of disrespect to be doing so.

She had not taken her hand from his thigh. They were a breath away from it becoming all that mattered.

Chapter Three

Four days later Erika and Harrison still hadn't heard back from Greg. Unless an email stating "will get back to you shortly" counts as a response.

When Erika returned from work that evening, a brown carton from Olivia Chatham plastered with FedEx stickers was waiting for her on the couch in the lobby, making up for Greg's neglect. She could hardly keep from ripping it open, but she wanted to discover its contents with Harrison. He was at a faculty meeting and would be back soon. Better be!

"The package came just after you and the professor left this morning," Kate called down from the first-floor balustrade. "I hope you don't mind that I left it on the couch."

"That's fine, Kate. How's Lucas?" Erika called back. She was already halfway up the stairs.

"He's good. In his highchair, about to have dinner." Kate smiled in response to Erika's sudden look of concern. "Grace is in the kitchen watching him." She anchored a wayward lock of flaxen hair behind her ear. "I'm guessing you'll be wanting to feed him."

"Of course! Give me a minute to wash up." Erika dropped her tote bag on the floor and made a beeline for the bathroom down the hall, calling: "Right with you, sweetie!"

* * *

Luc asleep. Adults fed. Kate and Grace retired to their private quarters.

21

Alone at last. "How did the meeting go?" Erika asked. She and Harrison were ensconced in his study, about to slit open the carton from Olivia.

"Fine." He speared the box at its seam with the point of his letter opener and slashed it open with the cold precision of a butcher. "The usual."

"Anything wrong? You seemed distracted over dinner." If he offered no explanation, she would let it go. Nothing worse than a nag.

"Really, I'm good." Let's get started here. Aren't you excited?" U-turning: "I got a disturbing call from Gretchen, Madame Denise Fontaine's receptionist." There. He'd ruined the moment. Couldn't hold off keeping it from her.

"Oh? What's going on?" Erika asked, concerned. She'd heard all about Madame D, the feisty nonagenarian who'd been Harrison's local historian and sidekick during his investigative sojourn in Paris. She'd spoken to the woman once over the phone, and that's all it had taken to produce a warm affection for her. "She's not ill, I hope."

"I don't know. Gretchen would only say Madame D wanted to talk to me tonight. She sounded deadly serious."

Prompting another "Oh?"

"I know. I'm just as confused—and afraid to guess." He checked his watch. "We're to expect an email alert from Gretchen before we talk. It should be coming through about an hour from now, so we have no choice but to wait." He waved at the neglected parcel. "Can we put our talk with Madame D aside and get on with this?"

"Of course," Erika agreed, the use of the word "our" not escaping her notice. She was glad he was including her in on the issue with Madame D. "In answer to your first question, yes."

"What was that?"

"You asked if I was excited to get started. I am."

Olivia's unexamined parcel was sitting on Harrison's desk chair, the desktop cleared to accommodate its contents. Erika pulled open the freed box flaps. A crumpled mass of brown wrapping paper covered whatever items lay beneath. She removed the paper, scrunched it, and tossed the wad into Harrison's wastebasket. The crinkling sound aroused Jake, snoozing in his man-pad under Harrison's desk, and he crept out from under to be a part of whatever they were up to, especially if it involved rubbing his belly. To make it accessible, he plopped down at their feet and presented it to any takers. Erika obliged by caressing his underside as Harrison removed the items from the carton one by one. When they were laid out on his desktop, Erika kissed Jake's graying muzzle and rose from her crouched position.

Harrison had piled the loose papers—from personal jottings to formal-looking documents—on one side of his desktop, a few sealed and unsealed envelopes on the other. In the center, he'd placed the pièce de résistance: a brown weatherworn leather journal. As for an accompanying note from Olivia, none had been enclosed. They were on their own.

"Do you think we need to wear gloves?" Erika asked, eyeing her pooch-contaminated palm.

"As long as our hands are clean and Jake keeps his distance, no," Harrison replied, digging for a packet of wipes in his desk's middle drawer. He pulled one out for himself and handed another to Erika. After tossing the used items into the wastebasket, they rubbed their hands until completely dry. "Let's sit on the couch and crack open the journal," he suggested.

"You have a couple of legal pads?" Erika asked, as Jake, sensing his diminished role in the proceedings, wriggled back to his retreat in the desk's knee hole.

Harrison fetched the lined pads along with a couple of ballpoints from one of his desk's commodious side drawers.

The cumbersome leather recliner that had once stood on the opposite side of the room had been replaced with a sleek upholstered couch. At the moment, its center cushion was occupied by a stack of papers. With the Barrett journal pressed to her chest, Erika sat down beside them. "Student essays," Harrison explained, moving them to the lid of the printer perched on a nearby table otherwise strewn with books. "Yet to be graded." He gave the stack a paternal pat and returned to the couch to sit close beside her. "Am I crowding you?"

"Never." She opened the journal and set it down on their abutting thighs.

He laid the pads and pens on the oak coffee table, miraculously free of clutter. "Here we go."

The first page identified the journal's owner and date of inception in neatly penned script:

Andrew James Dexter Barrett
Book One: 22 March 1897 – 17 August 1897

The subject of where Book Two and beyond might have gone off to was not raised because it would have been futile and, at least for now, irrelevant. Erika carefully turned the page to reveal the journal's first entry, thankfully in that same legible, script: *22 March, homecoming.* They read on, silently.

Hard to believe it has been less than ten weeks since the SS Malacca, cargo steamship refitted as a hospital ship, set forth for the Benin coast with me and my fellow medics aboard. It seems like a lifetime ago, perhaps because I have become a new man, or rather a newly awakened man, in the interim.

I have learned firsthand what history books and hearsay can only, at best, inadequately describe, and I will never again shut my eyes to the indignities and injustices we self-proclaimed entitled few, heap upon our brethren: those less fiscally sound as well as those of darker skin.

On Saturday, 20 March, when the ship pulled into Gosport, England, Father was waiting for me on the dock in top hat and frock coat, dapper as the nobleman he is. As I heave-hoed my laundry bag containing the rescued Benin treasures into our horse-drawn carriage, Father commented on its obvious weight. "What have you got in there?" he asked, with barely a trace of curiosity. "Medical books and instruments," I answered without hesitation, realizing as I uttered the words that I had no intention of bringing him into my confidence.

I had been getting about on my own for years and could very well have hired a carriage to take me on the sixty-six-mile journey home, but Father had been adamant about accompanying me, even though it meant that both he and his coachman must overnight at an inn to, and again from, Gosport. In retrospect, I wonder if his intention, perhaps not conscious, was to use our extensive time alone to reclaim his control over me, since he did, after all, spend a good deal of time speaking of his activities in the House of Lords and pressing upon me the certainty that I was "marvelously suited" to that rewarding life. Mid-point between Gosport and Hertfordshire, we rented rooms at the inn in Guildford, where Father and the coachman had stayed the night before. To dilute Father's lecture disguised as conversation, I must have consumed more ale that night than I had in the previous six months.

I awakened this morning well rested, but with a raging headache. Father must have taken pity on me because for the balance of our journey he eased up considerably on his mission to refashion me as a slightly taller version of himself. We arrived home late this evening, and Mother's embrace and smile of relief comforted me no end. Never mind my goals in life. All that mattered to Mother was my safe return to Barrett Farms.

"'The rescued Benin treasures,'" Harrison quoted, pausing at the end of the first entry. "It whets the appetite, yes?"

Erika was regarding the splotch of ink between the words '*my*' and '*safe*,' partially obscuring the words, as if a black teardrop had fallen on the page. She imagined Andrew's slender fingers—*why slender?*—grasping the pen and wondered if an expletive had escaped his lips. "Do you feel like we're invading Andrew's privacy?"

"Sure, but judging from his humanitarian point of view, he would have approved, given our ultimate goals." He smiled. "You're not used to prowling around people's personal documents like I am."

She reminded him of how, among other things, she'd *prowled* around Bertram Morrison's personal letters with him several years back, during what he'd dubbed their Cuban Caper. "But I guess letters are one step closer to the public domain than a journal or diary."

"Exactly."

"So, let's go on."

They read through the next two entries without stopping to comment.

23 March 1897, I am regaled

It came as a surprise. I suppose it was meant to, Mother and the cook having prepared most of the dinner beforehand so that there wasn't much of a scuffling about in the kitchen to give it away, although the aromas should have at least given me a hint of what was to come.

Father had taken it upon himself to invite a new, and I would assume politically useful, acquaintance of his to dinner, the barrister Samuel Worthington, an overbearing gentleman in tow with his doting wife, Rosalind, all frills and curls, and his raven-haired daughter, Lillian, whose penetrating brown eyes captivated me at first glance. Lillian wore her abundant hair swept up in barrettes that seemed hardly to contain it, and I was half-hoping they would lose the battle and her hair would cascade down her back and fall about her shoulders.

Shortly after being seated around the dinner table, we were presented the main course in all its glory, and it was then I realized that under Mother's direction we were to be treated to a most lavish traditional Christmas dinner, all the more welcome in its off-season staging. In his pre-prandial prayer, Father thanked the Lord and took credit for arranging this sumptuous feast in my honor. I acted as if the remark had escaped my notice and thanked Mother for all her efforts.

The start of the meal was mostly spent on praising the food, which out of respect for Mother as well as dear old Anna, our cook, I hereby duly record: Turkey with sage and onion stuffing, surrounded by sausages wrapped in bacon. Roast potatoes made with goose fat, parsley and thyme. Steamed Brussel sprouts. Yorkshire pudding. I know I'm missing something. Cranberry sauce, of course. Accompanied by a choice of wines—full-bodied white; red less bold.

Dominated by Father and Mr. Worthington, the conversation pivoted to the subject of petrol-driven automobiles, namely the Daimler and the Benz. Worthington was considering purchasing a Daimler, but Father attempted to change his mind, singing the praises of his newly acquired Benz as if it were his mistress, and in truth I had never heard him speak of Mother in such glowing terms. It's a mystery to me how he knows enough about the Benz to recommend it, since by his own admission he's brought it out from its custom-made shed only two or three times, and then only for gentle half-mile jaunts.

The subject of my recent experience in West Africa was bound to arise, although not by my provocation. For Mother's sake, I tried to remain non-combative as Father and his new friend opened with their laudatory views of the "tempered response of our generals" (Father), "inflicting no more damage to the environs than the occasion required" (Worthington). However, setting them straight soon took precedence over Mother's comfort when Mr. Worthington uttered the rhetorical,

*"The natives will fare better under our tutelage, eh what?" I could no longer hold
my tongue. "See here!" I began, but was cut short when Lillian, sitting directly
across from me, dealt her father a withering look and addressed me. "Tell me,
Andy," she began—and here, Mother blushed, so rarely is that sobriquet heard in
our household—"have you ever performed an autopsy?" "Yes, Lily, I unabashedly
replied. "To become a medic, one must perform at least one autopsy, but as it
happens, I've performed several." At this, she sat forward. "I don't suppose one of
your subjects happened to be a Negro?" she asked. I guessed where this was going,
and my chest pounded. If I am to reveal to anyone where I've hidden my Benin
treasures, it will be to Lily. "Yes, I have. On a woman." Lily (I shall always call
her Lily) cocked her head and posed: "And may I assume my insides would look
virtually the same as hers if you were to perform the same procedure on me, God
forbid?" I could not help but smile. "Head to toe, yes." She returned my smile, and I
felt we had begun a second conversation on a more intimate level. "Same intricate
convolutions of the brain?" she went on. I paused to allow our silent conversation
to progress. "The very same," I said. "My dear innocent girl," her father declared,
knitting his brow in loving consternation. "Not innocent, Daddy," she smartly
replied. "More accurately, un-warped." She bestowed upon him a smile that was
at once affectionate and demolishing, depriving him of a suitable response.*

*Shortly thereafter we were served my favorite dessert, mince pies. The majority
were filled with fruits (raisins, sultanas, cranberries) and the balance, with chopped
nuts and spices. It was during our communal pie-sampling that I learned of Lily's
work with the Liverpool Society for the Prevention of Cruelty to Children, modeled
after its New York prototype.*

If she will have me, I will marry Miss Lily Worthington within the year.

24 March 1897, the vision

*I am not one to attribute a visual occurrence as anything more than the
interaction of the natural world and our image receptors, along with the vagaries
of the mind and spirit, decidedly functions of the brain rather than emanations
from above. I therefore credit last night's bedtime experience as arising from the
confluence of several factors: the transition from wartime atrocities to ignoble
pampering, the sudden assault on my digestive system, and the precipitous and*

wholly uncharacteristic manner in which I have fallen in love.

Although what I experienced as a vision was in truth a vivid dream does not mean that it did not have as profound an effect on me as those purportedly bestowed upon the likes of Joan of Arc and Ezekiel. It was a life-changing event.

In my vision the woman I remember washing clothes by the river jumps to her feet and faces me. She holds out her hands like a child asking to be carried and her eyes are pleading with me to save her from the men with rifles bearing down on her and on all the village. She does not understand why this is happening and I am as useless as the clothes she'd been washing float away like drowned babies. I see the soldier beside me take aim at the woman and I try to stop him, but it is as if I am made of stone, and I am forced to watch a bullet fly from the barrel of the rifle to its intended target. As the woman falls to the ground, one arm flings away from her body and remains outstretched in death, as if still reaching for something. The soldiers freeze in their tracks, and as I gaze in horror at what I am convinced my passivity has brought about, my Benin treasures suddenly rise from the earth and hover over the woman's body. I hardly know if at that moment the objects change before my eyes, or if I had misidentified them. In any case they are or have become stone Tablets.

Harrison paused to note the "Tablets" reference and the date of its entry in one of the yellow pads. He turned to Erika. "I think Andrew's *treasures* may be a pair of plaques—Benin Bronzes."

Erika nodded. "So, in his dream, the plaques morphed into stone Tablets. It makes sense; their shapes are alike. Have you gotten to the part where he walks up to them?"

"Not yet."

"Read on. It gets interesting."

I move through an otherwise motionless world to read the Tablets' inscriptions and find they are undecipherable, yet I know what I have been called to do. The commandment comes from my troubled mind, but it is imperative just the same. I know what I must do to make up for my silence. If I am successful in this calling, many more works of art besides my precious two will be returned from whence they

came. I will find a sanctuary for my collection, or what will become my collection.
A collection of works that I will consider on temporary loan, a loan wrested from
the Edo people.

The day's entry went on for another few paragraphs, covering a squabble
between the Barretts' groomsman and the stable boy and a lament about
Lily having gone off to Switzerland to attend her friend's wedding, thereby
"rendering herself unavailable for a second encounter" until late the following week. Newsworthy from the standpoint of human interest, but Erika
and Harrison were on the prowl for references to lost treasures.

"We have our first glimpse of why we were asked to pore through Barrett's
journal and papers," Harrison commented before reading further. "Do you
suppose there's a collection of artifacts hidden somewhere?"

"Artworks," Erika corrected. "We don't classify our ancient Greek
sculptures of the gods as artifacts. Why not give African works the same
respect?"

"Yes. Point taken."

She smiled. "Lesson over. To your question, yes, I think it's possible there's
a hidden cache of artworks somewhere, but so far it's only wishful thinking
on our part. Andrew may never have carried out his plan. Or, during his
lifetime may have returned whatever treasures he collected. Or they were
sold privately, auctioned off or stolen. I'm sure there are other possible
scenarios."

"If there are, I know you'll come up with them."

"Don't make fun of me."

"I'm not making fun of you. I'm admiring you."

"That's better."

As they were about to return their attention to the journal, Harrison's cell
phone beeped from his desktop. He carefully laid the journal on the coffee
table before bolting to his desk. "Must be Gretchen's email alert, a little
earlier than expected," he said, grabbing the device. "It is," he confirmed,
after tapping the email prompt. He was expecting the worst—whatever *that*
might be.

Erika rose from the couch to join him. From the way his shoulders relaxed as he scanned the email, she knew the news was not dire. "What's happening?"

"This is an invitation to a Zoom meeting," Harrison replied, smiling. "'To swap news,' she says. I can't believe it. She was totally averse to this sort of thing. Gretchen must have set it up for her."

"When's it scheduled for?"

"Right now. I'm going to go to the link on my desktop computer." He started moving his desk chairs alongside each other and froze.

Erika understood. She, too, was struck by the memory of their last Zoom meeting's seating arrangement. "Let's go back to the couch. We can put your laptop on the coffee table, on top of a couple of books. It'll work fine."

When they were properly settled, Harrison clicked into the meeting. An enlarged segment of a cheek appeared on the screen. Harrison recognized the rose tattoo.

"*Bonjour,* Gretchen," he said. "Madame D?" he called, as if she might be hiding under the rug. "Are you there?"

"I'm here, yes!" came the disembodied voice of Madame D. "*Merci,* Gretchen. *J'ai ça! A bientôt!*

The cheek was withdrawn, replaced by what Harrison assumed to be Madame D's upper brow and neat fringe of gray hair. "You've cut your bangs," Harrison remarked. "Very flattering, Madame D—Denise," he corrected, remembering her stipulation—"but that's all we can see of you!"

Madame D fiddled with the lid of her—or Gretchen's—laptop. "Ah, yes, there's my image. Oh, dear. I worked on myself for an hour, and this was the best I could do?" She smiled, amused by the ludicrous gravity of it all.

"You look lovely," Erika assured her, and indeed she did. Sitting straight-backed in her wheelchair—Erika could see the cane-style handlebars at either shoulder—Madame D looked quite regal in her black ruffle-neck blouse and draped shawl. She had fine features, chiseled cheeks, and a bright smile revealing even teeth gently worn to opalescence.

"Thank you, my dear. I suppose I'm not quite 'sans everything,' as the bard observed, but I dare say I'm getting there." She leaned forward, filling the screen with a benignly stern countenance. "You know, I'm a little angry with you people."

"That's comforting," Harrison said. "From Gretchen's tone, I thought it might be something more serious."

"How delicate of you, Harry. No, I'm not at death's door, only at his front stoop. Gretchen's suffering through another one of her nasty break-ups, which explains her mood. Poor girl is drawn to control freaks. Her men are all the same. One person, different hat sizes. No, I'm a little angry, hurt, more truthfully, at you for promising to visit me with your new baby, who by now must be—"

"Wait, Madame D!" Erika cut in. "I'm the one—"

"Denise."

"What?"

"Call me Denise."

"Yes—of course! Well, Denise, I'm the one to blame for delaying our trip to Paris. I realize I'm being overly cautious, but I'm just not ready to fly with Lucas. I hope you understand."

"I do, and I'm sorry to have scolded."

"No, no, you didn't scold and—ah, I have an idea!"

"Hold your seats," Harrison grinningly advised.

Erika squinted a warning shot at him. "Denise, do you feel up to visiting *us?*"

"What a great idea," Harrison declared, wryness vaporized. "We'll charter a flight, hire a limo to take you everywhere you need to be. We'll make the trip so comfortable you won't know you've left the ground until you land!"

"Bring an escort to make the trip as easy as possible for you," Erika suggested, glancing at Harrison for his inevitable sign of approval, which he gave in the form of an arm- around-the-waist body squeeze. "Anyone—a friend, relative...Gretchen? How about it?"

"Thank you, my dears, but I couldn't *possibly* impose on your hospitality in..."

"Not *possibly*, Denise. *Absolutely!*" Erika replied emphatically. "In fact, *we* will be a little angry, hurt even, if you turn *us* down." She consulted Harrison.

"Won't we, darling?"

"We will, indeed."

"Well, I must say," Madame D said crisply, the elevated pitch of her voice betraying her emotion, "Your offer is almost too much to bear." With a palm pressed to her chest, she added, "You must give me time to digest it."

"We will, if you promise to take it seriously," Erika allowed, cocking her head against Harrison's to present a united front.

Madame D smiled, perhaps a bit longingly, at the portrait of companionship displayed before her. "Do you think I might say hello to your boy?" she asked softly. "Would it be convenient?"

"It would," Erika said, rising from the couch. "Lucas keeps late hours. We're trying to ease him out of his sleep-wake pattern, but right now he's a night owl." She bent back down so that her face would be visible to Madame D. "I'll be right back."

"Wonderful. Meanwhile, Harry will tell me what you two have been up to. Any mucking about in the world of art crime these days?"

"Where shall I begin?" Harrison asked, as Erika headed for the door.

"At the beginning. Tell me everything. You know you can't hold anything back from me."

How true. Madame D exerted the same irresistible power over him as his grandmother had. Two wise old women for whom he was, for all intents and purposes, genetically inclined to both please and protect. He began by explaining the mission of the fateful Zoom meeting, segueing into a watered-down account of Timothy Thorpe's murder. She insisted he spare her no details, and he was just doubling back to spill the redacted material when Erika returned with Lucas, asleep in her arms.

"He's sleeping," Harrison mouthed to Madame D, putting a finger to his lips.

Erika carefully sat down on the couch, angling the pajama-ed boy so that Madame D could have a good look. "He's made a liar of me," she said, her voice just above a whisper. "First time he's asleep at this hour."

Madame D steepled her hands as if in prayer. *"Mon Dieu, il est si beau,"* she murmured.

Harrison kissed Lucas on his cheek and the tot moved his lips as if he was sucking on a nipple or a hard candy and wriggled in Erika's arms. Erika raised his limp little hand and made a tiny gesture of bye-bye at the screen. Madame D replied in kind and blew him a kiss for good measure. Erika raised a finger and mouthed "one minute," before rising from the couch. Silence prevailed until she was out the door.

When safe to resume talking in a normal voice, Madame D could only focus on her meeting with Lucas. No matter how brief, wordless, remote, it was a one-of-a-kind experience for her. "This is the closest I've been to feeling like a grandmother, she said with a sigh. "*Great*-grandmother, more accurately. Harry, I seem to remember you and Erika promising me great-godmother status. Does the promise still stand?"

"A done deed!" He sat forward, shoving his grinning face at her. "*Now* do you feel compelled to come for a proper visit?"

Madame D laughed. "Don't brow-beat me, Harry, but yes, I believe it does tip the balance."

They were still nose-to-nose when Erika walked in on them. "I can't leave you two alone for a minute," she joked, plopping down beside Harrison. "What were you cooking up?"

"Our rendezvous in Manhattan," Madame D replied evenly.

"Do you mean—really?" Erika asked, hoping her delight wasn't premature.

"Really," Madame D confirmed, unable to keep a straight face. "My great-godson, Lucas, talked me into it." After a beat, she folded her hands in her lap in a decisive manner. "Alright, my dears, before I become overly maudlin, let's get back to what we were discussing. Harry was describing a murder that had taken place during a Zoom meeting you had attended. You must go on with the story. Either of you. Speak."

They obliged, each contributing to the narrative. They had just begun to introduce Andrew Barrett's journal into the sequence of events when Madame D cut them off.

"I'm going to help you," she stated, matter-of-factly.

An explanation was in order.

"You mentioned Pierre Jolet," Madame D opened. "I've met the man. His grandfather was a regular customer at my family's antique prints and maps establishment, that is, before hard times forced my parents to transform it into its present persona, a high-end tattoo parlor."

Harrison remembered it well. *"Rouge Tatouage,"* he recited. "You knew Jolet's grandfather?"

"No. At least I don't recall being introduced. I know of his patronage only from his grandson, Pierre, who stopped by my parlor about a year ago, looking to have the prints he'd inherited from his grandfather reappraised. He thought he'd come to the wrong address, seeing the shop's marque, but we ended up having a lovely chat and exchanging cards, and I referred him to a gentleman who could help him with the reappraisal. He admired the beautiful photographs of tattoos on my showroom walls—as you yourself did, Harry—and thought that he might come back for one himself. He never did."

Their concerted response *And...?* hung in the air before Harrison spoke. "We're on tenterhooks, Denise. How do you propose to help?"

"Patience, Harry. You said that Pierre Jolet made a curious statement about the tragic Zoom incident hitting too close to home, his parting remark something like 'If you only knew,' followed by, it appeared from your recitation, a rather pregnant ellipsis."

"Exactly like," Erika threw in. "His exact words."

Madame D nodded. "Words you suspect he won't be inclined to explain to any of the interrogators. Words which may throw some light on the case."

"Yes," Harrison answered. "And you think you can cajole this man, barely an acquaintance, into telling all?"

"Spilling the beans. Yes."

"Not everyone is as susceptible to your charms as I am, you know."

"True, but the odds are in my favor."

"I've no doubt you're right," Erika commented, with a chuckle of admiration, but Jolet is stationed at the French Institute's branch in Portugal. You're not thinking of tracking him down in Portugal, are you?"

"Not at all. He owns a residence here in Paris, where he often sojourns. I will reach him either here or at his number in Portugal. In any case, I will persuade him to visit me at my shop."

Erika was impressed. "How do you plan to do that, Denise?"

"Not all coercion is based on pheromones, my dear. Trust me. I still have a trick or two up my sleeve."

"I bet you do. I look forward to hearing all about your encounter. I'm also excited about your visit. When do you plan to come to New York?"

"If you'll allow me, I'd like to wrap up the Pierre Jolet mystery before I commit to a date."

"That's great. I do love your confidence, Denise."

"Thank you. It requires maintenance. One must keep up the guise."

The Zoom meeting was essentially over. Madame D, at a loss when it came to signing off, called for assistance. "Gretchen, *viens ici!*" Afterward, managing to get in a piping "*Au revoir, mes chéris!*" as Gretchen zeroed in for the kill.

"It was very generous of you to make that offer to Denise," Harrison said, in all earnestness, after the meeting had been adjourned.

"My generosity is all that surprising?" Erika teased.

"Not at all." Still serious. "Your kindness is impetuous is what I'm thinking. It's refreshing."

"Let's not overdo it," she said, feeling her cheeks redden. "Now, shall we go back to Andrew Barrett's journal or call it a day? You've got an early class tomorrow, and I've got to finish editing an *Art News* article due at the printer at ten a.m."

He waited a minute before answering, gazing at her with that look of his that made her go limp. "What would I do without you?" he asked quietly.

"Only you could pull that off."

"What?"

"Make a timeworn phrase sound like the opening of a sonnet," she said, her dreamy smile proving she'd bought it.

Chapter Four

Planting themselves on the couch in Harrison's den, the Wheatleys were about to take up their study of Andrew Barrett's journal from where they'd left off the evening before, when Harrison's cell phone signaled a call from Greg Smith. Harrison greeted him and advised that they were on speakerphone.

"Sorry, blokes," Greg began, right off the bat acknowledging his tardiness. "I was on my honeymoon and forbidden the use of my cell phone. It was a compromise."

"Between that and what?" Erika asked.

"My demise. As it is, Marcia's been fed up, for years with my shuttling back and forth between the Art Register's offices in London and New York. I won't give that up, so I decided I could at least give up my phone for a few days. Make her happy. But she's at me constantly about my work schedule, now more than ever."

"By the way, congratulations," Harrison wedged into the conversation, figuring it was as good a time as any. "I didn't know you were engaged." He checked with Erika with a raised brow.

"Me neither," she said, although she had heard a similar plaint from Greg about his off-and-on partner some time ago, while Harrison was in Paris working on their last case. The exchange had been uncomfortable, and she had no intention of bringing it up now.

"It was a whirlwind affair," Greg said. We flew to Hawaii and were married at the chapel at the Grand Wailea Hotel. We had two witnesses, a florist, and a masseuse. No time for pre-nuptial jitters until after the fact. I was a good boy, and when we got back to London my cell phone was returned and I was able to make inquiries into the incident at the British Museum. And here I am, just arrived in New York and at your service. We can discuss matters over the phone, but I'd love to hang out with you for a bit. I'm thinking of The-Hole-In-The-Wall. Their website says they're open until eleven-thirty. How about it?"

It was close to 9:00 p.m. "What do you think?" Harrison asked Erika. "Too late?"

"No, I'm good. It'll be nice to get together, and I'm up for a walk. We can be there by nine-twenty; nine-fifteen in sneakers. You?"

"Perfect."

* * *

The-Hole-In-The-Wall was Harrison's old haunt, where he would spend hours at a time grading papers in a corner banquette. Since his change in lifestyle, he and Erika stopped by on occasion for drinks and appetizers, but Josh, his long-time waiter, remained bonded to the image of the lone professor in the corner booth. The wife complemented but did not change the object of his loyalty. After greetings were exchanged with Maude, the ever-present coat-check matron, Harrison and Erika were installed in Harrison's dedicated corner banquette. Erika supposed that if other patrons had been occupying the banquette, Josh would have evicted them on the spot.

Greg appeared in a crew-neck shirt and tight-fitting blazer five minutes later, looking like a bronzed Olympian. Hard to feel sorry for the beleaguered groom. "Hello, there!" he declared, leaning across the marble-top table to give each of them a token hug before planting himself in the wrought-iron chair opposite their banquette. He allowed them to reply in kind, then hailed Josh, waiting in the wings. "What are we drinking? Beer for me," he directed at the waiter. "Say, I remember you—Jack, is it?"

"Josh, sir."

"Well, Josh, I'll have a dark beer, your finest. I'll leave it up to you."

Erika ordered a glass of wine—the house white—and Harrison, a Bud Light.

Josh passed out the menus and went to fetch their drinks.

"I love this place," Greg said, glancing at the menu. "Best chicken quesadillas, as I recall." He looked up. "It's where you and I first met, Erika, remember? The Cuban affair?"

Harrison smiled. "Sounds a bit racy, if I hadn't been there myself."

"Bad luck for me," Greg returned, with a laugh.

Hard to miss, Greg was in a manic mood, Erika thought. Same as when he was confiding his relationship problems to her. She hoped the beer would help tone it down. "So, what have you got for us, Greg?" she asked, diving right in.

"Give it a minute, let's order first," Greg replied, peeved almost. "I'm famished. First class fare was inedible this trip."

Not until the second round of chicken and vegetable appetizers had been brought to the table and Greg had chugalugged his second glass of exotic beer, did his characteristically staid persona regain its foothold. "That's better," he stated, sliding his glass away from him.

"Would you care for another, sir?" Josh asked, stepping in.

"No, thanks, Josh."

"Yes, sir." Directing his focus solely on Harrison, "Refills for you, Doc? Ma'am?"

With no takers for food or drink, Josh cleared the empty plates and glasses and withdrew. He would not be disturbing them until closing time—or later, if only it were up to him.

Greg scanned the room. The only other patrons in the establishment were a couple of young lovers huddled in the corner farthest from them. "Now then," he announced. He held open his suit jacket and plucked a couple of papers folded lengthwise from its inner pocket. "My gleanings," he said, unfolding the stapled papers on the tabletop. "Let me begin by saying I've got an excellent working relationship with the trustees at The British Museum. Most recently, I filled in the provenance gaps for several of their works, Renoir's *The Boating Party* for one. They had no problem putting me in touch with the detective in charge of the homicide investigation, Clive Hogarty. My lord, what a dreadful event to witness as a captive audience! It must have been very difficult for you to watch, no less have the presence of mind to record!"

Erika shifted in her seat. "Difficult, but better than being absolutely helpless. Press the camera icon, focus, get the right angle, you know, something to *do*." She felt Harrison's hand on her knee, squeezing it. "You agree, sweetheart?" *Don't take your hand away.*

"Yes, absolutely. I hadn't thought of that." His hand stayed where it was.

"So," Greg said, smoothing out the papers, "I had a talk with Detective Hogarty. He was remarkably forthcoming. I suppose I came on good recommendation." He produced a modest smile in keeping with the occasion. "I have a list here of all the folks they intend to interview, or already have. A work in progress, of course, but I'll get to that. Have they reached out to you?"

"Only to acknowledge they've received our recordings," Harrison said. "We haven't been questioned—well, except for right afterwards, on Zoom."

"They might not see the need. Hogarty had an in-depth conversation with the host of the Zoom meeting, Ikemar"—he glanced at his notes—"Umar. Umar gave him a rundown on the attendees, which may have satisfied him for the time being."

"Ah, yes," Harrison said, riding over Greg's last words. "Ike texted me yesterday while I was at a faculty meeting."

Erika sat up. "Really?"

"I was focusing on the worrisome call from Gretchen. It slipped my mind."

"Worrisome call?" Greg asked. "Never mind, none of my business. Hope it's resolved." He stretched his legs, his left foot accidentally coming into contact with Erika's, where he allowed it to remain. "Was the text from Ike—Ikemar, I assume—about one of the attendees, namely"...he checked his notes...

"Pierre Jolet," Harrison finished for him, as Erika's foot took shelter behind his left heel. Turning to her, he said, "Ike wanted to know if we had any idea what Jolet meant by that remark of his. I texted him no, we were wondering about it ourselves.'"

"'This, hits too close to home,'" Erika quoted. "'If only you knew.'"

"That's it," Greg declared, looking up from his notes. "Apparently Ikemar posed his question to all attendees, including Monsieur Jolet himself. No go. Hogarty fared no better, and Jolet was of course under no obligation to bare all."

"There's someone he might open up to," Erika said.

"You have someone in mind?" Greg asked.

The couple clued him in on their conversation with Madame D and swore him to secrecy, at least until Madame D decided to go public with the results of her tête-à-tête with Jolet, that is, if it ever came to pass.

Greg agreed to keep it under his *"chapeau,"* joking, in an aside, about Jolet's shuttling back and forth between Portugal and France. "I hope his wife is more understanding than mine," he said, punctuating the remark with a sardonic chuckle. "But seriously, Jolet's excuse for beating a hasty retreat is one of the few nuggets that stand out thus far."

"Another being...?" Harrison prompted.

"The custodial worker who performed CPR on the victim remembered seeing someone heading for the staircase as he himself was on his way to Thorpe's office."

"Anything remarkable about the person's appearance?"

Greg shrugged. "Wearing a black suit, black T-shirt. When they passed in the hallway the individual's head was lowered, his shoulder-length mane making it hard to get a good look at his face. Ergo sex and race undetermined.

"Did this person seem to be in a hurry?" Erika asked.

"Detective Hogarty didn't give me a blow-by-blow account of all that transpired. In any event, the chap—or lass—may have left the museum before the guards received their orders to seal off the exits and detain all museum visitors and staff members intending to leave. As you must know, the museum closes at five p.m. The murder took place around four-twenty or so and—"

"Four-twenty-four," Erika interjected. "Eleven-twenty-four a.m. in New

York."

Greg raised a brow, impressed. "Yes, well the exits weren't blocked until about four-forty"—he smiled—"or so. Giving this individual, who may be innocent as hell, time to amble out the door during the time lag. Of course, the museum's nooks and crannies were thoroughly searched, and surveillance camera records are being scanned to detect anyone and anything amiss. In the meantime, I've listed the names of all the individuals contacted or to be contacted by Hogarty, along with a word or two on each."

"All of them?" Harrison asked. "Including the young man with the backpack—as well as the guards themselves?"

"Let's not forget the night watchman and the engineer repairing the ventilation system. Take it from me, the list to date is complete." He placed the stapled papers between Harrison and Erika. "I've got copies. Now be discreet. For your eyes only."

"That's understood," Harrison said.

"There are some interesting data on individuals here," Erika said, scrutinizing the top page. "Thanks, Greg."

"No problem. There are additional notes on the sheets below. You'll share them with no one."

"We *got* it, Greg," Harrison assured him, as Erika flipped to the second page.

"What's this?" she asked, taken aback by the first line.

"What I was about to get to." Greg rested his elbows on the tabletop and leaned forward. Before continuing, he checked out the couple at the other end of the room. The young lovers seemed in no rush to leave their cozy cul de sac. "We should have met in private. Choosing to come here was selfish of me."

"No worries, we can't be heard," Harrison replied off-handedly, staring down at the paper. "What's going on?" he asked, his voice a husky whisper. "'Anonymous call to *The Guardian* re UDC affiliation'?"

"Keep it down," Greg cautioned, leaning in still farther. "The Movement for Unity, Dignity, and Courage. Founded in 2014 by the activist Emery Mwazulu Diyabanza of the Domestic Republic of the Congo." He waited for a nod of recognition. Receiving none, he continued. "Its primary goal, the return of art stolen from Africa during the colonial era. A couple of years ago, Emery was fined for removing a funeral pole from the Quai Branly Museum of Non-European Art in Paris. He never meant to steal it, he said. His action was simply meant to draw attention to the longstanding crime against the African people. Gestures of this nature have been made throughout the world by members of the group. These events have never started or ended in violence."

Erika, too close for comfort to Greg, tilted out of nose-to-nose range. "From your notes, it looks like *The Guardian* received an anonymous call from an individual claiming to be a member of the UDC," she stated in hushed tones to avoid rebuke. "And, in its name, took credit for the murder of Timothy Thorpe. That correct?"

"Yes. The call was untraceable, the voice electronically modified. The murder was a protest against what the caller claimed to be a series of empty promises made to pacify Africa's defrauded nations. Tim Thorpe was made an example of this hypocrisy and his murder was a call to arms."

"I mean, a violent crime committed by a member of a non-violent organization?"

"Out of character, yes. The editor contacted the British Museum immediately and was persuaded not to leak the story. Not only because it was premature, but because it would produce a backlash regarding the return of Africa's heritage, affecting the general public as well as the bigwigs involved in the actual negotiations."

"Are they assuming *The Guardian* is the only newspaper or news source out there?" Harrison asked.

"Not at all. They're hoping there'll be mitigating circumstances by the time the item hits the newsstands. Or airwaves."

Erika scanned Greg's notes. "I don't see the name of any UDC member the detective's planning to interview. You said it was a complete list."

"You're certainly holding me to task, Erika. Reminds me of home. Hogarty hadn't yet specified the UDC member he plans to interview."

"But he definitely will?" she persisted.

"Of course."

"And he'll keep you in his loop?"

Greg nodded. "And I'll keep you in mine."

Harrison sat back. "Meanwhile, what's the story on physical evidence? Any fingerprints, hair fibers, I don't know, cigarette butts, to speak of?"

"Nothing noteworthy. Fingerprints from Thorpe, of course. One of the guards, the student with the backpack—his prints on the door—the custodial chap."

Erika dug for a pen in her tote bag. On the top sheet, she jotted down this latest information. "Has the Medical Examiner completed the autopsy?" she asked, pen poised. "I assume the cause of death was asphyxiation."

"No surprises there," Greg confirmed. "Completed, with no correlating factors," he added.

From the far corner of the room came the sound of chairs scraping the floor as the young couple rose from their table. Greg stiffened.

Harrison gave him a quizzical look. "What's up? They're leaving."

"Leaving's not what worries me. What worries me is that they've been here all along."

Greg's agitation is returning, Erika thought. Beer's calming effect wearing off. "Maybe we should get going ourselves," she suggested in no uncertain terms. "You've had a long day—a seven-hour flight, was it? It was generous of you to give us this time."

"My pleasure, as always," Greg said, glancing at his watch. "But I did tell Marcia I'd give her a buzz, hell, a half-hour ago." He looked up at them, from one to the other, beseeching almost.

Greg's most vulnerable moment was also his most endearing, Erika decided. Harrison's smile indicated he was of the same mind. She laid her hand on Harrison's, the one that had not strayed from her knee. He turned his hand under hers so that they met palm to palm. Their fingers knit just as he was raising his free hand to beckon Josh, waiting in the wings, for the check.

Chapter Five

The man with a face easily forgotten took his seat on the train out of Waterloo Station, South London. If the posted time was accurate, he would arrive at Effingham Junction Station in fifty-six minutes, at exactly 1:34 a.m., not that accuracy mattered. He slipped the duffle bag's strap from his shoulder and held the bag close to his body, as if it were a child given to wandering off. He could feel the corner of the sledgehammer through the sailcloth.

A young woman was sitting diagonally opposite, purposely avoiding eye contact, which was just fine with him, under the circumstances. Well, if he was going to be perfectly honest with himself, he disliked her for her natural beauty; no sign of the plastic surgeon's heavy hand on that perfectly sculpted mug. He pictured her in forty years, wrinkled and wattle-necked, and smiled to himself at the thought of it. Bitch gave him a queasy look; got up and changed her seat. Good riddance, hag.

Once the obstruction was out of the way, he felt at leisure to lay bare his thoughts, no one looking over his shoulder, spying on him. Don't laugh, he reproached the world at large. You never know who's got the power of ESP. If a dog can anticipate a child's epileptic fit, who's to say I'm wrong?

He wondered now why had it taken such an effort to decide which of his plans to set in motion. Walking off with an artifact or two from Franks House, the British Museum's storage facility in East London, may have given him his political statement, but at what cost? The place was crawling with workers in lab coats and masks—conservators, project managers, photographers, interns, auditors, volunteers—the lot of them engaged in the end goal of moving 200,000 objects from the museum's collection of Africa, Oceania, and the Americas to its nearly spanking new World Conservation and Exhibition Centre. True, it would not have been an insurmountable task, entering the quiet road where the quaint redbrick warehouse lay and unobtrusively blending into the workforce, but *then* what? Would he have been forced to shoot his way out of the place at the risk of being gunned down himself? How sordid and at the same time mundane to mow down an uncalculated number of individuals, only to find himself a mere casualty sprawled among them. Hell no, he was neither a loony terrorist nor a crack-head martyr. The plan in place was the more sensible course, no question about it.

It was restful, hearing below his thoughts the rhythmic phrase of train wheels clacking against the tracks in lulling repetition. His calmness surprised him a little, given what lay ahead. His scenario had been well choreographed, but only on an imagined stage with players moving about under his ironclad direction. In real life, even the most meticulous plan is apt to be disrupted by unforeseen circumstances. He knew that it was exactly 1.6 miles from Effingham Junction Station to the mansion on Ockham Lane in Cobham, Surrey, but was he certain that he would not be accosted by a madman or struck by lightning on his walk to the place?

If he allowed his thoughts to ramble on in this manner, his nerves would start acting up. He must lean into the physical moment and move with it into his destiny. He looked out the window past his reflection and focused on the indifferent stars.

Chapter Six

"I'm calling to inform you that Monsieur Jolet and I have set a date," Madame D announced, three days after her debut Zoom meeting with the Wheatleys. They were speaking on the phone, so her staged smugness could be detected only by the sound of her voice. "You should not have doubted my prowess," she added, dropping the act.

"I'm impressed," Erika said, aiming her voice at Harrison's cell phone sitting on the coffee table. "You catch him in Paris?" She and Harrison were seated alongside each other on the couch in his study, where they'd been having another go at the Andrew Barnett material. Hearing the exchange on speakerphone, Harrison was smiling, shaking his head in amazement.

"No," Madame D replied. "I caught Monsieur Jolet in Portugal. He's making a special trip to Paris to meet me on Monday, two days from now.

"I admire your chutzpah," Harrison declared. "How did you woo him?"

"I'm not giving away any secrets at this time. I realize keeping you on tenterhooks is giving me a good bit of sadistic pleasure. Interesting how one may discover, this far on in life, one's latent tendencies."

The remark drew a chuckle from all three before Erika introduced a word of caution. "Remember, Denise, you are not to put yourself in any kind of jeopardy at this meeting."

Simultaneously Harrison demanded, "You must meet the man in a public place!"

Madame D's laugh returned full force. "Don't worry," she assured them, after catching her breath, "I won't be flaunting my décolletage for the occasion. I, and for that matter, the gentleman in question, will be perfectly safe!"

The Wheatleys were amused but needed to hear that Madame D was not going to put Pierre Jolet in a position where he might feel trapped or threatened in any way.

Seeing how deadly serious they were, she told them what they wanted to hear.

The call ended on a high note, with Madame D reiterating her intention to visit the Wheatleys sometime during the summer.

Their minds relatively at ease, Erika and Harrison got back to the business at hand: reviewing Andrew Barrett's journal and loose papers for leads on his hypothetical treasure trove. Among other news, they'd been privy to Andrew's courtship with Lily (spoiler alert: a pressed flower taped to the wedding invitation tucked among the papers); his honorable separation from Queen Victoria's military service to pursue a private medical practice, much of which was to be dedicated to *pro bono publico* care to those in need; his search for suitable quarters for his practice and details on its furnishings. By far the most promising entries they'd come across had been the ones prefaced: "*8 May 1897, and so it begins*" and "*10 May 1897, progress.*" The most tantalizing entry, surely the last: "*17 August 1897, Eureka!*" which terminated abruptly, and a tease if ever there was one. Between May 10 and August 17 Andrew had logged in much less frequently, but when he did put pen to paper, he expounded in detail. Erika and Harrison had printed copies of the pages containing passages that piqued their interest and rifled through the loose documents in search of supplemental information. Erika suggested they reread the passages before strategizing further.

8 May 1897, and so it begins

Up to now, I have been a passive rather than an acquisitive lover of art, knowing nothing beyond the literal definitions of art dealers, art galleries, and art auctions. The walls of our home bear a number of passed-down somber oil paintings, mostly of overripe fruit and forgotten uncles, but I doubt that either Mother or Father knows from whom they were purchased or by whom commissioned. In any event, I had no intention of arousing their curiosity by asking them questions related to the art trade.

As I knew from the start, in regard to my cause, Lily would be my best ally, both in temperament and incentive. How fortuitous that she should also turn out to be my mentor! Who knows how many blind alleys I might have been merrily led down without her gentle, but firm guidance.

The Worthingtons, unlike my family, have acquired their art collection by purchasing it. Most of their paintings are by a group of contemporary artists who call themselves the pre-Raphaelite Brothers, as they endeavor to bring back the style of the Italians practicing their craft in the 15th century: the Quattrocento, as my learned guide informs me. Of course, my favorite is a commissioned portrait of Lily by the renowned Edward Burne-Jones. It is a beautifully detailed fantasy, a woodsy scene saturated with color and romance. Lily is gracefully reclined beneath a tree, her blue skirt billowing around her, accenting her slender waist. A small bird is perched upon her index finger, and she is scrutinizing it as if it, not she, were the most precious creature on earth.

The Worthington collection is comprised of paintings and statuary purchased solely from The Italian Gallery on Bond Street. Although the gallery trades predominantly in Italian art, Lily assures me that they acquire works from all over the world. Apparently, there are galleries in town with all sorts of stylish names: The Belgian Gallery, The Flemish Gallery, The Continental Gallery, all imitating their progenitor, Belgian-born Ernest Gambart's, The French Gallery, which debuted in London at 120 Pall Mall some forty years ago. "Don't be fooled by their cosmopolitan airs," Lily advises. "They're not quite as niche as they purport to be. We'll be as likely to come upon an African art object at The Italian Gallery as anywhere else."

I have discovered that Lily's knowledge of the art world is broader than I had dared hope. Not only is she familiar with the galleries and auction houses about town, but she has friends who work in these establishments and is allied with struggling young artists who strive to find patronage through them. My darling is quite the bohemian, it seems, and not in the pejorative sense. She is by no means a poseur. She is an explorer.

Tomorrow morning, as close to the crack of dawn as possible, she will have us begin our search for looted African art by, of all things, researching the archives of The London Gazette, the United Kingdom's official public record for over two hundred years. Among the current newsworthy events, it publishes notices of art auctions, wills, accreditations, as well as bankruptcies in all their revealing (one might say lurid) details. Estate sales, in which the insolvent parties' furniture and art works are auctioned off to pay their debts, often follow the court hearings, and Lily believes that if we're lucky, African treasures may be included in one or two such auctions on the docket. I remark that it is unlikely we will come across the spoils of so recent an event as the Punitive Expedition. "Do you really think your African exploit was a singular event, Andy?" Lily asks, direct as ever. I answer that although my own experience was revelatory, of course I know of similar acts of aggression, and furthermore that such behavior was not monopolized by the British. For good measure, I add that I intend to restore whatever stolen objects I come across to wherever in Africa they originated. Lily thinks she has offended me and with the dearest look of contrition, touches her lips to mine. I have not been offended, but happily accept her apology.

Tomorrow afternoon, unless we chance upon an estate auction that takes precedence, Lily and I will be searching the London galleries and auction houses for stolen treasures in need of my guardianship.

Before going on, Erika flipped to a clean page in her legal pad and added a few lines of inquiry to those she'd made on an earlier read-through.

Harrison gave her an impish glance. "You've written more about Barrett than Barrett himself, and he's pretty darn verbose."

"What can I do? One thing leads to another."

"You want to talk?"

"Not yet." She returned her attention to the printouts.

10 May 1897, progress

Yesterday I had no time for a journal entry. I record yesterday's events herewith.

In the morning Lily and I visited the Gazette office and searched for postings of upcoming auctions and sales. We came across several scheduled for the weeks to come (an auction scheduled for 21 May at Goupil and Cie particularly struck our fancy), and I entered all events in my notebook for future reference. Finding none scheduled for that very day, however, we decided to try another approach, that is, to study the records of recent bankruptcies and seek inspiration there. Lily, it turns out, is as resolute as I in this undertaking.

After painstakingly recording the details of the last ten bankruptcy notices, we reviewed them to see which, if any, we might reasonably look into at once. We agreed to make inquiries about the two most feasible. These debtors' addresses were located nearby, in adjacent counties (ultra- posh) just outside London, and their cases were being handled by the same solicitor, one Michael Henry Ewing, whose office was a five-minute walk from the Gazette office. Without so much as giving fair warning, we boldly marched into Mr. Ewing's office. At first, he was reluctant to hear us out, but Lily's wiles are irresistible, and to boot, he was impressed by her lineage. "An admirable barrister, your father, the Honorable Samuel Worthington," he offered with a little bow, as if Lily were the praiseworthy man himself. "How can I help you?"

We told him a revised version of the truth, planned in advance, since I trust no one but Lily with my story. "I am a collector of antiques and vintage furniture," I said. "Are the contents of either of these estates up for sale?" With a polite nod in my companion's direction, I added, "Lillian, my good friend and advisor in such matters, has suggested you may be kind enough to provide me a look-about." Mr. Ewing advised that I wait for the estate auctions, both to occur within weeks. I countered with the lie that I will be leaving the country for an extended period of time. As I prepared to expand on my fabrication, he yielded. "I will see what can be arranged," he said.

In the end, the three of us traveled by hansom cab to first one, then the other of the two properties in foreclosure. The first occupant would not allow us to step foot inside the domain of which he was shortly to be relieved. Understandable. The second, one Daniel Edgerton, was wistfully agreeable, giving us a tour of his transitory world as if in a dream, his wife hanging on to his arm for dear life, as if she feared we might abscond with him along with his belongings.

I was under no illusions about finding an African treasure among the cabinets of figurines and miniature ships-in-bottles, but much to my surprise (Lily expressed hers with a tiny gasp converted to a delicate cough) as we were being led down a second-floor hallway and Mr. Edgerton off-handedly remarked that he had some years ago acquired at auction a group of artifacts from the West African Kingdom of Dahomey. The objects, he said, had been "procured" ("procured," indeed!) by the French in 1892, at the close of their "successful encounter" with the Dahomeans. "My wife did not much care for the pieces," he said, his wife vouching for his honesty with an affirmative nod, "but I saw them as ethnological specimens that would increase in value with the passage of time." I smiled pleasantly through clenched teeth as we came to the door of what our host introduced as "the ancillary drawing room containing my tribal ensemble." When I beheld the three wooden statues, each about a foot tall, standing atop a low bookcase, I cocked my head in a play of mild curiosity as my heart raced.

"The half-man-half-shark is in the likeness of King Béhanzin, whom the French subdued," Mr. Edgerton informed us. "I'm not sure about the half-man-half-bird or - lion hybrids," he added. "I've been meaning to have the figures analyzed by the British Museum, but unforeseen circumstances..." Here he glanced at his solicitor. "The objects on the two bookshelves are altarpieces honoring the dead," he gallantly went on. "They're made of iron and strips of wood. If you look closely, you'll notice the traces of pigment."

"Very interesting," I said, pretending I was just warming up to the exhibit. "I don't own anything remotely like these objects."

Lily touched my arm. "Perhaps this would be a good time to start," she cleverly suggested. Turning to Edgerton, she asked, "Did you purchase these items in France?"

Edgerton shook his head. "At the London branch of the French auction house, Goupil and Cie," he replied, suddenly restless. "Are you interested in buying the collection?" he directed at me. "Understand, I will not entertain the idea of selling any of the objects singly, and my asking price will be firm."

Needless to say, I was eager to strike a bargain, but pretended to give the matter some consideration before doing so. I also expressed interest in purchasing two upholstered chairs and a small table to deflect attention from my preoccupation, and arrangements were ultimately made for payment of all items as well as for their transport to my home in Hertfordshire.

After Lily and I were back on our own in London, we enjoyed a celebratory high tea.

No sooner had I returned home than I was summoned back to the East End to attend to a young boy suffering from dysentery, all too common in this part of London. I sanitized the environment as best I could and instructed the poor child's parents how to make certain that all food is thoroughly cooked, water purified by boiling, and above all that, any and all ingested matter remain uncontaminated by human waste. I advised that for the next twenty-four hours the child be kept on a liquid diet consisting mainly of water and perhaps a bit of milk. and before leaving I administered a small amount of castor oil. The boy's temperature was somewhat high but stabilized, and he was alert and coherent. I have hopes that if the parents are vigilant, the illness will run its course and their child will recover. I promised to revisit the family in two days' time. As I was about to leave, the father reached into his pocket, but I placed my hand on his forearm to deter him from further action. To have accepted compensation from him would have been nothing short of reprehensible.

And so ended May 9.

Today was momentous. Early this morning I hired a carriage from a London moving company to collect my purchases. The carriage was to arrive at the Edgerton estate this afternoon. To prepare for the occasion, I dropped by Parsons, Thomson and Company when its doors opened and had cheques issued to both Daniel Edgerton and the moving company. Afterwards, I purchased sufficient packing materials for the move and betook myself to the Edgerton residence, where I wrapped my African treasures to protect them both from the jarring nature of their carriage ride and the prying eyes of my dear parents.

Of course, I accompanied my precious cargo on their journey. They are now locked away in my wardrobe, along with their Benin companions, where they will remain until I find a more secure home for them.

The chairs and table served as a decoy for my parents' attention. I presented the items to them with some fanfare, claiming that I had seen them in an antique dealer's window and had decided that they would provide a most pleasing arrangement in the drawing room. Fortunately, they did not probe for details.

17 August 1897, Eureka!

At last, I have found proper quarters for my collection, and none too soon! After months of accruement, my treasure trove has completely displaced the contents of my room's storage space. Socks and undershirts lie flattened beneath my mattress, dress shirts and ascots are crammed in my narrow linen closet. Suits, coats, hats, footwear, in short, the accoutrements of daily life that once boasted residence in either my wardrobe or armoire, are draped over a chair, reclined on a chaise lounge, stacked in a corner.

Since the day I returned from Africa, I have allowed no one, including the housekeeper, access to my room, and I have seen to it that I am the only individual in possession of the key to its door. My excuse is that I will soon be moving to my own apartment and must learn to take care of myself. The housekeeper thinks it is admirable of me. My parents, I suspect, fear I have acquired a mental quirk or two since my tenure in the army, and in fact, I have done everything in my power to nurture this belief.

My parents will be gone on a short holiday next week and at my insistence, they have given the housekeeper and the cook the time off as well. I will take advantage of this interlude by having my collection transported to its secure location. The necessary documents have been signed and notarized, the moving company alerted. Admittedly, despite their monopolization of my living quarters, I will miss having my treasures near at hand. ~~*Most important is*~~

Erika's coming upon the significant crossed-out words at the bottom of the page was as frustrating the second time around as it was on the first. Remembering the raw edge of the page that had been ripped out following that final entry, was equally disquieting. She was sure that Andrew had continued writing, then had thought better of it. "What was on that page?" she wondered aloud.

Harrison, who'd been waiting with clasped hands for her to complete her study, waited for her to answer her own question.

"I think Andrew must have specified the hiding place and then regretted having done so," she said. "What do you think?"

"I think you may be right, but of course we can't know for sure. What's equally puzzling is that he stopped writing at this point."

"Stopped writing in *this* journal," she qualified. "Who says there's no Book

Two?"

"A moot point if it's nowhere to be found."

"That goes without saying, but the fact that the loose documents included with the journal refer to things that occur after August 17, 1897, make me believe—*want* to believe—that their journal counterparts exist. Plus, why didn't he cross out 'Book One' from the journal's title if he'd decided to stop there?"

"He forgot?"

She shook her head. "The date of the journal's last entry is noted in its title. He would have known it was the final entry on that very day, or at some point afterward. That's when he added it to the title. If he had intended it to be the last of his recordings, he would have crossed out 'Book One' then and there. At least that's what I figure. Who knows?"

"No, you're right." He stroked her thigh. "As usual. It's the most logical conclusion."

She shrugged. "Sounds good, anyway." She placed the printouts on the coffee table and flipped back to the first sheet of her yellow pad. "Where do you want to start?"

He smiled. "Probably by booking a flight to London."

She smiled back. Clearly, they were on the same page. "I'm thinking the answers to most of my questions are buried in that city's archives, and I don't mean the ones on Google."

"You mean the ones in dusty bins."

"Surrounded by cobwebs. Those, yes."

He nodded at their cell phones perched on the coffee table. "No harm in giving the sedentary method a shot at it."

"Of course not. The internet's the first source we'll explore. In fact," she added as an aside, "I've already done a little of that already." To his *so-what-else-is-new?* grin, she elbowed him in the ribs. "Okay, shall we get down to business?"

"You begin. What are the areas you want to research?"

"I've made a mental list."

He smiled. "You love lists."

"I'm an addict."

"Does your list take into consideration all the loose documents included in the Barrett material?"

"Yes."

"What was I thinking? Of course, it does." He sat back, ready to marvel at her performance, predicting the only thing of substance he could add at its conclusion was his applause.

"For argument's sake," she began, "let's assume there's a cache of African treasures stashed away somewhere, no question about it. Not in a hideaway like an attic or basement because it would have been discovered by now. Nowhere far-flung because Andrew would have wanted access to it. Let's go with London or its environs. Assumptions, I know, but to discover the truth, we've got to start out with a hypothesis, even to knock it down.

"So, while our treasure map doesn't mark the spot with an 'x,' it does have signposts. Number one. Parsons, Thomson and Company, AKA Oxford Old Bank, a private bank, I looked it up. Now, Andrew says that on May 10, 1897, he visited that bank and had checks made out to Daniel Edgerton and to some unnamed moving company. And again, on August 17, he mentions that he's made arrangements with a moving company, again, nameless, this time to transport his collection to a secure location. Maybe it's the same moving company. What moving company? On that same date, he alludes to legal documents he's had drawn up for the occasion. Who's his lawyer? Are there any other documents this lawyer has executed for him over the years? Wouldn't it be great if we could have a crack at answering these questions? For instance, if we knew the name of the moving company, you think maybe we could find"—she smiled—"in its dusty bins, the destination of Andrew's precious cargo?" She waited for Harrison to comment, but his lips were sealed. Probably figured a punchline was coming and didn't want to step on it. She hugged him inwardly. Love expands with surprisingly small prompts.

"Well, it just so happens," she went on, "in 1900 the Oxford Old Bank amalgamated with Barclay and Company, and listen to this, the records for the Oxford Old Bank, including those made after it merged with Barclay, are held by Barclays Group Archives on Oxford Street. The archives run from 1802 to 1925 and include account ledgers, registers, and waste books—whatever they are. Made to order, right? We can pore over records from 1897 to 1918, the year of Andrew Barrett's death." She fixed her gaze on Harrison. "Well?"

"I'm blown away. And you're only at number one!" He grabbed her arm before she could land another jab at his rib cage. God, how he loved working with her.

"Number two," she pronounced, freeing herself, but with less conviction than her tone, had it been authentic, warranted. "Among Andrew's loose papers and documents, there's a bunch of receipts from auction houses and galleries. We need to go over them carefully. The major establishments can be researched long distance, but the smaller ones require footwork. Number three. Among the items there are photographs. Pinning down names and locations may turn up unexpected leads. Number—whatever. *Next.* We contact Olivia to see if she knows anything about the missing journal page. By the way, you don't know how much I want to search that desk of hers for more hidden chambers, things stuck between drawers. Oh, well. The list goes on, but let's stop here for now—wait, one more: Brian Latham, a curator at the British Museum, who helped us with our Michelangelo search. Let's touch base with him, see if he has any inside dope that may prove useful."

"In our search for Barrett's treasure trove or in Tim Thorpe's murder investigation?"

"Both."

"We've got a lot of balls in the air, don't we? You think it'll all come together?"

"We can only do our part," she cliché-ed, as a little grunt sounded from under Harrison's desk, prefacing Jake's emergence. Their cue. "You want to go out, boy?" she asked.

It was a rhetorical question. Jake uttered an affirmative bark to humor her. Whatever was transpiring in the inexplicable world of human endeavors, it was time to take a break on his behalf.

Chapter Seven

Next day, Sunday, began before dawn, with a languorous love fest followed by breakfast in bed prepared by Erika, tiptoeing around the kitchen before the rest of the household was up and about. It was a delicious interval.

And ended as Harrison was topping off their coffee cups, spilling a little in his saucer at the sudden warble of his cell phone. He steadied the bed tray, set the coffee pot on his night table, and grabbed the phone beside it. "It's Amilah Adamu!"

Erika reached for her nightgown. "FaceTime?" she asked, pulling the garment on over her head.

"No, darling you're fine." Nevertheless, influenced by her modesty, he folded the comforter over his naked pelvis before accepting the call. "Hello there, Amilah," he greeted pleasantly, disguising his apprehension for reasons that escaped him. Why was she calling, and why at this hour? "How have you been doing after...?"

"I still can't believe what happened," she replied, more appropriately somber. "I hope this isn't an ungodly time for you and your wife, Professor."

"Please. Harrison. And no, the time is perfectly convenient. By the way, you're on speakerphone."

"Hi, Amilah, it's Erika," Erika said, registering her presence.

"Erika, hello. I'm glad I'm able to speak to both of you."

There was nothing remotely "glad" in her tone. In fact, it reflected the antithesis of the beaming smile Erika associated with the woman. "What's wrong?" she asked, jumping in where Harrison apparently feared to go.

"There have been further developments. Ikemar called from London to give me the news, and we agreed that you should be informed as well. Moreover, we decided that you two should be the repository of *all* news and updates relating to our group's mission, either in its advancement or obstruction." After a pause: "You do consider us Zoom attendees a kind of, well, organization, don't you? Tied together by our shared goal?"

"Sharing a tragedy, the double knot."

"But Amilah," Harrison balked, "are you counting on us to come up with all the answers? That puts a lot of pressure—"

"Excuse me, Harrison, of course, your experience in solving crimes—"

"*Helping* solve."

"Let's not get technical," Amilah replied, dittoing Erika's unspoken thought. "Your experience does play an important factor, but you are also at the center of things. You're working on the Barrett material, plus Ikemar tells me that you said you're in touch with someone important in the art field who's got an in with both the British Museum's board of trustees and, by association, the detective investigating Thorpe's murder."

"All true, Amilah, and we accept your faith in us and are honored to be the group's repository," Erika summed up, negating Harrison's demureness in one fell swoop.

"Erika is more direct than I am," Harrison admitted, without a trace of resentment. "I concede. What have you got for us?" With one hand holding on for dear life to the flap of the comforter covering his pelvis, he reached to get a pad and pen from his night table drawer with the other.

"Two days ago, there was another murder," Amilah stated bluntly.

"What? Another one of *us?*"

"Oh, no. But the same person claiming credit for Thorpe's murder, or so it appears. The local police station received the call, and although the voice was again electronically altered, the analysts agree that it probably belongs to the same person who called in to *The Guardian* after the Zoom tragedy."

"Exactly what happened?" Erika urged. "Tell us everything you know."

"There are two parts to the story. The first took place two days ago, in the small hours of the morning, according to the coroner and corroborating evidence. The location, an estate on Ockham Lane in Cobham, Surrey. The homeowners, private investors, and art collectors Joanna and Keith Ashton, a couple in their mid-fifties. The wife was out of town for the night visiting her parents. When she returned at about nine a.m., she found her husband shot dead in the foyer. An initial finding of the investigation, just underway, is that her husband's voice had been recorded by their alarm company at one forty-seven a.m. He was telling the agent that his alarm system had gone off by accident."

Harrison jotted down the incoming facts.

"What was it, a robbery, a revenge killing?" Erika asked, unable to keep silent.

"A robbery. But out of all the valuable art works and unsecured jewelry in the home only one item was taken, a Picasso study for *Les Demoiselles d'Avignon.*"

"Probably what he came for," Harrison remarked, adding the detail to his notes.

"Yes," Amilah agreed. "And everything I've said so far was included in yesterday's news coverage. I can send you a link to the most detailed newspaper article, but I've told you the essentials."

"Thanks," Erika clipped. "We'd appreciate that. What about part two?" she asked, unable to feign patience. "What went on after the incident took place and the caller claimed responsibility for it?"

"I'm getting to that," Amilah said, a smile in her delivery. "I like your intensity, Erika. I can tell you put your all into things you commit to. We need that kind of tenacity here."

Harrison looked up from his notes and directly at Erika. "Good read. Dedication is my wife's motto." He studied Erika with a sudden, calculated intensity. Her tousled chestnut hair brushing her shoulders, her sheathed body, bared to him only moments ago, her lips still pink from contact with his, her hazel eyes, flecked with gold, bright with longing, no longer for him, but for facts about to be revealed. *Record what you see precisely as it appears,* he commanded himself. Driven, in that moment, by the fanciful certainty that every fleeting portrait is unique, but that a few must be saved intact so that all may one day be recalled in brilliant clarity.

"Part two," Amilah continued, her words coming mid-Harrison's digression without impeding it, "began yesterday, when a popular, somewhat incendiary YouTuber displayed the Picasso drawing on his vlog, 'No Holds Barred.' The drawing, he announced, had been overnighted to his home address, arriving in a FedEx tube along with a typed letter allegedly from the anonymous individual who'd stolen it. The vlogger read the letter and made a couple of remarks you will agree were designed to rabble-rouse." She paused. "I'm texting you the link so you can see it for yourselves. Here it comes. The video is only a few minutes long. I'm curious to get your feedback while we're still on the phone, if that's all right with you."

"Absolutely," Harrison replied, fully back in attendance. Holding the phone so that Erika had a good view, he clicked on the message icon. "Ah, here it is." He tapped the blue text and instantly a pasty-faced man teetering on middle-age appeared on the screen. He was wearing loose jeans and a black T-shirt emblazed with the name of his vlog. "Mick Ross here, starting the day with a dose of righteous indignation," he heralded in Beatles English. "Don't turn away." He stepped aside and there, pinned to a bulletin board propped on an easel, was Pablo Picasso's study for *Les Demoiselles d'Avignon*.

Erika sat back. "Amilah, you didn't warn us what'd been done to it!"

"I thought you should experience the full impact."

The dimensions of the drawing, judging from the relative size of the surrounding objects—a chair, a bridge table, the host himself—looked to be about 24 x 20 inches. It depicted the artist's concept-in-progress of two of the five nude women later to appear in his imposing painting housed at the Museum of Modern Art. Their faces had bold African mask-like features, demonstrating the inspiration Picasso had derived from such masks. Sprawled over the drawing in crude uppercase letters had been painted the words **PICASSO THE PIMP OF AFRICAN CULTURE.** The first four in black; the last two in bright red, the paint allowed to drip from the letters in a blatant reference to blood. Every segment of the drawing had been defaced by the message except the mask-faces.

"Message received?" Mick asked his unseen viewers. He went on to explain how he had acquired the drawing and, to prove that he had done his research, gave his audience a tidbit of history: "This is one of Picasso's many studies for the finished product, a huge oil painting weighing down a wall in The Big Apple's Museum of Modern Art. Picasso originally called it—that's along about 1907—*Le Bordel d'Avignon*, pardon my French. This refers to a whorehouse on a street in Barcelona famous for them. In 1916, a finicky poet, André Salmon, cleaned up the title for an art exhibition he was arranging, and the name stuck. *Les Demoiselles d'Avignon*, he called it. Presto-chango, from prostitutes to damsels. So, are you beginning to understand the layered meaning in the message plastered across this drawing? Picasso started what is touted as a bold movement with his use of the African mask—with the African style of depicting the human figure in general. He loved these masks, collected them, as did his less influential artist friends. And where did these masks come from? Why, they were looted from Africa by all those out-of-towners who thought they owned the place. To learn more, look up the colonial era in Africa, Picasso's African period, and throw in Cubism, when you have a free moment."

Mick picked up a sheet of paper from the bridge table. "As you know, on 'No Holds Barred' we feature tough men and women who shout out their views no matter what opposition they face." He held the paper in front of the camera long enough for his viewers to see that it contained a typewritten message. "This is a call for action. It was sent along with the drawing. I'll read it." He cleared his throat to mark the start of the quote. "'Picasso prostituted his looted African masks to portray his whores and kick off a new age in Western art. With barely a nod to his African inspiration, he took full credit for the avant-garde movement. The arrogance continues. The West's half-baked initiative to return Africa's stolen art to Africa is moving at the pace of a handicapped snail. I ask that you join me in a united demand that our high-and-mighty museum executives and private hoarders return all of Africa's looted art objects immediately or suffer the consequences. There are times when only force can bring about justice. No great cause was ever won without spilling a drop of blood.'"

Mick lowered the sheet of paper to his side and waited an amen moment for the message to sink in. "I should warn you," he went on after the pause, "you will hear on the news, if you haven't already, that the person who composed this note, the person who scrawled the message on the Picasso drawing, is also a cold-blooded killer. Thought for the day. If evidence proves the murder rap to be true beyond a shadow of a doubt, will that affect your opinion about the ideas addressed in this document?" He waved it in the air. "Even tougher, will you consider the possibility that this act of violence may have been justified in the commission of a moral exercise?" Another moment to contemplate the depth of the message bearer, this time yours truly. At the end of it, he bid his viewers what sounded like a ritual "Think big, be strong," although the pale white fist rising in a victory salute may or may not have been part of his usual sign-off.

"Well, *that* should fan the flames," Harrison summed up.

"That, plus this morning's outing of facts previously withheld regarding Tim Thorpe's murder," Amilah declared. "Specifically, the anonymous call to *The Guardian* from someone claiming credit for it. It's presumed a staffer overheard a couple of insiders talking about the repressed news and decided to pass it off as a scoop to the *Daily Express.* I get this paper delivered online every morning, so I'm a bit ahead of you. It's already hit the web, where it'll be acquiring a life of its own."

"Any reactions at this stage?" Erika asked.

"So far there's been some fiery chatter from the sympathizers, but hardly a call to arms. Minorities have more immediate, quality of life issues to focus their passions on. It takes a massive effort to create a movement with formidable clout. On the other hand, it only takes a couple of scary outliers to awaken the old tropes characterizing the group with which they're associated. You know, us primitive, uncultured Blacks? Unequipped to care for precious relics, even our own? It doesn't require a massive effort to slow down the process of restitution, only a bit of carefully phrased bias dressed as caution from a select group of administrators-slash-negotiators. But I'm preaching to the choir, aren't I? Even before you've had your morning coffee, I bet!"

"You're not preaching to us, and we've had our morning coffee," Erika assured her. "Besides, neither of us can carry a tune."

"Oh good," Amilah replied, her tone a notch brighter. "Is there anything I can do to help you piece together all the information coming at you? Anything at all?"

"Yes," Harrison replied at once. "Do you happen to know any of the higher-ups in the organization the confessed killer claims to represent? The Movement for Unity, Dignity and Courage, that is?"

"As an officer in the Federal Ministry's cultural branch in Benin City, yes, I have in the past made it my business to meet with its leader, Mwazulu Diyabanza. The last time we spoke was in July 2020, shortly after the Quai Branly Museum incident. I wanted to hear his side of the story before he went to trial. I agreed with his philosophy but had serious reservations about its implementation. We parted on excellent terms, but we haven't had contact since."

"Do you suppose you could get his thoughts on the perpetrator in question? For instance, is there a specific member of his organization he suspects? You think he'd open up to you? I'm sure the detectives investigating the two homicides will be interviewing Mr. Diyabanza, but I'm guessing he might be more forthcoming with you."

"I think so. After all, he did take me into his confidence pre-trial about his motivations regarding the Quai Branly affair, and he knows I've never leaked a word. Yes, I will try to speak to him, although you should understand beforehand that I'll be perfectly honest about why I'm reaching out to him and with whom I'm sharing his input."

"Of course. Erika, do you agree with the tactic?"

"I do. In fact, he should be made aware that any information he reveals to you will probably be passed along to those detectives, unless he strongly objects. In which case he can rest assured that we'll respect his confidentiality or, if it's sufficient, his anonymity."

"Good point. I'll lose credibility if I don't inform him of this, and later he hears that his revelations, if there are any, have been relayed to the authorities without his consent. Please keep in mind, if he stipulates that I tell *no* one, including you, of some fact or other that he wishes to remain between the two of us, I intend to honor his wish."

"Understood."

"Absolutely," Harrison underlined.

The conversation ended with the mutual promise to stay in contact and an agreement that despite the tragic outcome of their first Zoom meeting, another should be slated in the near future with Ikemar at the helm.

"We have another reason to fly to London," Erika proposed, the second the call ended.

Harrison put his note-taking material and cell phone on his night table. "Let me guess. You want to interview the victim's wife."

"Yes, Joanna Ashton. I want to know how the Picasso drawing was acquired, was a broker involved, and who transported it. It's inappropriate for us to give the detectives a list of questions we want answered, and we can't very well ask Greg to pump them for every single detail they acquire on their own, can we?" She shrugged. "I just want to be on *location*, Harrison."

"I get it. Things have a way of, well, evolving when you're in the country of origin."

"I want to walk the streets where Andrew Barrett walked with Lily Worthington. I want to search Olivia's desk. I want to chat with Brian Latham over a cup of tea and see if he's got any useful dirt on any of the British Museum staff. It's always good to talk to an insider."

"Thing is, right now will a cold cup of coffee do the trick?" He raised the coffee pot in preparation for the answer she was sure to give.

* * *

Thirty minutes later, Harrison was out walking Jake and Erika was prolonging her shower, tilting her head back to allow the pulsating stream to massage her scalp long after the shampoo had been rinsed away. Chin forward at last, she closed her eyes to exist fully within the experience, turning in stages to feel the water strike different planes of her body, all the while, in the fullness of her ease, Amilah's words seeping into her reverie and, in the absence of a fixed context, their import becoming fluid, open to interpretation. Erika's take on events, up to now axiomatic, became unmoored, debatable. And with a sudden shift in current, capsized.

There was a certain thrill to this up-ending of ideas, a sign of mental flexibility, if nothing else. She decided, though, while toweling off, that she would not prejudice Harrison's view of things by bringing up her new, frankly counter-intuitive, outlook until they'd heard back from Greg, Madame D, and Amilah.

Facing her image in the still foggy mirror and about to pick up her comb, a word capturing the essence of her new line of thought came to her. For some reason, maybe only for the shock effect, she felt compelled to trace it in the fast-disappearing mist: CHAOS.

Chapter Eight

He sat in the beat-up leather lounge chair that reminded him of his wife's favorite, bless her pitiful soul, and took stock. An okay alliteration, "Picasso Pimps," he grudgingly gave himself, but the rest was shit. Maybe he was being hard on himself. Maybe it wasn't the words themselves, but the way Mick had read them aloud, no bite in them, more cocky than inspiring. Maybe it was the limited platform. "No Holds Barred" had a major fan base and sure, his message had received some intense commentary since its showcase the day before, but this was a far cry from the stir he'd have created if he'd been able to put a knife to the super-sized whores of Barcelona kicking ass at the Museum of Modern Art.

Right. Who was he kidding? Here he was, a loner sitting in his rented rathole, dreaming he could star in one of those action-packed movies, capers they call them, shimmying up the sides of buildings, dodging laser beams, escaping through the sewer system. Deceiving word, capers. As in panty-raids, more like. Even if by some miracle he could pull it off—guards dozing, tourists off gawking at an installation of Daffy Duck—the authorities would find him on the flight's manifest and he'd be done for.

Too bad about the skirmish with the man of the house, but what could he do? The chap had seen his face, he had to be eliminated. In the end, the operation had received better news coverage because of the fatality, so it had worked out for the best, after all.

He studied the dingy wall opposite. The color photo of the completed *Les Demoiselles d'Avignon* was tacked more or less at its center, slightly askew, he noticed, but no matter. It served its purpose, kept his blood on a rolling boil.

Next to it, another mask-inspired opus, a George Braque. *Tête de Femme.* Head of Lady iteration number two or three, he couldn't remember. Above it, Henri Matisse's daughter, *Marguerite,* poor thing grossly distorted in like manner. And over to the left, Amedo Modigliani's portrait of *Jeanne Hébuterne,* her elongated face plagiarizing a mask of the Fang People of Equatorial West Africa. By her side, he'd pinned a photograph of one of those masks just to remind himself, as if he needed reminding. Other samples of those avant-garde busy bees of the early 1900s were impaled here and there, adding to the revered crowd of posthumous millionaires.

Whatever. The next move on the agenda had better pick up the pace. It needed refining and he needed to quit twiddling his thumbs and come up with a few clever ideas to bounce off, hah, *himself*!

It would be an obstacle, he knew, but shit, he wished he had a partner to brainstorm with, never mind a friend.

Chapter Nine

Madame D had Pierre Jolet where she wanted him. On her own turf and on edge. "Tea?" she asked, swinging her wheelchair around to face him squarely. "I've given my staff the day off, but my receptionist has left us with her unsurpassable *mousse au chocolat*. I suggest you indulge."

"Thank you, but no, Madame," Pierre declined, his glance once again helplessly grazing the large, bulging leather art portfolio perched beside him on the couch like a mysterious guest, exactly as Madame D had staged it.

"Ah, well, your loss, monsieur. Another day, perhaps." Poor thing was tugging at his collar, the knot of his lovely silk tie holding its ground.

"I was much intrigued by your call," Pierre stated, pulling himself together, surprised by his need to, no doubt.

"I do hope I didn't alarm you," Madame D replied, with the smallest grin designed to put him off guard. *Here's a man used to running the show*, she mused. *Well, we shall see what we shall see.* "Did I alarm you?"

Pierre had another go at his collar. "Well, there did appear to be a degree of urgency in your desire to speak with me in person. When I reminded you of my professional status, that I am in no way equipped to advise you on the distribution of your estate, you nevertheless insisted my help was required." He looked at her expectantly, as if he'd posed a question.

"Have you forgotten that there was a decided benefit for you in this matter?" she replied, scanning the wall opposite, tacitly inviting him to do the same. "Or that I mentioned that I was eager to distribute my assets, shall we say *prematurely*?" She watched his glance roam left and right, up and down the collection of framed artwork. She'd had one of her tattoo artists remove the television screen from the wall for the occasion so that she could add two more engravings to the display. Her sitting room occupied a small portion of her modest living quarters in the rear of her *tatouage* establishment, but for Pierre's benefit, it now flaunted as many antique etchings, engravings, woodcuts, and the like as any exhibit of its kind at the Louvre. Harrison, who had sat with her in this very room, would be proud of her resourcefulness, or at least amused by it.

"Am I mistaken, or is that a Matisse linocut?" Pierre asked, in lieu of an answer to her question. He rose from the couch to have a closer look at a framed portrait of a dancer on the northeast area of the wall.

"Yes, it is," Madame D replied. "No need to wander. Please sit down." She clasped her hands in her lap. "It's the original, by the way. The others have been destroyed I've been told. "It's dated 1947. Thank you," she added, as Pierre, taken aback by her command, nevertheless obeyed it.

"Let's not beat around the bush," she firmly suggested. "When I met you a year ago, I was taken by your genuine enthusiasm regarding the art works you had inherited from your grandfather. I thought, here is someone with depth and sensibility. You reminded me of my father, ironically enough—you, a young man, at least fifty years my junior. I never forgot our encounter." She unclasped her hands to genteelly slap her thighs. "And now, I believe we can be of service to each other."

Pierre sat very still, although from his strained expression, it seemed to take some effort. "I don't understand, Madame Fontaine. You must explain."

"Certainly. I have two very dear friends who are deeply invested in solving—or I should say *helping* to solve—the murder of James Thorpe."

Pierre flinched.

"Exactly. You witnessed the murder yourself. Well, as you surely are aware, you hastily exited the meeting with a remark that was bound to arouse curiosity."

Pierre raised his eyebrows.

"Don't feign bewilderment. It wastes time. Quote: 'Too close to home. If you only knew.'"

"Meaning?"

"Possibly nothing. But if it were not relevant, you would not have remained averse to explaining it." With a grandmotherly smile: "Up to now."

"I'm not obliged to report to you, Madame Fontaine."

"Indeed, you are, Monsieur Jolet. That is, if you wish to be memorialized in the archives, of art history."

With a strained titter: "Is this a bribe, ma'am?"

"Absolutely not, sir. It is a quid pro quo. Heavily weighted in your favor, morally as well as materially."

"And what if nothing I say advances the murder investigation? What then?"

"The terms of our agreement remain in force."

"Terms of agreement? Have I missed something?"

Getting cheeky. Good sign. "I'll elucidate. Are you sure you won't have a cup of tea?"

Pierre sucked in his breath, nostrils aflare.

"Understood. Moving on, there are several key factors governing my decision. First and foremost, I have no heirs. Second, although I wish to leave my worldly goods"—a sweeping wave took in the display wall and leather portfolio—"to the community at large, I have neither the need nor remote desire to have my ego propped up after its demise. I am therefore prepared to donate my treasured art works anonymously to your *Institut* or the museum of your choice, with the stipulation that it be called 'The Pierre Jolet Collection' in your honor, and that it be on view to the public permanently or at reasonable intervals anywhere in the world. I will also permit you to choose two works for your personal ownership from either the wall hangings or the grab-bag beside you. An original hand-tinted engraving by Jean-Honoré Fragonard, 1778, and Pablo Picasso's original linocut of a bullfight, circa 1955, are among the items in the bag that may pique your interest."

A tentative, testing-the-waters sort of smile greeted Madame D's remarks, then vanished. "I fear for my life."

"Don't we all. No, I apologize, that was insensitive. I mean to say only that one must be willing to take a modicum of risk when it comes to preserving one's moral core. Wouldn't you agree?"

Pierre shrugged. "Looks good on paper; I'll give you that."

"I can promise you that I and my friends will see to it that your name will never be publicly associated with what I know your conscience is urging you to disclose," she said, trying her best to convince him, as well as herself, of the ironclad nature of her promise. After a pause: "Are you on board?"

From his look of fearful resignation, she knew what his answer would be. A wave of guilt hit her full force as she waited for it.

Chapter Ten

Y ou look upset, Denise," Harrison observed, his knit brow mirroring hers. "You were going to meet with Pierre Jolet earlier today. How did it go?" Once again, Gretchen had facilitated their connection and retired from the scene. On this go-round, FaceTime was the receptionist's recommended mode of communication. If Madame D had been feeling herself, she would have been wisecracking about modern technology or her own ineptitude in regard to it. Bad sign.

"I *am* upset. I may have put Pierre in danger. A small chance, I believe, but there it is."

"He must have told you what he's been keeping from everyone," Erika suggested, sitting beside Harrison on the couch in his study.

"Yes."

"You are something else, Denise," Harrison praised, hoping to lighten her spirits.

"Nice try, Harry, but ill-timed." She double-checked that Gretchen was out of hearing by calling her name in a moderately raised voice. When there was no response, she headed straight into her account of her tête-à-tête with Monsieur Jolet, making a full stop at the point where he'd accepted her offer of a quid pro quo. "Quid pro quo *mon pied!*" she scoffed. "It was a bribe, pure and simple."

"If it was a bribe, it was certainly a generous one," Erika encouraged, her smile so affectionately conspiratorial, Madame D could not help but smile back, perhaps longing for a sense of inclusion more than she was willing to admit.

"It happened a few years ago," she began. She reached for the glass of water on her coffee table, took a sip or two, and placed it back on the table. "The incident Pierre has been so reluctant to speak of, that is. I'm going to try to keep his perspective in mind so that you won't be too harsh on him. Now then. Picture this. The scene is an exhibit hall at the *Institut francais du Portugal*. On display is a collection of art and artifacts from Mozambique confiscated by the Portuguese during their rule of that country from the 1890s to the 1930s. Pierre has put together this special exhibition with great care, mindful of the security and preservation concerns of the institutions and private collectors who entrusted him with their treasures.

"It's a half hour past closing time. Pierre is in his office just off the exhibit hall writing an article for the *Institut's* newsletter. He hears what sounds like someone moving about in the exhibit hall. He knows the staff has left. He should be alone in the building. He picks up the nearest object that might serve as a weapon, a brass replica of Brancusi's *Bird in Space*. He is terrified of engaging in physical combat, but the need to protect his exhibition overrides his fear. He opens the door a crack."

"Why doesn't he call the police?" Harrison threw out.

"Good question. I asked him that myself, and he said he acted on the notion that the police would either arrive too late or cause a ruckus and damage his display. Sorry, *mes chers*, my fault for not conveying to you the urgency with which the snap decision was made."

"You're doing great," Erika said. "What happens next?"

"The man's back is to him. He is dressed in trousers and a white shirt. His sleeves are rolled up above his elbows exposing his dark skin. He must have picked open the lock to the vitrine because no glass has been broken. Its lid is raised, and the intruder is removing the items from within, small statuary, some carved from wood, others ivory, and placing them in a canvas bag sitting by his right foot. Pierre's fear vanishes as his plan materializes. He approaches. He is light on his feet and moves more quickly than he has foreseen. The man is reaching toward the display case to pluck out another object. Pierre acts with a deliberation that surprises him, raising the *Bird in Space* and striking the man on the right side of his head as if he'd

73

practiced the act a thousand times, refining the trajectory and force that would knock out a well-built opponent without cracking his skull. Having been intentionally struck on the right, the victim falls left, away from the canvas bag.

"Pierre says what he does next feels like an out of body experience and at the same time, the most *present* he's ever been. Without a moment's hesitation, he fetches the roll of duct tape from the bottom drawer of his desk. He has used it only once, almost a year ago, to seal a box of books he was donating to the local library. He thinks providence has kept it at his disposal. He binds the man's wrists with the tape and gently places a throw pillow from the office couch under his head for comfort. There is no blood, and minimum swelling. He expects the man will regain consciousness quickly."

"At *this* point, he calls the police," Harrison could not help interjecting.

"*Mais non*, Harry. At this point, he retrieves the objects from the canvas bag, checks their condition, and carefully sets them back in their assigned spots in the vitrine. In fact, at *no* point does he call the police. Despite the pride he feels in having mounted this exhibit, he is conflicted with some degree of guilt for what he admits has been his exploitation of looted goods. He wants to give the man a chance to explain himself. I may be reading between the lines, but I think Pierre thought he could perform an on-the-spot rehabilitation. He did say his decisions that day were due in good measure to the heightened awareness of racial injustice. This was just after the murder of George Floyd, you see, and there was a great outpouring of sympathy and outrage. Demonstrations and marches were taking place all over the world, including in the streets of Portugal, literally right outside his door. Indeed, how could Pierre *not* have been touched? I myself had Gretchen push me in my chair down the Champs-Élysées during one such protest. 'You are too old for this,' Gretchen scolded. 'Why are you exposing yourself to risk now?' There was only one answer to that. 'If not now, *when?*' Forgive me, children. This is not my story, it is Pierre Jolet's. Where was I? Yes, he has removed the items from the canvas bag and has put them back in the vitrine.

"I marvel at the sang-froid of Pierre's next move, even as the man begins to stir. He whips his cell phone out of his pocket and snaps a photograph of him, thinking it might be useful at some time in the future."

"Useful for the man who lies unconscious on the floor," Erika surmised.

"Explain," Harrison requested, before the light dawned. "Ah, yes!"

Madame D nodded. "You're a quick one, Erika. It was only later, after he'd given the man a good talking-to and let him go, that Pierre realized he had no proof an attempted robbery had taken place, only that an *assault* had occurred, and that he himself had been the culprit!"

"Is this why he's so fearful of having his story go public?" Harrison asked. "Afraid that the man will seek a reprisal of some sort?"

"Yes, but there's more to it than that. You see, the man was so grateful to be let off the hook, he forgot to recover his canvas bag when he scurried out of the place. The tool he used to pick open the lock remained tucked inside the bag, and since no gloves were worn during the commission of the crime, his fingerprints on the tool's handle remain intact to this day."

"Wait a minute, Pierre kept the bag?" Erika asked, thrown for a loop.

"He did."

"And the intruder has never come back for it? Has never bothered Pierre?"

"That's right. Understandably, Pierre would prefer to let sleeping dogs lie. Especially now that he's fixed on the idea that the man may in fact have murdered Jim Thorpe. I told him his notion was as far-fetched as can be, but I failed to convince him. The man told him that his grandparents had been killed during a Portuguese military campaign in Mozambique and that his only motive was to return the looted art in his relatives' memory. Pierre now believes he fell for the story because he badly wanted to. He said the intruder had a distinct Cockney accent. From this, he leaps to the conclusion that he was in London when the crime took place and therefore must have committed it. He admits he's probably got a misguided bug in his head, but *tant pis*, it appears that a similar bug has taken up residence inside *my* head. What do you think? Are there grounds for my concern? Have I put Pierre in harm's way?"

"There's a better chance he'll get hit by a bus," Harrison assured her, projecting more confidence than he felt. "But we'll take every precaution that his name will not be publicized in association with the man in question. Unless, of course, in the unlikely event the man is brought to trial and Jolet is asked to take the stand, which is even more unlikely. By the way, did Jolet email you the photo he took of the fellow?"

"While he was here with me, yes. You're going to ask me to send it to you, aren't you?"

"Of course. We'll have to pass it on to the people handling the case."

"You'll have to walk me through it, Harry. I don't want to involve Gretchen."

"Of course. Did Jolet happen to get the man's name, by the way?"

"No. Intentionally not."

"That's okay. I can tell you a couple of ways the photo can be used to track down his ID."

"Don't crowd my brain, Harry."

Erika raised her hand. "Do you think Pierre will agree to ship us the canvas bag and whatever it contains? Lifting fingerprints off the items might be useful in pinning down the ID."

"I asked. For the present, he's not willing to go quite that far. *Maintenant,* will you people walk me slowly, very slowly, step by step through the process of transmitting Pierre's photograph to you?"

"Yes," Erika volunteered. "First, let's clear the screen and tap on your email icon."

"My what? Oh dear, it's going to be a long night. I hope you've brought your camping equipment."

Chapter Eleven

Harrison looked at the photograph one more time before pressing the "send" button. "Too bad his eyes are closed. Think this'll be enough to find a match?"

Erika shrugged. "Hope so. The man's got strong, distinctive features, and the clenched fist tattoo on his neck should help." She took his phone from him and spread her fingers on the image to enlarge it. "One of his incisors is chipped. You know, either or both of these distinguishing marks may have been made too recently to show up in his file." She handed him back his cell. "If he's even *got* a file."

"Right. So,"—he pressed the button—"one down, one to go." He turned to her on the couch. "By the way, you showed great patience with Denise last night. What an ordeal."

Erika smiled. "My only worry was that she would accidentally delete the photo. Actually, it was Denise who was the good sport, putting up with all my commands." She looked down at her notepad and put a checkmark next to Amilah Adamu's name on her "timely" list. They were emailing Jolet's photo of his anonymous intruder to two people, each accompanied by a personalized note. John Mitchell was next. They were not sure John could obtain access to the UK's police records, but he was a seasoned operator and well within six degrees of separation from any law person on earth. Didn't hurt to give it a try. They'd thought about sending the photo to Clive Hogarty, the detective on the Thorpe murder investigation in London, but decided to leave the timing of that to Amilah, since it might directly impact her dealings with the leader of the activist movement and his trust in her.

"Ready with John's email address?"

"All set."

Side-by-side they composed the text to send John, Harrison typing it on the screen as their thoughts coalesced. They implored him to keep his motivation for ID-ing the man in the photo as vague as possible when communicating with his contacts, suggesting that, if need be, he fudge it altogether. "We good?" Harrison asked, before sending the message on its way.

"We are."

"Done."

Erika checked her list. "Not yet." She rose from the couch to retrieve from Harrison's desk the loose documents accompanying Andrew Barrett's journal. "Let's photograph Andrew's auction-house receipts," she said, replanting herself beside Harrison. "A couple are from Christie's and I'm hoping Greg can track them down. I'd say we could make a stab at it ourselves, but I just discovered Christie's closed off its auction archives to the public in 2021." To Harrison's quizzical look she replied, "Google and I are on intimate terms."

He smiled. "I should have guessed. Anyway, I thought we decided the descriptions were too sketchy to research. Altar figure, carved tusk, brass plaque. No distinguishing features."

"Right. Which means Greg couldn't determine if the items had subsequently changed hands. But if Christie's has a record of any of the initial purchases, maybe they'll show to what mysterious hiding place they were shipped." She began sifting through the papers, plucking out the receipts and placing them on the coffee table. "Humor me."

Fifteen minutes later copies of the receipt photographs had been emailed and acknowledged.

"Any more balls to toss in the air?" Harrison asked.

Erika scanned her to-dos. "Nothing that can't wait for London." Eliding Harrison's look of surprise, she added, "I asked John if he'd come along, and he said yes. I'm going to ask if he can be deputized by the FBI's art theft team. It would guarantee access to the UK's records." She grinned. "And no,

I haven't yet booked our flights."

Chapter Twelve

Easy to say, and confidently to boot: "Let's book our flight!" Not so easy to anticipate—for a whole week, no less—the agony of leave-taking. There were distractions, to be sure—composing those treatises of dos and don'ts, expanding lists of contacts, local and abroad, itinerary minutia—but whenever Erika was in close contact with Lucas and sometimes, in the still of the night, spooning against her sleeping husband, a wave of prophetic longing for her son would overtake her, as if there was already an ocean between them.

But just as beds are made and floors are swept on the morning of one's last-ditch chemo-therapy session, so the ordinary chores prior to an impossible separation get done: suitcases packed, bills paid, meetings arranged.

And before she knew it, the day had come—and gone. She, Harrison, and John had left JFK five hours ago, at 11:00 p.m., scheduled to arrive at 11:05 a.m., British Summer Time, at Heathrow Airport. In the dim light, she could just make out the time on her watch. It was now 4:00 a.m. in New York. Lucas should be sleeping soundly. The thought that he could live without her was comforting. She moved the watch's hour hand five hours ahead. *Think 9:00 a.m.* Harrison stirred beside her, his head dropping to rest on her shoulder.

She looked across the aisle to check John's state of wakefulness. He was sound asleep, stretched out on his commodious business class seat, pillow beneath his head, blanket pulled up to his chin. An imposing, confident man in his mid-fifties, at rest he looked like a contented puppy. The sole seat beside him was unoccupied and he'd used it to accommodate his laptop, cell phone, tissues, hand wipes, and the glass bowl that had contained an assortment of warm nuts. John had vehemently resisted being treated to business class but had finally relented. Harrison's generosity was a force impossible to overcome.

Erika's first appointment in London was scheduled for 2:30 and she hadn't slept a wink. She rested her head against Harrison's and closed her eyes to give it another try. No chance of success, but no harm in pretending.

* * *

The threesome piled out of the limo and stood facing the entrance of the Kimpton Fitzroy Hotel—the Russell up until a few years ago— a splendid brick edifice with turrets and arches and all the trappings of a castle decked out in rich *thé-au-lait* terracotta.

"Will you take a look at these prom queens," John chortled, referring to the four life-size stone images built into the hotel's grand façade. "I feel underdressed for the occasion." He played at straightening out his sweatshirt. "Sorry, girls."

"Elizabeth the First, Mary the Second, Anne and Victoria," the chauffeur recited, with a whiff of pride as he began removing their luggage from the trunk of the car, the others hastening to help.

Almost at once, a smartly uniformed bellhop pulled up alongside the vehicle with a polished brass trolley that dazzled in the mid-day sun, and the travelers and their escort were presently gliding within the lavishly appointed marble-and-wood lobby on route to the reception area.

The check-in process went without a hitch, and the trio was transported via lift to the fourth floor and ushered to their rooms—John's three doors down from Erika and Harrison's—with Harrison managing to tip the bellhop and sending him on his way before John had to chance to retrieve his wallet.

"Impossible," John complained, with a helpless shrug.

"Let's meet in the front lobby in twenty minutes," Harrison responded, unheeding. "Erika has us on a tight schedule. I've got an appointment at Barclay's Bank in exactly"—he checked his watch—"forty-six minutes. You two are off to the British Museum, also pushing the envelope."

"Sure thing." John took a look at his Breitling, a gift from his wife on his fifty-fifth birthday, cringe-worthy expensive, but treasured. "I've got twelve-forty-five. See you at one-o-five on the dot. You guys hungry at all?"

The Wheatleys were good. The hearty brunch served on the plane would hold them until dinner. John said he'd grab something from the room bar, which the receptionist had mentioned was provided, and the travelers withdrew to their respective quarters to freshen up before the day began in earnest.

"This is *our* room," Erika said prayerfully, once they were alone.

Harrison slipped his hand around her waist as they stood motionless, taking it in. "I didn't tell John, did you? It's our secret."

"Of course, I didn't. I feel guilty enough, reveling in it when I should be thinking exclusively about the business at hand."

He drew her closer. "Don't feel bad. I'll comfort you tonight."

She smiled. A few years ago, they'd made love for the first time, here, in this room. It seemed like yesterday—and forever ago. She'd come to him from the room next door, seeking comfort after a nightmare. How tightly she'd knotted the belt of that terrycloth bathrobe! The room had been renovated since then, its ambience at odds with the opulent Victorian style of its past and with the hotel's common areas, where it still prevailed. Yet, the clean lines of contemporary design, enhanced by warm, neutral tones and plush upholstery, were equally inviting—unless, of course, she was investing the space with images of what had transpired in it.

"We better get moving," Harrison said, snapping them out of their shared memory.

"It'll take me ten minutes to wash up and change clothes. That leaves a few minutes to call home." She grabbed her cell phone from her tote bag before he could object and called Kate's cell number on FaceTime.

"How's everything?" she opened. Translation: "How's my baby?"

"Lucas is fine," Kate said, reading the subtitle. "He just had breakfast and Grace has taken him out for a walk in his stroller. It's a beautiful day."

"That's nice. We'll FaceTime later tonight so we can see him."

Kate's lips puckered. "He wants to see you, too. He's been looking all over for you!"

Erika winced. "Oh, no." She drooped against Harrison's side.

"Don't you want Lucas to miss you, sweetheart?" Harrison asked seconds later, after the call had ended.

"Only a little. I want him to say, 'I miss you guys, but I'm good with it.'"

Harrison smiled. "The kid's got a limited vocabulary; mama, dada, and milk."

"'Mook,'" she corrected. "I want him to be tough, to be able to live without us. You know what I mean."

"Of course, I do. But I promise, nothing's going to happen to us. Now, let's get going."

* * *

John was waiting for them in the lobby, laptop carrying case in hand. "Ready to roll?" he asked, as Erika and Harrison approached.

"You clean up good," Harrison commented on arrival. He'd never seen John in a suit and tie. He was almost unrecognizable.

"Was that a compliment or an insult?" John asked, mugging perplexity. "Figured I should raise my game to fit the venue." He made a point of looking them up and down—Harrison in gray pants, blazer, and tie; Erika, in fitted navy suit, and stylish but presumably comfortable heels. "I see we're on the same page."

"Let's hope," Erika said, patting the oversized tote that contained her and Harrison's collated notes and queries, the papers Greg had given them, lists of addresses and phone numbers with every person or institution they might have occasion to contact during the course of their stay, and a pad and pen for additional data and insights.

"You're prepared," John commented. "What have you got in there?"

"Crib sheets," she replied, with a tight little smile, all business now.

Harrison was carrying his own set of notes and note-taking supplies in the slender leather briefcase usually filled with such matter as lecture outlines and student essays. "It's a short cab ride to Barclay's. I guess you two will be walking to the museum. We'll touch base during the day, but the basic plan is that we'll be having dinner at the hotel restaurant at seven, yes? I made reservations."

Nods all around.

"My first assignment, as I understand it," John said, "is to keep my eyes and ears open. My next stop, I plan to take the initiative, guys. I've got it down pat. I've been deputized by the FBI as instructed"—crediting Erika with a glance in her direction—"so I'm ready for any and all undertakings. I've done my best to find a match with the guy in the photo you sent me but came up empty-handed. I'll be taking an alternate route, along with my FBI credentials, which I figure will open up more avenues of research."

"Oh, there'll be matters that only you will be qualified to investigate," Erika assured him. She smiled inwardly. She was well aware Harrison harbored a secondary motive for wanting to have John along, and that was to serve as her bodyguard. Harrison would have invited John had she not preempted him, no doubt about it. She didn't bring this up since he would only deny it and John would stick up for him. Besides, if circumstances arose that she needed to act alone, she could always give John the slip.

Chapter Thirteen

"Looks like an enormous space capsule," John commented first thing on entering the sprawling Elizabeth II Great Court and struck by the Reading Room at its center.

"Good Call," Erika said. "Take a look some time at an aerial photo of its interior. The arrangement of tables and bookshelves looks like the spaceship from Kubrick's *Space Odyssey*. This your first time at the British Museum?"

"My first time anywhere." He grinned. "You think because I know my way around the world's criminal database, I've been around the world?"

"I guess this is as good a place as any to start," Erika said, returning the smile. "After we speak to Brian, let's take a look at the Benin Bronzes." She pulled her cell phone from her tote and punched in the curators' office number in her contacts file.

"This is Erika Shawn-Wheatley," she replied to the abrupt "Curators!" prompt as softly as possible so as not to disturb the museum visitors circulating in the area. "I have an appointment with Brian Latham at two-thirty."

"Erika *who*? Shaughnessy, did you say?"

"Wheatley," she repeated, simplifying things. "Erika Wheatley," she clearly enunciated, raising her voice out of necessity, noticing, as she did so, someone in a green jacket off to her right, maybe five yards away, spin around at the sound of her voice. "Right," she replied to the anonymous being on the phone, focusing obliquely on the man who'd turned toward her and hadn't moved on. He was wearing aviator sunglasses and a peaked cap that further shaded his eyes, so it was impossible to tell if he was looking directly at her. "Thanks, we'll be right up," she said, feeling the man's eyes on her despite the uncertainty.

"What's up?" John asked, sensing her unease.

"I think the man to my right—don't look—is staring at me," she said, just above a whisper.

"You're a beautiful woman, what do you expect?" John said, hardly disguising his worry. He studied the man out of the corner of his eye. "There, he's waving toward someone. Now he's walking toward—"

"Was there anyone waving *back*? Forget it. I'm being paranoid. Let's go meet Brian."

"Wait, I'm going to check out this guy." He took a step in his direction.

She grabbed his sleeve. "No, John. It's just me, freaking over what took place right here in this building. What we're here to talk about. Come on, let's do it."

* * *

Erika's uneasiness resurfaced as she and John stepped from the elevator onto the floor where Timothy Thorpe's murder had taken place. Heightened by the cold reserve of the young woman who corralled them at the elevator, introducing herself as "Cherry-Ames-projects-assistant-we spoke-on-the phone" and marching them down the hall to Brian Latham's office like they were about to catch hell from the school principal.

Cherry departed wordlessly after delivering her charges to Brian's small but accommodating quarters, and Brian, flashing a knowing smile, rose from his desk chair to greet his guests and lock the door. "Cherry's full of herself, but quite capable," he said, taking Erika's hand in both of his, then offering John the traditional handshake. "You must be private eye John Mitchell—and I must be Brian Latham," he went on, giving John's hand one vigorous pump. "By the way, you look splendid, Erika; haven't aged a minute. Marriage and motherhood clearly agree with you."

Erika could see that Brian had put on about twenty pounds and had gone bald since they'd last met. "You're looking terrific yourself," she said.

86

Brian patted his paunch. "Right. Ah, well, love is blind, I suppose," he quipped. "Come sit, the two of you." He gestured at the two leather straight-back chairs across from his own swivel bucket chair. When the three were settled in, Brian sat forward, elbows planted on the desktop, hands folded under his chin. "Enough of this. You're here to discuss Tim's murder, not pretend nothing's happened. Forgive my freneticism. I hardly know how to handle it. My mood swings. Talk to me."

Erika withdrew a bunch of papers from her tote and plucked out the ones Greg had handed over to her and Harrison at The-Hole-In-The-Wall. Before sliding the remainder back inside the tote, she retrieved her pad and pen.

"You came supplied," Brian said, sliding the pad and pen he was about to give her over to John.

"Thanks," John said, shifting in his seat, his features bearing the classic ill-at-ease expression of the third wheel.

"I don't mean to sound like an interrogating officer, Brian," Erika said, pen in hand, "but is there anything you can think of about that morning—sorry, afternoon for you—anything you can think of that I might want to know?"

"In what capacity, *know*?" Brian asked, rocking back in his chair. "Are you acting as an agent of the London police force, or behind their back? Forgive my bluntness. Call me dense, but I think I should know in what capacity you're functioning. No offense."

"None taken. It's a perfectly legitimate question, Brian." She crossed her legs and her tight skirt rose to mid-thigh. "Let me explain," she said, uncrossing her legs and clamping them together. "First, everything we're doing or intend to do is perfectly aboveboard. Second, anything we discover that's relevant to the murder case we'll share with the local authorities."

"Clive Hogarty is the detective in charge," John offered, if only to join in.

"Nice chap," Brian said. "*He's* interviewed me as well."

Erika noted the sarcasm in his tone, but it was hardly off-putting. A few years ago, Brian had been helpful to her and Harrison in their search for a putative Vittorio da Lucca drawing and she, in turn, had written a lively article featuring Brian's curatorial theories and practices for *Art News* magazine. The article had brought him a modest degree of fame in the niche world of museum administration, which had led, for one thing, to a position as guest lecturer at Sotheby's Institute of Art; for another, a jump from assistant to associate curator. It had always been apparent that Brian was at heart a political animal and given the positive impact her article had had on his career, she was sure he believed she still wielded some form of karma over him, which might work for either good or ill. She had no proof of this, but there was a subtle obeisance in his demeanor toward her, even at his snappiest—the tilt of his head, the lowering of his gaze—that was convincing enough. He'd be cooperative. She knew it in her gut.

"Let me set things straight," she said. "Harrison and I don't pretend to be criminal detectives., but we do feel an alliance—*an allegiance*—to a group of individuals with a mission we believe in. We witnessed one member of the group brutally murdered in front of our eyes, and we feel a certain responsibility toward him. We want to be part of the effort of tracking down his killer, and we intend to use any resources at our disposal."

"Yours truly being one of them."

"Yes, and as ever, we'll be truly grateful." She paused, let that sink in. "Shall we start over?"

Brian dropped eye contact. "No need."

"So. Do you remember anything unusual about that day? Seeing any unfamiliar faces on this floor, for instance?"

"It was a Saturday. I was attending a charity affair emceed by my wife." Eye contact restored: "It ran all afternoon and into the early evening. 'Literacy United' is the name of the organization, perhaps you've heard of it? Its mission is to eradicate illiteracy worldwide." He chuckled. "A tall order, but admirable all the same."

Erika slid the papers from Greg across the desk to him. "Would you take a look at the list of people who were interviewed as of—well, a while ago. Anything jump out at you?"

Brian turned the papers, so the print was right side up. "I know a number of these people. Nothing jumping out. You want a run-down?"

"If you wouldn't mind, Brian. You never know what may turn out to be useful."

Brian pressed his fingers against his forehead as if he were a psychic calling forth the spirits.

"I know Freddy Leach," he imparted. "He's a student, working on his master's degree in Pre-Columbian art and a permanent fixture around here. We've got a research room on this floor and when he's not at London U, he's holing up in that room. It's my theory he has a crush on Cherry, if you can believe it."

Erika jotted down the information. "Does he generally carry a backpack with him?" she asked, matching him with the confused-looking young man tagging along with the medical team in the aftermath of the assault.

"The backpack is a permanent appendage," Brian confirmed. He put a checkmark next to Freddy's name; a good sign he meant to be thorough. "Let's see...the security guards. Don't know this name"—*check*—"nor this one"—*check*. He looked up. "That's not to say I wouldn't recognize either of these fellows," he qualified, addressing Erika, with an inclusive glance at John. Looking back down, his eyes lit up. "Peter Holmes, now *there's* a sweetheart. One of the guards on the late shift. Always inquires after the Mrs. and progeny—remembers the names of the lot of them." *Check*. "Here's an odd one—Martin Maclevy. Nightwatchman, on duty only on weekends. Keeps to himself. I challenged myself to draw him out. No luck. The fellow's polite enough but keeps his distance. He's either aloof or shy; I never determined which." *Check*. He ran his finger down the list, checking off names he didn't recognize, including the HVAC engineer and individual members of the medical team tending to Thorpe. "Ah, here's a familiar name." He tapped on it. "Clifford Dean. On the custodial staff; comes in a.m. Wednesday, Thursday; p.m. Saturday. Gave poor Tim CPR with your remote help. Cliff, another chap not given to mingling. Nice enough, I suppose, but...no, I should stop here."

"Why stop?" Erika asked, dittoed by John's knit brow.

"I don't want to put any ideas in your head; more precisely, to mislead you."

"Let us worry about that. John and I are not all that quick to judge. Trust us."

"It was just one time, you understand. I caught him rifling through my wastebasket. Out of simple curiosity, surely. No harm done." Brian gave a remorseful shake of his head and immediately began scrutinizing the remainder of Greg's notes, deflecting from his perceived gaffe by going on about the dynamics of the Movement for Unity, Dignity, and Courage—the UDF—and the laudatory behavior of its leader, regrettably so often misunderstood.

"Did Timothy Thorpe have any enemies that you know of?" John asked, at once cutting to the chase and becoming a full-fledged participant in the conversation. Cocking his head, he gave Brian a pointed look, easy to interpret as accusatory.

Erika flashed John a quizzical look in lieu of a kick in the shin.

"I can think of no one who could even remotely be considered an enemy of Tim's," Brian stated flatly. If he'd taken John's question personally, he was hiding it well. "Is there any way I can be of further assistance?" he asked, addressing Erika with a glint of hope in his eyes.

"Actually, yes. Do you have access to the museum's personnel files? Our list obviously includes the basics—present addresses and such—but if we could take a look at a more detailed profile of staff members, it might be of use." She had no idea what kind of use, but how could she pass up the opportunity to crack open an off-limits area of research just within reach?

Brian visibly squirmed. "I do have access to the files, but not for the purpose of opening them up to the public."

"We're not exactly the public," she cajoled. "And if it should lead to anything, shall we say *tangible*, I know our group of academic, museum, and organizational leaders, would be most grateful—and you know I mean what I say."

He did. Still, he hesitated.

John pulled out the document deputizing him as an FBI agent from his breast pocket and held it up in front of Brian's face. The dates of its limited duration were on the reverse side, hence not in immediate evidence.

Brian acceded before the document was fully tucked back inside John's pocket.

Erika would have been content to review the histories of the staff members she provisionally deemed as key, in particular the prying custodial worker and the taciturn night watchman. But Brian, probably because it was less complicated than extracting individuals from the group, downloaded the entire file, photos and all, to both of them, taking their word that it would be deleted when no longer needed and forwarded to no one.

Erika promised Brian she'd keep him informed and, as she and John were preparing to leave his office, she casually inquired where the custodial supply closet happened to be located on the administration floor. With a nervous catch in his voice, Brian asked why. Was she out to cause trouble? "Of course not. I may just want to bump into Clifford Dean to thank him for his efforts that day," she answered, so disingenuously it could hardly merit Brian's concern. And so, throwing caution to the wind, he told her what she wanted to know.

* * *

John's attitude was not so cavalier. "You're not 'bumping' into anyone," he advised Erika on their elevator ride to the ground floor. "Not on my watch."

Making an issue of his meddling would only increase his watchfulness, and by default, Harrison's. "Just a passing thought. No worries."

John appeared to be mollified. "Let's find a place to sit and talk about where we go from here. I know where I'm headed. Not so sure about you. I need to be briefed."

She reminded him of her wish to take a look at the Benin Bronzes. "You familiar with them?"

"I've read an article, seen photographs. They're plaques decorating the royal grounds of Benin City back in the day. From the 1500s, as I recall. I thought Benin City was in the country of Benin, but I was wrong. It's Nigeria."

"Easy mistake to make."

Once back in the Great Court, they proceeded down the stairwell to room 25, where the Benin Bronzes were on display. John went straight for the pamphlets explaining the history and fabrication of the plaques, while Erika stood before the array gawking.

"Interesting," John commented, poring over the reading material, occasionally glancing up at the artwork itself as if only to verify the text's accuracy. "Another reference to mislead me. The 'bronzes' are made of brass. Using what's called the 'lost wax casting technique.' The craftsman formed a wax version of the finished work, then covered it in clay," he paraphrased. "Then he fired the piece to harden the clay. In the process, the wax melted away—aha, why it's called the lost wax technique!" He looked up, marveling, not at the works, it seemed, but at the brilliance behind their creation. "Finally," he said, briefly checking his cheat sheet, "the molten brass was poured into the clay mold. It cooled and hardened, and the clay was removed. The plaques were cast as matching pairs, though each was individually made. Sorry, I don't mean to lecture. I remember facts a lot longer if I say them aloud." He folded the pamphlet and inserted it into his breast pocket, behind his FBI document. He was ready to view the display for its own sake. "They're amazing," he commented, moving closer beside her. "Thanks for taking me here. Too bad Harrison couldn't come along."

"Harrison's off on another tack. Checking things out at Barclay's Bank and nosing about *The Guardian*'s archives."

"Looking for leads to your storehouse of treasures."

"Assuming it exists. Yes."

For some minutes—too few, they concluded afterwards— they circulated the room, commenting on the scenes depicted by the plaques crowding the walls from top to bottom.

"Hold it," John declared toward the end of their tour, his look bordering on revelatory. "I'm seeing kings—obas as you pointed out—kings with their attendants, priests, warriors, European traders with their swords and pikes, court officials, acrobats even. And then there are the animals—the crocodiles and leopards—"

"Symbols of the oba's power," Erika offered. "The leopard, especially, symbolizes the oba's triumph over nature."

"Bears, lizards, fish, chickens," John went on.

"Chickens were thought to predict the future," Erika tagged.

John turned to face her head on. "So where are the women and children? What are they, chopped liver?"

Erika laughed. "Behind the scenes. The plaques commemorate the obas—their power, their history, their dynasty."

John shook his head. "My wife's ultra-woke. She would not approve." He gestured toward an unoccupied bench. "Let's go sit and discuss the agenda."

From the moment they sat down she saw there was something troubling him. "What's wrong?"

"I don't like the guy."

Taken by surprise: "Who, *Brian?*"

He nodded. "There's something about him. He's got airs. Bugs me."

She slid farther apart to regard him more fully. "Really, John. He loves his work and he's

basically a nice person, generous with his time. So, he's got airs. Live with it."

"Trust me, I will," John said, the words loaded with meaning.

"You're not thinking of checking him out, are you?"

"We'll see."

"John!"

"He seemed awfully keen on besmirching the character of one or two of his staffers, don't you think? Plus, counting on your wife to provide an alibi for your absence from a crime scene is as old as the hills." He gave a dismissive wave. "Drop it for now. I'm heading over to Tinworth Street, looks like about two and a half miles from here. National Crime Agency headquarters. I was planning on working with the City of London Police or the more inclusive Metropolitan Police, but one of my FBI pals put me onto these people, suggested I go straight to them. This was news to me. I'd never heard of them."

Erika decided arguing with John about Brian's innocence at this moment would be equivalent to beating a dead horse. "What about this agency?" she asked, moving on. "What do they do?"

"For starters, their jurisdiction is the United Kingdom. Broad enough for you? I'm told the media's dubbed them 'the British FBI.' That's already a good thing, given what I want from them."

"Which is, I take it, the most complete background material on a couple of individuals on staff at the British Museum, like Clifford Dean and Martin MacLevy. Not that there's any evidence of guilt attached to either of them."

"I may look into a number of others, if given the chance. Can't hurt. I also want to see if I can find a match for the guy in the photo you sent me—from the Frenchman."

"Pierre Jolet, right. And you'll tell your source that this is highly sensitive information, that it can't be leaked. Until we get the go-ahead from my contact, Amilah Adamu, we are not to release the man's identity to the detective in charge of handling Thorpe's case. You got that, right?"

"Multiple times. I told you I've got a good memory for the spoken word," he reminded her, reaching over to pat her arm.

"Sorry for repeating myself."

"You're forgiven. Getting back to the NCA—the Brit's FBI wannabe—this is a relatively new organization, established in 2013. It may be naïve of me, but I think they'll be impressed with my FBI credentials, eager to be of service."

"Good for their street cred. You may be right. Did your friend give you the name of a particular person to contact?"

"Sure did. Monica Evans. Works in close contact with the Director-General. We've got a date in"—he glanced at his watch—"a half-hour. And what will *you* be doing while I'm currying up to the NCA?"

She recited her plans as succinctly as possible.

He eyed her warily. "I don't know. Shall I let you out of my sight?"

She thought of the addendum she'd just tacked onto tomorrow's agenda that she had no intention of disclosing to either of her travelmates. "You have no choice, John," she said blithely. "Let's meet back at the hotel a half hour or so before dinner to sum up our day, discuss what we've all been up to." She rose to go, John following suit.

She was feeling good—hopeful—leaving the museum and off to her first unchaperoned appointment. That is, until she felt the same pelvic tug of alarm she'd experienced earlier. A false alarm, she realized several seconds later, when the man in the green jacket and cap turned her way and proved to be a woman.

Chapter Fourteen

Erika was well prepared for her interview with Joanna Ashton on Ockham Lane in Cobham, Surrey. The present trip to London was barely in its planning stages when she'd begun scouring the web for references to Joanna and her husband Keith, from whose home the now infamous Picasso study for *Les Demoiselles d'Avignon* had been stolen, along with what would have been the remainder of Keith's life.

She and Harrison had been informed by Amilah that the Ashtons were private investors and art collectors. What Amilah had not told them was that the couple were also mega-philanthropists and that at the time of his death, Keith, along with Joanna, were in the process of overseeing and funding the construction of a major exhibition center at the Royal College of Art in Kensington. Almost instantly, from this single seed of information sprang the idea for an *Art News* essay. Erika had run it by her boss, Sara Masden and she'd approved. "You exploit your vocation for good cause," Sara had said, gracing the remark with her signature staccato laugh. "Go to it."

And, indeed she had. Most of the research for the project had been done before she'd stepped foot onto the plane bound for Heathrow. It only needed Joanna Asthon's input to round it out.

However, as she stepped from the taxi at the end of the Ashtons' tree-lined driveway (which she'd mistaken for a boulevard), her confidence was momentarily shaken. Still adapting to the splendid accommodations of the Wheatley residence, still ill-at-ease with the reality that her lifestyle was at odds with those less fortunate but equally deserving, she was both awestruck and dismayed by the grandeur of the Greek Revival palace that stood before her. She tugged at her skirt, which suddenly felt too short, and proceeded to the portico entrance of the dwelling. As she timidly struck the bronze lion's head knocker against the oversized wooden door, she heard the taxi begin its retreat, abandoning her.

The door slowly opened to reveal the hostess—"Hello, Erika, I'm Joanna"—and the world turned upside down: Joanna, the abandoned; Erika, the lady of the domain.

Without thinking, Erika embraced her. "It's okay, I'm so sorry." She could feel the woman's shoulder blades beneath the shapeless blue dress; would not have guessed she was so thin.

"Oh my, oh my," Joanna murmured, drawing away. "What's gotten into me? I haven't been like this in days. I'm mortified." Her eyes were red and swollen from the crying, and though she appeared to be over it for now, it had left her looking ravaged and worn. "Do come in. Please."

She ushered Erika into the entryway and swung the door shut behind them. "Let's start over, shall we?" she said, leading her into the central living area. Her spirit seemed to have improved, either through Erika's warm embrace or the exercise of British restraint.

Erika, meanwhile, having returned to the more appropriate role of interloper, found herself standing in the middle of Downton Abbey, season five. There they were, the wingback chairs with their carved wood feet and armrests, the great stone fireplace, the ornately patterned rugs, the beveled glass mirror in a decorative gold frame, the crystal chandelier. Yet the most curious feature of the space was its welcoming comfort and hominess, despite the inescapable aura of wealth. The next most curious feature was the discrepancy of taste between the room's furnishings and its exhibited art.

"It's not *us*," Joanna said, responding to Erika's surveillance. "The house came furnished. It was essentially a fire sale. We'd fallen in love with the grounds, you see. We so valued our privacy." She beckoned Erika toward a grouping of decorative side chairs upholstered in jade velvet. "Although in the end, we did come to cherish the furnishings," she added, with a gesture indicating Erika take a seat. "It broadened our taste, we believed. Belongings foisted on us occasionally have that effect, don't you think?"

"Yes, I do," Erika said, understanding now the discrepancy in taste between the inherited portion of the décor: traditional, and the displayed art: experimental. "Although I take it the paintings are all imports from you and your husband."

"Straight from the heart, yes. Primary rather than acquired taste. You're observant, Erika. Now, please take a seat."

"Mind if I have a walk-about first? For my own sake as well as for the article's? You have quite a gallery here. It rivals the Museum of Modern Art. At a glance, the modern era seems to predominate. Am I wrong?"

Joanna smiled. "Not predominate. Monopolize. Keith and I concentrate... " She paused. "We *concentrated*," she went on, forcing acceptance of the new grammar, "on the dawn of experimentation, from the impressionists with their interpretation of reality determined by the fleeting play of light—to the fauvists with their use of bold colors overriding their adherence to reality"—she seemed to be soaring off on her own—"to the analytical cubists and their multiple perspectives of things—to the expressionists and the objectification of their subjective states." She came to a halt; a forced landing. "What am I doing? I've been babbling a lot lately, only in my head, not before a captive audience. We used to have long talks about the nature of art, its function, its purpose. I miss them, so I talk to myself." She shrugged. "Forgive me."

"Nothing to forgive." Erika reached into her bag for her pad and pen; held them up. "You mind? I don't use a tape recorder; it tends to make people nervous."

"Perfectly fine."

Erika jotted down a few of Joanna's remarks verbatim before they slipped her mind. She kept her writing supplies in hand as she walked toward one of the walls displaying a fraction of the Ashtons' collection, art created roughly from the mid-nineteenth century to the mid-twentieth. There must be lots more in other rooms, she thought greedily. She hoped an invitation to view them was forthcoming. If not, she'd take the initiative. "Would it be okay to photograph a few of the paintings?" she asked.

"Certainly. But I would like to consult my lawyer and insurance agent before I give you my consent to publish them. I'm sure you understand."

"Of course," Erika said, coming to a dead stop before a grouping of expressionist paintings. "In fact, no word or image will be set in print before you review those passages of the article that reference you and your husband," she added, unable to tear her gaze from the Vincent van Gogh oil painting at the center of the arrangement. It was a relatively small canvas, maybe ten by twelve inches, but it was as if the whole of humanity's rowdy dance of life had been compressed within this small space, like a universe shrinking in size without losing a particle of energy. "It reminds me of his *Dance Hall at Arles*," only..."

"Only more so," Joanna supplied. "Denser, more compact."

"Exactly. The thickness of the paint contributes to the effect." She exchanged the pad and pen for her cell phone, snapped a photograph of the painting, and finally forced herself to move on to another portion of the exhibit. If she didn't pick up the pace, she'd never get to the substance of the interview, no less fulfill the covert purpose of her visit.

"I see you have an interest in the women impressionists," she remarked, coming upon an Eva Gonzalès portrait of a woman sitting in an opera box, opera glasses in hand, and adjacent to it, a Berthe Morisot portrait of a woman gazing lovingly at an infant in a cradle. A Mary Cassatt painting of a girl with a parasol hung above the Morisot, and Erika described the Wheatleys' own Mary Cassatt of a young woman in a blue dress. "Knitting," she added. "A sweet domesticity, or at least ladylike propriety about the paintings, yes? But then, women were excluded from patronizing the dance halls and such, unlike their male counterparts."

"Absolutely," Joanna agreed, suddenly animated. "Can you imagine if a woman had painted anything resembling that iconic Matisse masterpiece, *The Dance*? Those bold nudes, hand-in-hand moving in their joyous circle? Matisse himself created quite a stir. Cassatt would have been tarred and feathered!" She uttered a grunt of exasperation. "Do you know that the art academies fashioned their courses for women to adapt to what they considered their limited capacities? What am I saying, of *course* you know!"

The perfect segue. "I know how passionate you are about the plight of women," Erika remarked. "In *all* spheres of life, judging from the charities you and your husband have supported so generously over the years." She dropped her cell phone into her bag and pulled out her pad and pen. "Shall we sit and get down to it? If you allow me to wander about at my leisure you may never be rid of me."

"That would greatly please me. In fact, you must stay for dinner. My mother is staying with me for now, and she insists on lavishing me with the most extravagant meals. It's her way of cheering me up, she thinks, and I allow her to believe it. Our housekeeper was a wonderful cook, but she left us to take on another job shortly before Keith's death. We had but one live-in employee. As I said, we cherished our privacy." Staring off into space, she added, "I'm not sure what I'll do when my mother returns to her own life." She brushed her hand across her face as if she were removing a film. "You'll stay for dinner?"

Erika gracefully declined the dinner invitation, but accepted the one offering tea and pastries, realizing as she did so, that she was famished.

A short time later they were seated together in the two jade green accent chairs, the tea tray (prepared by the hostess refusing help from her guest) between them on the delicate carved wood table. "I've agreed to this interview to commemorate my husband's body of charitable work," Joanna announced as she lifted her teacup to her lips. "In business, Keith was an aggressive negotiator and deal maker—*out* there, as they say—but when it came to his charitable work, he preferred to remain behind the scenes. I want him to at last be noticed—*lauded*, if you will." She took a sip of her tea. "As for myself, I wish to be underplayed. I'm not being coy, you understand. I simply want you to tell it like it is. Keith was the prime mover in our charitable enterprises."

Erika assured Joanna that she would abide by her wishes as she delicately plucked a scone from the tea tray and warned herself not to scarf it down. "I see now why it was so difficult for me to come up with references to your philanthropic achievements. You might have at least tooted your own horn a time or two!" She took a ladylike bite, followed it with a spot of tea, then polished off the pastry. Her writing materials had been balancing on her lap. She took them in hand. "Shall we?"

"Fire away."

The object of Erika's proposed magazine article was to examine the artistic and philanthropic inclinations of a select group of art collectors and see how, or if, they were related. In the Ashtons' case, she already knew the answer, at least partially. "I can see your interest in women's issues is reflected in both your selection of art and charitable causes. "How did this interest arise?"

"It was a given right from the start. Keith's mother had been an artist herself and had encountered a good deal of male chauvinism from art dealers and from both private and museum collectors. Not that the problem has been eradicated," she added as an aside. "Keith never formally stated that his interest took shape as a result of his mother's difficulties, but I suspect they played a good part. He was not a strident feminist by any means, but he was a devoted one."

Joanna elaborated on the women's issues that she and her husband had been particularly involved with, including medical research in the areas of breast cancer and post-partum depression, as well as a host of autoimmune diseases, more prevalent in women than men. She went on to cite the student art study scholarships her husband had initiated and lastly, described in detail the major building project they'd both been engaged in at the time of his death, making sure Erika understood that she would remain committed to the project going forward.

Once Erika had obtained all the information she needed for her article, she felt morally justified to switch hats. "It's hard to broach the subject, Joanna, but you do of course know how I discovered that you and your husband were major art collectors."

"By hearing of our tragedy. How else?"

"Yes, and when I contacted you for an interview, I also mentioned that my husband and I are part of a group interested in accelerating the repatriation of looted African art. So, you must also understand why I feel compelled to ask you about that terrible day. Not as a subject for my essay, but for a purpose outside it."

"You're referring to the matter of the Picasso drawing, the motivation behind its theft. I've been expecting you to ask me about that—counting on you!" Her words were uttered in as animated a manner as when she'd spoken her mind on the treatment of female impressionists. She cracked a smile. "You look relieved, Erika."

So relieved she grabbed another pastry. "I was afraid you would be reluctant to talk about, well, the actual circumstances."

"I'm not surprised. I was a sniveling wreck when you first set eyes on me. I do fall into these terrible states, but then I'm good for a while. I'm not sure how it works, maybe my anger upstages my grief, but there you have it." Joanna rose to her feet. "Come, let me show you where the Picasso was displayed. The placement is important, I believe, but the detective—Detective Hogarty—clings to his simple theories."

Erika had waited a discreet second before taking a bite of the pastry. At Joanna's summons, she laid the remainder on the edge of her saucer and leaped to her feet.

Joanna led her through an arched entrance to the adjacent room—sitting, drawing or parlor given its cozy but unspecified character—where another twenty or so artworks adorned the walls. At a glance, there appeared to be no glaring space where the Picasso might have hung.

"Right here," Joanna beckoned, pointing to a pleasant country landscape whose style was unfamiliar to Erika. "Replaced with one of my mother-in-law's oils. I took it from upstairs. I'd take you up to see more of her work, but my own mother is taking a much needed nap and is a very light sleeper. This was one of Keith's favorites."

"It's lovely," Erika said, realizing at its utterance the thinness of the praise, especially in the context of the neighboring canvas, another astounding Van Gogh and a landscape as well. The word "lovely" went up in flames in its presence.

"You understand what I mean about the placement of the Picasso," Joanna said quietly. "It's obvious, isn't it?"

Erika nodded, studying the turbulent Van Gogh countryside. "Why would a thief choose a drawing, even a Picasso drawing, over an oil by Van Gogh?"

She turned abruptly to Joanna. "Why would he choose to turn down a *Picasso* oil, for that matter? There are two—I saw them—hanging in the first room he walked into. Why did he leave the main room to search elsewhere for a Picasso of lesser value?"

"Because he was after that particular drawing."

"Exactly." Erika, along with Harrison and Amilah, had come up with that theory a week ago, but being on site where the crime had taken place made their theory virtually incontrovertible. "Wait. Did he access the premises through the window in this room?"

"No. He hacked open the lock to the front door. I've had the door replaced."

Erika rested her hand on Joanna's shoulder. "You hate this. It's selfish of me to make you go over it."

"But I want to go over it. I must understand what happened here—*why* it happened." Joanna patted the hand resting on her shoulder, then broke away. "Forget first impressions. I'm more resilient than you think."

Erika smiled even as her brow furrowed in consternation. "I don't understand why Detective Hogarty didn't pursue this line of reasoning. Did he at least give it some thought?"

Joanna shrugged. "Who knows. Maybe later, after he interviewed me. But no, not while he was here. While he was here his main concern was collecting physical evidence, overseeing the crime scene experts, and going over the general area on his own, inside and out. As for motivation, he was sticking to his theory until the evidence proved otherwise. He believed the perpetrator had intended to rob the place of whatever art he could lay his hands on and that was that. He assumed that he had arrived in a transport of some kind, and that the lack of tread marks on the driveway did not refute the fact. Although my husband had called off the alarm company, Hogarty stuck to his idea that the perpetrator had feared the company's operator had heard the nervousness in Keith's voice and had decided to activate the local police to be on the safe side. You'll have to allow him that point, Erika. The detective played the tape for me, and there was no mistaking the terror in Keith's voice. It was very difficult to listen to."

"I can only imagine," Erika said, cringing from the inadequacy of the phrase. Snuffing out the pause that followed, she asked, "Hogarty must have reassessed his theory after what happened to the drawing, don't you think?"

"You're referring to its desecration," Joanna said, closing her eyes as if to shut out the sight of it.

"Disclosed on Mick Ross's vlog, yes. Hogarty must have realized then that the motivation behind the crime could not have been that of the stereotypical art thief. This individual had not only destroyed a valuable artwork, but he'd given it away in the bargain."

"The destruction of the drawing is unforgivable, but the political message is even worse," Joanna adamantly declared.

"I'm going to quote you on that," Erika said, making note of it in her pad, inadvertently catching sight of her watch as she did so. Time was marching on. Switching gears to broach the subject she needed to cover without fail, she asked, "Joanna, would you mind telling me how you came into possession of the Picasso drawing? At auction, was it?"

"Not at auction, no. Although we did acquire a sizable number of our pieces at auction. From Christie's and Sotheby's most often. The Picasso was acquired in quite a different manner." She hesitated.

Is Joanna wondering in what manner to deliver the information, or if she should deliver it at all! Erika was on tenterhooks.

"Ah yes, Brian," Joanna declared, the proverbial bulb lighting up. "I couldn't remember the first name."

It was a common name, Brian. So why did John's reservations about Brian Latham pop into Erika's mind so readily? "Brian?"

"Yes, Brian Latham. He's a curator at the British Museum and a longtime ally of Keith's. Mates at Oxford they were, not that they carried on a close friendship after college, but if push came to shove, they had each other's backs."

Suppressing any outward sign of surprise, Erika considered mentioning that she knew Brian. Decided it might prejudice Joanna's story. Admittedly, not quite an honorable excuse, but honor was not the theme of the day, knowledge was. "I'm curious; go on."

"Well, we had always wanted to own a study—in *any* medium—for

Picasso's *Les Demoiselles d'Avignon*, but we were never able to find one either through auction or private dealers. Once we came close, but were finessed by an oil baron from Gujarat, India, for whom money was no issue. You know how it goes," she added almost airily. "If you can't have something, it becomes an obsession."

"I know," Erika replied agreeably. Generically she knew, yes. But to covet a must-have work of art by Picasso? Not a clue.

"About six months ago we approached a number of museums to see if they had what we were looking for in storage and if so, would they be willing to part with it? We have the closest ties with the British Museum and the trustees were willing, if tepidly, to think about it. De-accession is a controversial subject for museums. Many have codified rules about it. For a museum to sell off art for any other purpose than for the acquisition of art is frowned on. Latham went the extra yard for us. He searched the records of the museum's storage facilities and came up with the Picasso drawing listed in the records of one of them—Franks House in East London, I believe. He suggested to the board that they transact an exchange rather than conduct an outright sale. In the end, we traded one of our Braque oils for the drawing and everyone was satisfied," she concluded. Stripped from the narrative bubble, Joanna's demeanor suddenly darkened. "I wish we'd never done it," she said bitterly. "Keith would still be here."

In blaming her husband's death on the Picasso drawing, Joanna had spoken the truth. The felon had broken into the Ashton home to take possession of that particular drawing. Anything that contradicted that, no matter how comforting, would be an insult to Joanna's intelligence. "You can't know what might have happened," Erika elided. "You can never know."

Joanna thanked Erika for the gallant try with a wan smile. "I'm glad you came today," she said. "I never would have opened up if we had spoken long distance. I do wish you'd stay for dinner. My mother tends to suffocate me. You're a breath of fresh air."

Polite regrets were repeated, and the unconventional interview was brought to a close with the formulaic rituals of those less so: summarizing the facts gathered, reviewing contact information, setting the date for a follow-up conference. Before Erika called for a taxi, she asked Joanna if she would give—or lend—her a few photographs of herself and her husband. Joanna gave her only one, a formal portrait taken of the couple on their thirtieth wedding anniversary two years prior. "This is what Keith would have allowed," she said. "Anything else he would have considered an encroachment on his private life."

A short while later, reviewing things on her own in the back of the cab on the way to Olivia Chatham's flat in south London, Erika found herself dwelling on the means by which the Picasso study for *Les Demoiselles d'Avignon* had found its way to the Ashton residence. With growing certainty, she believed that because the process had been conducted within the orbit of the British Museum—even the transfer of art had been made by a museum-owned van, she'd learned from Joanna in their last-minute wrap-up—the theft of the drawing, if not actually committed by an insider, had at least been *enabled* by one.

What did she plan to do with this knowledge? There was one more action she must take before making that crucial decision. The decision would have to wait until tomorrow.

Chapter Fifteen

O n clear days such as this, Ikemar Umar made it his business to find time to stroll along the Thames River, sneakers hitting the now familiar stone pavement of Victoria Embankment, covering the same two-point-three miles before treading back along the same route, up Aldwych to Kingsway, where his temporary quarters, the sleek Virginia Woolf Building, awaited his return. The repetition of the trip—every now and then recognizing a jogger or two or feeling that same pinch in the pit of his stomach on passing a couple of young people sitting atop the stone barricade, fearlessly dangling their legs over the river—made him feel he knew the place; he belonged here.

Although on entering the building, as he did now, there was always that introductory moment when he felt like an intruder, when that slightly spooky wax statue of Virginia Woolf in the lobby would look at him askance, or so it seemed, containing in that glance the whole of Continental and English History, which was, not surprisingly, one of the courses Virginia took at the King's Ladies' Department in Kensington in her teens; the others, no great news, Latin and Greek. It was only after a natural relaxation of his senses, often hastened by a friendly nod from a student or fellow professor, that Virginia's look appeared to be directed inward, or at least past his shoulder. Anyway, he might brightly rethink, as now, what was he here for, if not to expand the cultural horizons at King's College? Wasn't that worth a bit of discomfort?

"Bloody hell, yes!" he quietly Brit-mimicked, strutting off to his office in high spirits, taking the stairs three at a time to the second floor, feeling his impressive stature as an agent of his intellect, this feeling new to him and, come to think of it, pretty damn tolerable. Once inside his temporary lair, by rights that of a French lit professor presently on sabbatical, he peeled off his blazer and hung it over his desk chair. Functional-contemporary, he'd describe the chair, like most of the furnishings in this all-accommodating building where he lived, taught, studied, and played an occasional game of table tennis. Indeed, this was a building where an unadventurous professor or postgrad student might enjoy a relatively comfortable life as an agoraphobic.

Ike sat down in the chair, loosened his tie, and took a look at his anachronously non-digital calendar, a twelve-page collection of animal babies sent in return for a ten dollar or more donation to the World Wildlife Fund. Today, Wednesday, Harrison and Erika Wheatley had arrived in London for a short stay. Harrison had asked to meet with him this afternoon, but Ike had stated his preference for the following day, and Harrison had readily agreed. "HW 11am KF Htl" had been duly noted in tomorrow's square. Ike had explained that his classes were held on Monday, Wednesday, and Friday mornings, and that he liked to leave those afternoons free for student conferences, scheduled and/or spur of the moment.

This afternoon there was only one conference scheduled, with a student named Bradan Yusuf. Ike knew the name only by its association with a record of exam and essay grades. His lecture course was vastly over-enrolled, and he was able to identify by sight only those students who were inveterate class participants, eager to turn lectures into conversations, an activity he found to be both flattering and self-instructive.

As he was checking his laptop for his latest emails, he heard a knock on the door. He glanced at his watch. Bradan—he assumed it was Bradan—was ten minutes early. "Come!" he called, rising from his chair to greet his guest.

He was expecting a young man to enter the office. This fellow, from what he could see of him, given the peaked cap, aviator sunglasses and upturned collar of his Windbreaker, seemed somewhat older. Not unusual, really. One often came across a middle-aged, even an elderly individual, bent on attaining an advanced degree or simply improving his knowledge of the world. This gentleman, done up in this manner, was either going for what he imagined was a cool look or trying to conceal the fact that he was no longer a bloke in his salad days. A bit sad, either way. "Shut the door, will you, Bradan—you are Bradan, are you not?" He offered a cordial smile.

"Yes, sir. Bradan Yusuf." Smile returned.

Up to now, Ike had only been able to make out the slightly lax jawline. Now he could add to the list a pleasant voice and an even set of teeth. The visitor turned his back on him and shut the door. A single snapping sound followed, like a lock clicking into place; an extra twist of the knob, no doubt. Even Ike had never locked the door from within. "Take a seat, Bradan," he directed, sitting back down himself. "You called to say you wanted to discuss your essay. How can I help you?"

The petitioner slipped off his backpack and dumped it beside the chair he was assigned to, across from Ike's. "I'm writing about the rise of Boko Haram in Nigeria," he recited, remaining on his feet. "I started off focusing on the unrest caused by the gap between national wealth and poverty of the individual, but I got caught up contrasting the protocol of the terrorist group with a pacific interpretation of the Islamic faith."

"You might want to consider changing your central theme," Ike suggested. "Do you see another theme taking precedence? Can you summarize it? It'll help you organize your thoughts."

"I guess," the man answered, eyes wandering.

"Let's hear it," Ike encouraged. "Take your time." Probably Irish-Nigerian, he randomly thought. Back home his dentist's surname was Yusuf. He was due for a checkup, actually. He supposed he'd call the individual's skin color olive—more olive than tawny. "Have a seat," he urged.

"I'm okay," the man said, directing his gaze to a spot behind Ike—the wall bookshelf, must be.

"You see something that interests you?" Ike asked. *What happened to the thread of our conversation?* "Why don't you take off your glasses?" he suddenly asked, more boldly than he'd intended.

"Got an eye condition," the man said, his hip brushing the side of the desk as he stepped toward the wall. "That book," he said idly, arriving right beside Ike.

I'm twice his size, Ike thought, as if there was a reason to take the man down.

And then, of course, it was too late. Too late even to cry out. No sound uttered even as the blade sliced across his throat, only an odd gurgling noise coming afterwards—from *himself*, his intact being observed from without.

He pressed his palm to his throat to stop the flow; not too late for a last try. His detached self, knowing better, moved away, his image of the dying man fading.

In his final clutch of life, Ikemar Umar was overcome with a sudden effusion of faith, which startled and calmed him, and with a voice he no longer possessed, to a killer he could no longer see, he cried, unheard, *"Ki olorun dariji."* May God forgive you.

Chapter Sixteen

"Y ou first," Erika cheerfully advised John, after the trio had settled in for their pre-prandial conference. She and Harrison had just been FaceTiming Lucas and she was still on a high. Sitting astride Kate's lap as she held onto his waist, the boy had shot forward, screeching with glee, his chubby little hands reaching for his mommy through the screen; satisfied with the remote connection, not wailing for more; what a relief.

"I'll pass," John replied. "I want to hear what you people have to say first." He patted the laptop propped up against his stomach and directed a tentative smile at his hosts, contentedly perched across from him on their hotel room's sofa.

"You okay?" Harrison asked.

"Sure." The eyes saying otherwise.

Harrison gave him a quizzical look but proceeded. They were booked for a table forty minutes from now at the hotel's popular seafood restaurant, the Neptune, and he did not intend to be bumped by a party of stand-bys. Never mind the seafood; he hoped they were still featuring their Spaghetti Alla Vongole. Was it his memory of the dish or the woman he had shared it with giving him hunger pangs? "You start," he advised the beloved culprit sitting beside him. "You learn anything from your visit with Joanna Ashton?"

Erika gave them a rundown on all that had occurred at the Ashton residence, focusing on her conclusion that an individual associated with the British Museum was a dealer in museum-sensitive information or both source *and* felon.

"A jack of all trades," John offered half-heartedly. "Sorry."

What's up with him? Erika wondered. Hoped he was just missing his wife. "I visited Olivia Chatham afterwards," she went on. "As you know"—with a glance at Harrison—"I had a compulsion to search the nooks and crannies of Andrew Barrett's desk. Deep down, I figured I was only in for a pleasant conversation and another spot of tea, but I had to see for myself."

Harrison sat forward. "You're kidding. You found something?"

"I did." Her tote bag, with which she was inseparable this trip, was lying at her feet. "Drum roll, please." She reached into the bag and drew forth an unmarked manila envelope, lifted its flap, and carefully withdrew a slip of paper about five by seven inches in size. It was obvious from its maze of wrinkles that it had been restored from a severely crunched-up state. She handed it to Harrison. "It's a nineteenth-century receipt for a bracelet," she clued John in. "It has to do with our research on Andrew Barrett, a medic in the Royal Army."

"This is about your treasure hunt, I take it."

She nodded. "Related by circumstance to Timothy Thorpe's murder."

"This is interesting," Harrison remarked, with less enthusiasm than Erika had predicted. "How did Olivia manage to miss it?"

"I removed the drawers. The paper must have slipped out the back of one drawer and gotten jammed in a seam between the back and side walls of the desk. Easy to miss, although Olivia was pretty hard on herself. What do you think of our find?"

"As I said, interesting, certainly for its human interest. I imagine the bracelet was bought for Lily. Six-hundred fifty pounds. That must be equivalent to about twenty-thousand dollars in today's market." He smiled. "Found out the inflation then to now from my connection at Barclay's today."

"Harrison!"

"What?"

"Read it carefully."

He did so—aloud, from top to bottom. "'L. P. Sutton, Goldsmith, Nettles Road, Brentford, Sixteen August 1897. Solid twenty-four karat gold handmade chain link necklace, eighteen inches. Six-hundred fifty pounds.'" He looked up. "Sutton's signature below. Am I missing something?"

"Only the connection."

"Sweetheart, our reservation's at seven. *Tell* me."

"Do you remember the date of Andrew Barrett's 'Eureka' entry? The day he says he's found a safe place for the treasures he's holding on behalf of their countries of origin?"

"I don't, no."

"August *seventeenth!*"

"The day after he visits the goldsmith!"

She smiled. "The light dawns."

Harrison slapped his thigh like he'd just heard a riotous joke. "Here I've been toiling away at Barclay's," he began, suppressing a full-fledged grin so he could get out the words, "rummaging through the old ledgers of Parsons, Thomas and Company for the express purpose of finding just such a clue! You're amazing, Erika. Isn't she amazing, John?"

"Sure is," John replied, his mind clearly elsewhere.

"Hold it," Harrison put forth with sudden deliberation. "Let's take a look at some papers I've got here." While he searched the contents of his briefcase, lying within reach on the coffee table, he gave them his backstory. "My appointment was with the Barclay bank manager, but when the man heard what I was after, he directed me to the pensions financial accountant, Jill Mortimer, who, he said, was their resident historian, unofficial, of course—ah, here's what I'm looking for." He slipped two sheets of paper from his general collection. They were copies of pages from the record books of Parsons, Thomson, and Company, the private bank at which Andrew Barrett had written a number of critical checks.

Harrison passed the sheets to Erika. "Not that they're for Erika's and my eyes only," he explained to John, "but they're not related to the criminal activity you're digging into. Anytime you want to have a look, though, you're welcome to."

"Appreciate it," John said, holding his laptop against himself as if he was afraid someone might snatch it from him.

Erika examined the pages. The generic printed matter on each appeared below spaces filled in in ink with numbers and names written in longhand.

On one of the pages, two of Barrett's checks were recorded. The first was the check he'd made out to Daniel Edgerton for his statues and altarpieces from West Africa, along with the furniture grouping meant to divert his parents. The second was the check he'd made out to the moving company that had transported the Edgerton purchase to Barrett Farms in Hertfordshire. Both had been written on May 10, 1897. "Packard's is the name of the moving company," Erika commented. In Andrew's journal, no name is given."

"Don't get your hopes up there," Harrison said. "Ms. Mortimer informed me that the company went out of business a hundred years ago, leaving no records. Saved me from going on a wild goose chase at least. But it's something else that's key here. Before I tell you, take a look at the second page."

Two checks were recorded on the second page, both dated August 17, 1897. One was irrelevant, having to do with a G. Holmes purchasing a cow from one Nelly Paxton. The other was a check from Andrew Barrett written to Packard's Moving Company. Unlike the other check to Packard's, no notation as to the destination had been made. At Andrew's request, no doubt. "What's the catch here, Harrison?"

"Alright then," he stated solemnly.

The professor's time to shine. Why did she find him so damn adorable when he turned tutorial? "I'm listening."

"So, as you can see, in the case of both trips, the mileage, the estimated cubic feet of space allowed for the articles to be transported, and lastly, the cost to transport the articles are all recorded. The first trip is from the Edgerton's home in— Buckinghamshire, we discover here, since Barrett's journal did not specify the county—to Barrett Farms in Hertfordshire. The second trip is from Barrett Farms to an undisclosed destination, which we're now assuming is the safe haven for Andrew's treasures." He paused, leaning toward her.

She imagined him hunching over his lectern. "You want me to check out the numbers; compare them."

He nodded. "For what purpose?" the professor queried.

She needed to get this right. "Let's see. If we *only* know the distance from Buckinghamshire to Hertfordshire, but we *also* know the cost and approximate bulk of *both* shipments, then we ought to be able to calculate the approximate number of miles from Barrett Farms to the unknown destination—the secret hiding place. Am I close?" Of course, she was. She just wanted to hear it from him.

"Exactly right, good! So now let's take a look." He took his cell phone from his breast pocket and punched in his question. "The distance between Buckinghamshire and Hertfordshire is eighteen miles. Got a pen?"

John handed him the one clipped inside his jacket pocket.

"Thanks." He reached across Erika to jot down the number in the margin of one of the pages lying on her lap. "Eighteen miles," he repeated.

"The cubic feet estimates are both fifty," Erika said. "We can scratch that variable. We have only three *knowns* we need to play with. The two payments—thirty-three pounds sterling for the trip in May from the Edgertons in Buckinghamshire to Barrett Farms in Hertfordshire and fifty-one for the trip in August from Hertfordshire to destination unknown. Our *third* given is the distance between Buckinghamshire and Hertfordshire, eighteen miles. If I remember my algebra correctly—"

"Twenty-seven point eight one eight one eight one et cetera," John blandly put forth. "Not taking into account varying costs of packing materials, detours, delays."

From Erika: *What?*" accompanied by a cartoonish stare.

"Miles from Hertfordshire to destination unknown. Isn't that what you wanted to know?" John shrugged. "It's a talent. They made fun of me at school for it. Since then, I try not to let it get around."

"I'm impressed."

"That's what I was afraid of." Waving off the topic, he asked, "Shouldn't you check to see how far from Hertfordshire your goldsmith was doing business? See if it's in the realm of possibility that it's where your guy Andrew shipped his treasures?"

Harrison had already been working on it with his cell phone. "Wow," he commented, retyping on Google Maps the names of the English counties under discussion. "Yup, here it is again. Twenty-eight and a half miles."

He looked up. "Uncanny, yes? I know where I'm headed tomorrow after my brunch with Ike. Either of you want to join us—and me, on my trip to Brentford— or do you have other plans?"

"It's more efficient if we work independently," John suggested, saving the day for Erika, who was already plotting and planning her own itinerary.

"Good thinking," Harrison agreed. "You know," he added almost reminiscently, "Jill—at the bank—was trying every which way to talk me into telling all. I felt rather guilty, being so closemouthed about our project, seeing she was putting herself out for me, spending time foraging for records, educating me on the customs of the 1890s." To John, abruptly: "You have that problem yourself, John? I mean with the Metropolitan Police, or whomever you talked to today?" *Had John just flinched?* "John?"

"Maybe I did at that!" John replied, his tone bordering on combative. He flipped open his laptop; found what he was looking for. "Put that thought aside for a minute. Let me sum up. First of all, sorry, Erika, but I don't care for your Mr. Latham. I'd keep him on my watch list if I were you. Just saying." Before going further, he told Harrison about the organization from whom he had sought help. "As I explained earlier to Erika, the National Crime Agency's jurisdiction is the United Kingdom. Quite a broad sphere of operations compared to the Metropolitan Police."

For the most part, John was keeping his eyes glued to his laptop screen—*to avoid making eye contact with* us, Erika reluctantly concluded. John reported that he'd learned a great deal from his newly formed connections at the NCA, information that he would not have been able to uncover without their help. Erika remembered he'd mentioned in particular a Monica Evans, a person who worked closely with the agency's Director-General. No names were mentioned at this telling, oddly enough. He was holding back, keeping something from them. Totally out of character. *What's up with you, John?*

Meanwhile, what John had learned from his new colleagues was eye-opening. To begin with, from the personnel list Brian had shared with John, there was one—*only* one—name that had set off John's alarm, and that name was Clifford Dean: the custodian who'd been caught rifling through Brian's wastebasket, and who had tried to breathe life back into Timothy Thorpe.

"At first scan, Dean's personnel file looked good, no problem," John said, briefly glancing up from his screen in the general direction of his audience. "However, due to Latham's sketchy remarks about him, I wanted to dig deeper and needed help big time. In the process, I was clued in on how folks living in the UK go about securing a National Insurance Number, or NIN—more or less the equivalent of our social security number. Seems it's issued a couple of months before your sixteenth birthday if your parent fills in what they call a child benefit claim. Sure enough, Dean's personnel file goes back to 1991, the year he turns sixteen and gets his first job, part-time working in an auto repair shop. Records are scant after that. A couple of jobs listed, with letters of recommendation, but there's something out of whack there. His letters of recommendation, they're f-ing *glowing*, and on top of that, they all seem to be written in the same..."

"Voice?" Erika suggested.

"Voice," he came up with simultaneously. "The computer whiz thought I was reading into the letters what I wanted to see but went along with my foolishness. Ended up doing an in-depth probe of Dean's NIN and happened to find relatively few records before the year 2015. In 2015 the records fattened up, took on a more lived-in look. This did not seem to ruffle any feathers, especially since there were no arrests on record, nothing you could call newsworthy. I realized, like in the case of the Frenchman's would-be thief, you might want the information to go no further than my laptop, so I down-played it, told them there was nothing to see here, that I'd let my imagination get the better of me."

"Good idea," Erika said, gliding into the subject that interested her more: "What was the first thing registered in 2015?" she asked, curiosity piqued.

"An incident that amounted to next to nothing. Took place early May. The Liverpool police received a call from a woman alleging that a man had been parked in front of her house for a long while and was possibly stalking her. She gave them the license plate number. Turned out to be a vehicle rented to Clifford Dean. By the time the cops arrived, the car was gone. Looks like Dean came up with a good enough excuse to satisfy the lady, and she dropped the charge, such as it was."

"Did you happen to make a note of the woman's name and address?" Erika asked, rummaging for her writing tools. Despite her casual tone, she noticed Harrison's features take on a worried expression. She wanted to tell him not to fret, that she was not about to go gallivanting off to some potentially perilous location, but of course that would only convince him that that was exactly what she intended to do.

John dictated the information. She scribbled it down almost illegibly, as if this would render it harmless. Harrison, she noticed, was quick to jot it down as well.

"So, John," Harrison began, his features still bearing his premonitory look of concern, not for the first time in their sleuthing history. "What about the man in the photograph taken by Pierre Jolet? Have you found a name to go with the face?"

"Yes, I have," John countered, as if Harrison had thrown down the gauntlet. "For this one, I got help from the acknowledged expert on the NCA team. He didn't have much to work with, you realize. Forgetting the chipped tooth—a non-entity, sorry to say—the clenched-fist neck tattoo was about it. The face in the photograph did not appear in any easily accessible criminal data file or internet site. However, with a little more...*digging*, the ace was able to find the individual on the dark web, hosting what basically works like a blog site. What he does is invite disgruntled Blacks to air their encounters with racism and submit their ideas on how to end it. The range goes from prayer to outright revolution. What the NCA expert also found was that in 1995 the individual was detained in Mozambique during a protest against the country's having elected to join the British Commonwealth. He was released the next day."

"His name, John?" Harrison asked gently, not quite knowing what to make of John's slightly querulous tone but counting on him to reveal the cause in his own good time.

"Jacob Tembe. Mother, English. Father, Mozambican. Presently resides in London."

Don't ask for his address! Harrison's first thought, lasered at Erika.

Erika's interests were elsewhere. "John, you did, didn't you, tell the people at NSA to consider this top secret until you gave them the all-clear," she said, her question delivered as a statement to will it into fact. "Our relationship with our friend Amilah, a federal administrative officer in Nigeria, as well as *her* standing with the head of the Movement for Unity, Dignity, and Courage, depend on us sticking to this one promise."

"Yes, of course, I told them," John declared adamantly. "Don't blame *me* if the promise wasn't kept!" He slapped shut his laptop. "Easy for *you* to say I should alter the facts—no fudge, *fudge* was the word you used—but do you understand that in order to conduct a search and come up with decent results, a minimum of reliable input is required? I love you guys, you know I do, but I was stuck between a rock and a hard place."

"Oh, no," Erika said, her heart sinking for Amilah and breaking for John, "you allowed them to share this information with the people in charge of the Thorpe murder investigation?"

"*Allowed* them to? Like I have authority over a crime-fighting organization whose bailiwick is the United Kingdom? What I did was strongly request that they withhold the information until further notice. I said it was critical that they do so, that they wouldn't regret it, that they'd understand why very soon—*all* that malarkey. I thought they got it."

"What makes you think they didn't?" Harrison asked, glad he at least knew what had been bothering the man. It was bad, yes, but his imagination was taking it to places beyond bad.

"I was on my way out," John said. "On route to the exit, I thought I'd take a leak you want the truth. Guess they thought I'd gone. When I came out of the men's room I overheard my contact, Monica Evans, spilling the beans to Detective Hogarty. And no, I didn't let on I'd overheard, I didn't give them hell. What I did was tippy-toe the hell out of there."

"I'm sorry you had to experience that," Erika said while trying to predict the fallout. "Don't take my reaction personally."

"I'll try not to," John said, cracking a smile.

"Thank you."

"Before we head to the Neptune," Harrison said, breaking into the peace negotiations, "I think we should give Amilah a call. She was going to speak to the head of the UDC about his ideas on which member of his organization might have claimed responsibility for Thorpe's murder. She was going to show him Jolet's photo, see if he recognizes the man. If he hasn't already, our information may be of service, and possibly offset any resentment for its premature release."

The agreement being unanimous, Harrison put a call through to Amilah. The call went straight to voicemail, and he felt comfortable enough leaving a nondescript "Photo ID-ed, reply at your convenience" message. It was exactly 6:54 p.m. when he terminated the connection.

John rose to his feet. "I don't know about you guys, but I sure as hell need a drink. This meeting is over."

Chapter Seventeen

The interlude before the day officially began—before they *allowed* it to—was a deliciously self-absorbed reunion of the present with the past. "Was it better for you the first time?" Erika asked, snuggling up to Harrison in the heap of what had once been a tidy arrangement of bedclothes.

"Is this a trick question?" he asked, reveling in their after-play.

"Only if you want it to be," she replied, lying across his lap in her twisted-around nightgown, giving him an eyeful; she, too, enjoying their meaningful nonsense.

"Are you referring to the first time this morning or the first time ever?" he asked, his hand roaming the landscape presented to him.

"Whichever." She reached up to stroke his chest.

"Hmm. This is like asking which facet of a perfect diamond I like best."

"Good answer," she said, just as a staccato rap sounded at their hotel room door. "Breakfast is here," she announced, tearing herself away from him to grab one of the two terrycloth robes from the pile at the foot of the bed. "Coming!" she cried, as she trotted barefoot to the door, securing the belt on the way.

"I'll take it from here, thanks," she advised the room service attendant as he was about to wheel the breakfast cart further into their quarters. On his departure, she threw off the robe, tossed it over a chair, and pushed the cart to the side of the bed.

It was only 7:15. Plenty of time to improvise before their first scheduled events of the day. Harrison was meeting Ike at 11:00 at the hotel's Palm

Court and afterwards hiring a driver for the ride to Brentford to piece together the history of L. P. Sutton's goldsmith establishment, including the possible survival of an underground storehouse and/or the fate of its contents. Erika's plans were down pat as well, only hers had been redacted to minimize Harrison's concern for her safety. First, she was going to pop by the British Museum when it opened at 10:00 and make it her business to bump into Clifford Dean. She would either manage to pry some information out of the custodial worker or determine just how unwilling he was to cooperate; useful information in and of itself. After her interview with Dean, she planned to head off to his alleged stalking address, which John had acquired from the NCA. Given the sparse notations in Dean's records before this incident in 2015, it looked to her like his life had, in a sense, *begun* at that time. Something was fishy about this, and judging from his account, John was of the same opinion.

In the meantime, she and Harrison would continue entertaining themselves in their honeymoon bubble.

They were all set, sitting at the edge of the bed, the cart in front of them, the smells of bacon, eggs, and coffee competing for dominance, when their bubble burst at the sound of Harrison's cell phone.

He reached for it, then angled the device so Erika could take a look at the name of the caller: Amilah Adamu.

"Déjà vu," Erika commented, referencing the last time Amilah had crashed their breakfast party in bed.

"We were expecting her call."

"I know. Take a breath. You're about to make her angry—justifiably."

"Hi, Amilah. Thanks for returning our call so qui—" He popped onto speakerphone so Erika could catch the remainder of Amilah's interruption.

"—and I can't believe it. How *could* you?"

"Hello, Amilah," Erika responded. "I missed the first few words. How could we *what*?"

"Report Jacob Tembe's identity to the police before Emery—the director of the UDC— had a chance to give his input. I thought we had agreed to that!"

Erika explained how Tembe's identity had been released prematurely without directly blaming anyone—not John, the NCA, Harrison, herself. "I think you can understand how it happened, Amilah. Tim Thorpe's murder took place at the British Museum and someone claiming to be a member of the UDC confessed to having committed the crime. His motivation, fury over the mismanagement of repatriation of looted art to the African nations. Jacob Tembe's profile comes up. Not a bad fit, I think you'll agree. It's not hard to see how a well-intentioned individual might decide that promptly relaying this profile to the people in charge of a murder investigation takes precedence over an agreement that's political in nature."

"It's not as if the man's been arrested," Harrison offered in support of Erika's argument. "There's no evidence that would warrant that drastic a move!" The eggs were cold, the bacon was calling to him. He snatched a strip and turned away to dim the sound of his crunching. If they'd been FaceTiming he wouldn't have dared. *Say,* he suddenly thought, *who told Amilah that Jacob Tembe's identity had been leaked?*

"Of *course,* Tembe's been arrested; how do you think I discovered his identity had been leaked?" Amilah retorted, trespassing his thoughts. "It's all over the Internet!"

"What? We haven't been checking the news. How is it possible? It's not like he was there, at the *museum.*"

"Oh, but he was! He was caught on the museum's security camera. In fact, he admits he was there, and his explanation sounds too crazy to be true. Which in my opinion, and more strongly in Emery's, means it probably *is* true. Don't ask me to explain. Read about it yourself."

"I'll do more than that," Erika said, beating Harrison to the punch. "I'm going to the museum this morning and I'll make sure Detective Hogarty is motivated to meet me there. I want to look at those security camera videotapes and—"

"Digital video recordings," Amilah corrected.

"Right, whatever." Harrison had poured their coffee. She sipped at hers. It was still hot, but not steaming. She polished it off. Give it a minute, she'd be wired. "I promise to get to the bottom of this, Amilah."

"That makes me feel a lot better. I'll pass on the news. I know Emery will appreciate your efforts. He recognized Tembe from the photo, you know. Tembe had been a member of his activist group but had been ousted from it some years ago because of his incendiary blog, or I should say the incendiary ideas his blog aroused. Emery swears the man is a provocateur, a loudmouth, but not a killer. The only crime he committed—*almost* committed—was the theft of a few articles from Pierre Jolet's Mozambique exhibit."

"Emery knew about that incident?"

"Yes. Tembe told him about it after the fact. He was trying to impress Emery, get back into his favor."

"Even though his robbery attempt had failed?"

"Yes. *Attempt* is the operative word here."

The caffeine was kicking in; Erika felt unstoppable. She scooped up a clump of scrambled eggs with her fingers and stuffed it into her mouth. "I'll let you know how it goes," she said, when she was able to speak without giving away her rudeness. Inwardly, she was adapting her plans for the day to accommodate this new priority; foreseeing herself punching in Detective Clive Hogarty's cell phone number they'd been given at the close of the Zoom meeting.

Chapter Eighteen

With the excuse that she wanted to have another look at the Benin Bronzes before their meeting with Detective Hogarty, Erika was able to dash off to the museum on her own. "Meet you at eleven in the research room, administration floor," she old John via the hotel room phone, her tone chipper but firm.

At 9:50 she was waiting for the museum doors to open. By 10:15 she'd already been loitering in the general area of the custodial supply closet, waiting to accidentally run into Clifford Dean, if only for a quick read of his demeanor.

Three minutes into her operation, Cherry Ames, the cold-fish projects assistant, sallied forth from Brian Latham's office and seemed downright alarmed at Erika's presence.

"Are you here to see Brian—Mr. Latham?" she asked, nose in the air to compensate for her brief loss of control.

"Hi, Cherry, no. I have a meeting with Detective Hogarty. I'm a bit early."

"Would you care to wait in the research room?"

"That's okay. I'll probably go for a cup of coffee or something."

"As you wish," Cherry replied tartly, continuing to somewhere down the hall, hopefully for an extended absence.

Erika meandered in the opposite direction, then returned to her point of origin. Began the routine again. When she turned to retrace her steps, Clifford Dean was headed her way from the stairwell, its door thudding along with Erika's heart. "My gosh, you're him!" she exclaimed, beating him to the punch, if one was coming, extending her hand as she approached.

He took her hand, despite his obvious bewilderment. "I'm sorry, do I know you?" He studied her, his deep brown eyes—intelligent, honest, her instinctive appraisal, taking her aback—focused directly on her. "Oh! You're the woman who guided me through my failed try at CPR...aren't you?"

"Yes, it's me. I'm Erika Shawn-Wheatley, and I'm honored to meet you. Your try may have failed, but it was a gallant one. You wouldn't give up. The medics practically had to pull you off of Mr. Thorpe."

"Thank you. I couldn't help thinking that if I'd been a little more...*capable*, I could have made a difference. I'm Clifford Dean, by the way. They kept my name out of the news." He brushed back a wisp of dark brown hair from his forehead. "You did a good job yourself, by the way." He took her hand for another shake.

"Erika!" came a greeting from behind. She spun around just as Brian was upon her, heading in for a collegial hug. "What are you doing here so early? Your meeting, with Hogarty's not until eleven. Come wait in my office." To Dean, off-handedly: "Morning, Clifford, don't let us keep you." He tugged at Erika's arm, a bit too forcefully for comfort. "Come."

"I was thanking Mr. Dean for his efforts that day," she said, standing her ground.

"Good of you," Brian commented, growing impatient.

Dean dug a loaded key chain from his pants pocket and grasped one of the keys from the lot. "Nice meeting you, Erika." He unlocked the supply closet door, revealing a tidy-looking area the size of a modest walk-in closet, and gave Erika a salutatory palm-up gesture before entering it and shutting the door behind him.

To avoid appearing unfriendly, Erika felt obliged to spend the next half hour conversing idly with Brian in his office. Cherry showed her face mid-point in their chat, bestowed the pair with a killer look, and departed.

* * *

Erika had persuaded Detective Hogarty to meet her and her "associate, FBI-deputized Detective John Mitchell" (it had a distinctive ring), at the British

Museum rather than at police headquarters. "In case we decide we need to reenact any of the activity presumed to have gone down at or around the time of the murder," her reasoning.

"Pretty presumptuous," Hogarty now commented with pointed good humor, referring to her somewhat imperious request.

"I'd say *dedicated*," John corrected, loyal friend that he was.

Semantics aside, the threesome were now convened in the research room. Request granted is all that mattered. Brian Latham had hung a "Do Not Disturb" sign on the door handle, adding the bonus of privacy.

In outward appearance, Detective Hogarty brought to Erika's mind the mischievous Puck in *A Midsummer Night's Dream*. She imagined the demeanor would stand him in good stead in the interrogation room, where he could play the role of bad cop to off-putting perfection. She wondered if that were in fact the actual case.

"So, what do you know that I don't?" he asked, boosting the case for bad cop by impaling her with his gaze.

"You've got a man in custody that maybe shouldn't be," she politely suggested, matching his gaze with her own bad-cop version. "I've heard on good authority that although Jacob Tembe may have provoked acts of violence with his fiery language, he is not capable of committing violence himself. Definitely not cold-blooded murder."

Hogarty's lips formed an impish smile. "That's what Mrs. Bundy said."

John cast him a withering look. That, plus Erika's subsequent elaboration of her recent talk with Amilah Adamu containing reliable hearsay from Emery Mwazulu Diyabanza, pitched Hogarty into a more serious state of mind. "I'd like you to take a look at what was captured on the museum's security cameras. You can decide for yourselves if what you see supports my department's consensus of guilt or not. I've got your Zoom videos on file, too, if you'd care to review them." His closed laptop was sitting before him on the conference table. He shoved it closer to Erika and John's side of the table and rose from his chair. "We should be sitting alongside each other."

Once the group had rearranged itself, with Hogarty sitting between Erika and John, Hogarty flipped open his laptop and logged onto the relevant file.

"Of course, I don't have every camera's digital record of every minute of the day on tap here, but I do have what I think is key, and anywhere you want to fill in, we can go directly to the source."

"Sounds good," Erika said.

"Any location or time where you want to begin?"

"You decide."

"Okay, sure," Hogarty replied, with an instinctive brow raise at his taskmaster's abstention. "After the NCA transmitted the photograph of the chap ID-ed as Jacob Tembe, along with a history that dove-tailed with our composite profile of the killer, we went right to it, looking for a match in the recorded videos. The neck tattoo—the clenched fist—was the defining feature. It didn't take me long to pick up several images of him. Let me show you the first one I came upon. Tembe was on his way out of the building." It took Hogarty a moment to fast forward to the action he was looking for. "Here." He paused the video. The time recorded in the lower right corner of the image was 4:37. "The exits to the museum were blocked at 4:40. Tembe just missed being detained." He enlarged the image of the man dressed in black frozen in the act of finger-combing his shoulder-length hair away from the side of his face. "You see the tattoo? At least ninety percent exposed. Clear as day."

Erika dug for the cell phone in her tote. "Hold it there, would you, Detective? I want to compare this image to the photo that started it all."

"You mean the photo taken by Monsieur Pierre Jolet?" Hogarty queried with mock innocence. "If you're thinking of keeping his name a secret, think again. Mr. Tembe enlightened us on his misfired robbery attempt in Portugal. We've already spoken to Jolet, and he was very cooperative with us." Like a quick-change artist, a mischievous grin appeared for a split second before turning dead serious. "You got your photo?"

Erika was punching in her photo app, when John came up with the Tembe photo on his own laptop. "Here you go."

Erika shoved her device into the pocket of her black linen blazer and brought John's laptop closer to her; looked from one screen to the other.

"What are you looking for?" Hogarty asked sarcastically. "Checking if the tattoo is on the same side of the neck?"

"That, and if the thumbs of the clenched fists match up—both should be either anterior or posterior."

The detectives' reactions were identical: wide-eyed, slack-jawed. Hogarty opted to speak. "You've been watching too many movies, Erika."

"Or you haven't been watching enough of them."

Smiles were exchanged between the two. John breathed a sigh of relief.

"This is most probably Jacob Tembe, alright," Erika concluded. "Sorry, I felt I had to check."

"Erika," Hogarty stated, "you are aware, are you not, that Jacob Tembe has admitted to being in the building? I mean, it's not as if we're trying to *prove* that he was!"

"Of course, I'm aware. I just needed to prove that this particular likeness of him is really *him*. I don't know much about tattoos, but I'm betting the clenched fist is a stock image."

"Erika, what are the chances that another person—"

"Slim," she answered, anticipating the inevitable question. "I also feel obliged, for Amilah's sake, to leave no stone unturned in this matter. Bottom line, Tembe may have admitted to having been in the building, but by no means has he admitted to killing Timothy Thorpe!"

Hogarty threw up his hands in frustration with this confounded woman; looked to John for testicular accord. Got none.

"If you have what you believe is an image of Jacob Tembe on the administration floor, may we see it?" Erika requested. "I suspect he denies ever having been there."

"He does," Hogarty said, high speeding the video in reverse. He slowed down as he approached the critical moments; paused when he arrived. The time registered on the image was 4:25. "That's one minute after the murder occurred, as your Zoom records indicate. "We're looking at the hallway, yards from Thorpe's office. Tembe is walking toward the stairwell, just about the time Clifford Dean, the custodial worker, says he saw him."

"He didn't say he saw Tembe," Erika corrected. "What he said is that he saw a man in a black suit, black T-shirt, with shoulder-length hair—a *mane,*

I think you quoted to my colleague, Greg Smith of Art Loss Register. Am I correct?" *Good time as any for another name drop.*

"Yes, you are," Hogarty conceded, with renewed respect.

"Whose forearm and hand?" she asked, pointing to the left border of the frame. "Looks like someone may have been walking across the hall from the alleged Mr. Tembe, and in the opposite direction."

"Good observation. The surveillance camera captures about seventy percent of the hall area, which explains the partial image. The segment belongs to Freddy Leach, a regular, I'm told, of this very room. He doesn't remember seeing anybody, but they say his head is either in his books or in the clouds."

Erika was considering bringing up Freddy's possible crush, Cherry Ames, but something in the frame suddenly took precedence. She spread her fingers on the putative Tembe, targeting the visible hand and jacket cuff. "I'm going to take a photo of this to compare it with the first image you showed us, of the undisputed Jacob Tembe. Okay with you, Detective?" She was already removing the cell phone from her jacket pocket.

"Anything you say." He waited for her to take her photo then fast-forwarded to the image of Tembe about to exit the museum.

From her photo app, Erika selected the shot she'd just taken, and it instantly filled her screen. Heart racing, she glanced from her image to the one on Hogarty's laptop screen. Couldn't believe her eyes—but of course she could. "Detective, John, do you see what I see?"

"I was never good at finding Waldo," John demurred.

"John!"

She waited for the aha moment. Shamelessly delighted in the delay.

John was the first to turn wide-eyed. "The ring!" he declared.

"Yes!" Hogarty promptly agreed, either with or without the aid of John's cue. "In your enlargement, Erika, there is no ring on the man's finger, left hand. In the photo of Jacob Tembe on his way out of the building there's a ring on the fourth finger—there, on the hand brushing back the hair—exposing the neck tattoo. Same hand—the left."

"Anything else?" Erika posed.

Hogarty pulled the laptop nearly up to his nose. "There's more?" He sat up abruptly. "Erika!"

"What?"

"I'm either going to have to kill you or hire you."

She hammed a helpless shrug, relieved to see what a good sport he was.

"Fill me in," John demanded. "You're monopolizing the screen."

"Compare the jacket cuffs, Detective," Hogarty advised, facing the screen toward John.

"Come on," John commented dismissively before actually taking a look. "Well, I'll be damned!" after his review. "There's one button on Tembe's cuff. None on mystery man's."

"Yep," Erika said. She turned to Hogarty. "When you questioned Tembe, what did he say was the reason for his museum visit?"

"He was in a real huff about that, asked me did I think he was incapable of visiting a museum to see its exhibits, that he had to have an ulterior motive. Overdid it, which of course raised my suspicions, but he didn't budge from his story. I'm thinking the look-alike on the administration floor must have had something to do with Tembe's showing up."

"I think so, too," Erika said, as John nodded his agreement.

"Alright, then," Hogarty said, suddenly fidgety. "I think it's time we call it a day." He slapped shut the lid of his laptop and went for the cell phone in his pants pocket. "Excuse me for a minute." He punched in a phone number. "Danny, listen. Get Jacob Tembe to interrogation. I'm coming right in." After a pause, "Sure, let him finish his bagel. See you in ten."

"Will you let us know how it goes?" Erika asked as they rose from the table. She hoped she was not pushing her luck.

Hogarty seemed surprised at the question. "What do you think? I have you to thank for the breakthrough. Of course, I'll notify you." With that, he headed for the door.

* * *

Erika glanced behind her before jumping into the cab, her tight skirt tested to its limit. "Twenty-seven Margo Lane, Liverpool!"

"That's over a four-hour drive from here, Miss. I can get you to the train station on Euston Road in five minutes. A high-speed train will bring you to Liverpool in two hours."

"Great. Let's do it!"

The driver, a pleasant young man in a denim Newsboy Cap turned around in his seat to face her. "The trains run pretty frequently. You shouldn't have much of a wait. Maybe none at all."

"Thanks, I hear you—go!"

Only after the cab had pulled away from the front of the museum did Erika feel a twinge of guilt for having given John the slip. After their meeting with Detective Hogarty, she'd suggested they have a bite to eat at the museum's Court Café on the ground floor. "Their chicken salad is great," she'd added for effect, without a clue if it was, or had ever been, on the menu. John had thought it a splendid idea, and she'd said she'd meet him there—"go get us a table, it gets crowded this time of day!"—while she made a pit stop at the "ladies' loo." He'd gotten a kick out of her use of the word "loo," and it had been a cinch after that to leave him in the lurch.

In her mind's eye, she saw Harrison berating John for having let her out of his sight, but there was no way she was going to be deterred from going off on her own. What would worry Harrison would, of course, be her fearlessness under select circumstances. He knew her well enough to understand that although she had a more than healthy fear of potential natural, medical and mechanical disasters, when she was at the helm, or perceived herself to be, she was, as he put it, "unsettlingly brave."

She fetched her cell phone from her jacket pocket and sent a short text to Harrison and John saying she was perfectly fine and would meet them back at the hotel in due time—"yes, today, Lol!" Then she turned off the phone and sat back to contemplate the inescapable possibility that she had just embarked on the wildest goose chase of her career.

Chapter Nineteen

At 11:15 Harrison had succumbed to the waitress's third inquiry if he'd like to order something. "My friend will be along in a minute" would not have worked again. The poor girl had looked as if she'd been personally rejected. "Thanks, I'll have a Perrier," he'd answered instead, watching her mood brighten.

Now it was 11:23 and he was nursing his glass of sparkling water and taking in his surroundings. The hotel's Palm Court was a perfect place to have chosen to meet Ikemar, he thought. Who could not be uplifted by the light flooding in from the soaring glass ceiling, the playful greenery lacing through the trellises all about the room, here and there tickling the marble busts too close to escape the random shoots. He was looking forward to catching up with Ike, filling him in on what he and Erika had been up to, hearing what Ike had been up to himself. The ambience of the place would surely favor an optimistic view of their endeavors, shared and personal. In fact, it was already working. He was feeling a surge of hope about this afternoon's planned trip to Nettles Road in Brentford, erstwhile site of L.P. Sutton, Goldsmith, and, possibly, preserved hideaway of Andrew Barrett's treasure trove. Earlier this morning he'd Googled the words "Brentford England" and had been greeted with an announcement of the "Brentford & Chiswick Local History Society," urging one to "explore the rich history of the West London riverside towns of Brentford and Chiswick." It was the boldface ampersand that now stirred his hopes of discovery. A society sporting that self-important symbol must surely be steeped in local lore. Maybe Ike would like to join him on his expedition.

Where was Ike, anyway? Even his needy waitress was sneaking worried looks his way, as if she herself might be on the verge of being stood up. Harrison reached into his pants pocket for his cell phone and punched in Ike's cell number. When the call went to voice messages, he left one: "Harrison here. Tell me you're about to walk through the door. Looking forward." He placed the cell phone on the table and waited for a response.

Five minutes later he left another phone message: "You okay? Got the time, place wrong? I'm here at the Kimpton Fitzroy, Russell Square, Plaza Court." Then texted a shortened version of it.

At 11:45 he gave up. Paid for his Perrier, gave his waitress and the maître d his cell phone number, and told them to call him if his friend, Ikemar Umar showed up. "Tell him I'm cabbing it straight to the Virginia Woolf Building to find him. I'll be there at noon. Wherever he is, tell him not to move, to give him a call and we'll decide where to connect."

* * *

At 12:03, Harrison was averting the gaze of Virginia Woolf's wax figure and looking for someone to button-hole. "Excuse me," he directed to the back of a gray-haired woman with sensible shoes, who was headed toward whatever her destination was at a more leisurely pace than the two presumably less receptive young men striding toward each of theirs more purposefully.

"Yes?" the woman answered, turning to Harrison with an anticipatory smile.

Harrison briefly introduced himself and related his present quandary. The woman, Rachel Stein, English lit professor, happened to be at her leisure and would be happy to help him find his colleague, Ikemar Umar. "Lovely man," she said. "We often sit together at lunch or dinnertime, here, in VW's cafeteria. We've had our share of exchanges on the ailing state of staff diversity, I dare say. Brilliant; I wish he were here to stay, not on visiting status. When did you last try to reach him? Have you checked your email and texts?"

"Minutes ago. And yes, I've checked."

"Now that I think of it, I didn't see him last night at dinner. He takes his breakfast well before I do, so that's of no help. His room's on the third floor; office on the second. I say we try both. What have we got to lose?"

"Rachel, I don't want to trouble you. If you'd tell me the room numbers, that'll be fine."

"You have me worried now. I'm coming along. I say we try the office first. We'll take the stairs. It'll be quicker than waiting for the elevator. Follow me."

"You think he could have forgotten about our date and just gone off somewhere?" Harrison asked, trailing after her. "Somewhere where he had to shut off his phone—like a conference?"

"I thought of that," Rachel replied as they arrived at the staircase. "I didn't want to suggest it. I thought it would hurt your feelings."

"Do I look that sensitive?" Harrison joked, trying to ease the tension in his belly—to no avail.

Rachel emitted a token laugh as they began their ascent. "I was being polite. You look perfectly macho."

"Wait...wait," she expelled with effort, on reaching the summit. She moved aside to let him step up beside her. "I'm...a little out of breath." She held onto his arm.

"We should have taken the elevator," he chided himself, guilt adding to the tension in his gut. "Are you okay?"

"I'm fine." She let go of his arm, apparently recovered. "Aren't there any old ladies in your life, son? We catch our breath and then we move on." She nodded toward the right. "This way. Three doors down."

Arriving, Rachel lightly rapped on the door. There was no response from within, as Harrison expected would be the case. Rachel rapped again, less genteelly, then tested the doorknob. "The door is unlocked," she said.

"He's not here," Harrison replied, surprised by the edge of irritability in his tone.

"I understand your impatience," Rachel said, "but perhaps there's a calendar on his desk. We can see what he's marked for today."

"Sorry, you're right, of course," Harrison agreed, hope glimmering. "Go ahead."

Rachel gently turned the knob, and at the door's cracking, they were assaulted by the unique odor of putrefaction, source known without the confirmation of sight. Rachel's hand slipped from the doorknob, knees buckling. "Ay!" she cried weakly, falling into Harrison's arms, forcing him out of his own stumble to brace her, muscles tensed to keep them both on their feet, the effort a distraction, but only briefly, very briefly, from the inescapable truth. Reaching out from their clumsy embrace, he closed the door.

"Can you stand without my support?" he asked her, his voice cracking. "I have to get my phone, call the police."

"Maybe it's a mouse," she said, quiet as one.

"Rachel, please."

"We should go in."

"We can't disturb the scene. Rachel, please. Do you want to sit on the floor? Will that be okay?"

A sorry little laugh. "I'll never be able to get up." She freed herself from him, stood on her own. The belt of her dress had slipped to the right. She took hold of the buckle and re-positioned it mid-waist. "It's unusually quiet on this floor today," she observed.

Harrison was already punching in a call to emergency—9-9-9, he remembered Olivia Chatham saying it was—and he made no response to Rachel's observation. Who cared if it was a quiet day?

"Emergency. Which service?" the deep voice registered.

"I'm not sure. Police. Ambulance."

"What's the situation?"

Harrison explained.

"An odor, sir? You need to verify. Open the door, but do not step inside. Tell me what you see."

"Move away, Rachel. I'm opening the door."

"Pardon?" the operator said.

"I'm talking to—"

"I must go to my room," Rachel said. "Room 303. I'll be there if you need me. Ikemar's room is 325." Her hand went to her stomach as she turned to walk away. "Sick."

"Sir!"

"I'm sorry. Just a second. I'm opening the door." Just as he was pulling open the door, steeling himself, or trying to, someone came from round the bend in the hallway—a boy, maybe fifteen years old, some genius maybe—and cried "Shit! What's that fucking smell?"

"Go away!" Harrison barked. "I've got the police on the line. Get the hell away!"

The kid fled back to where he'd come from; fear conquering curiosity.

And now there was only a door's arc-swing between them, Harrison and Ikemar, for of course it was Ikemar he would be seeing in a millisecond, Ikemar, who in an alternate universe was chatting with him in a duplicate Palm Court, their hearts beating, lungs expanding—*Oh God oh God is it you?*

It didn't matter about the smell, a universal indignity, but the wanton exposure of the man's last suffering—eyes wide open in pitiful innocence, gaping neck wound caked with dried blood, like the mouth of a vampire who'd drunk more than his fill—this Harrison could do something about. He could close Ike's eyes, wash his neck, cover his face. Surely Ike would want Harrison to grant his remains a simulation of gentle repose. But he could not, he could not.

Nor could he rip from Ike's lower torso the flag of his homeland, Nigeria, its green and white stripes blasphemed by a slathered-on black swastika. The killer must have been eerily calm to have draped the flag so neatly over Ike, especially after he'd taken the time to arrange his body on the floor, arms at his side, legs stiffly together, soldier mocked.

But no. The site and the decedent must be left intact. All he was permitted to do was stand guard and take in the gruesome scene in ever-demanding immediacy.

By the time they came, ten minutes later—police, detective, photographer, coroner, Queen Mother for all the good it would do—a small crowd had gathered in the hall. From what rooms or holes, they had crawled out of, he knew not. His fiercely protective look had not sent the theatergoers away, but it had kept them at a safe distance. They'd asked him questions, which he would not answer, and they'd left him alone. He'd stood in front of the doorway, blocking their view so they were unable to take cell phone photographs of the scene's silent star.

The authorities performed an initial examination of the site and of Ikemar himself. After Ikemar's body had been removed, Harrison was next in line for review. The detective who questioned him turned out to be Clive Hogarty's underling, a stocky young woman with a face like an angel. He told her all she wanted to know and more, hoping that she, in turn, would furnish him with information that she needn't have. He asked her if there was a calendar on Ike's desk and she said "Yes, here's the appointment you two had scheduled for today, 'HW 11am' at the 'KF'—Kimpton Fitzroy, like you told me."

"What about yesterday?" he asked, passively as he could. He noticed her focus kept switching to a paper in the center of Ike's desk. It was hard to tell the nature of the document from his vantage point just outside the doorway, and she, across the room.

"Only one appointment yesterday, with Bradan Yusef," she said. "To discuss an assignment, looks like. You know this person?"

"The name is not familiar," he said, pretending to give it some thought. He supposed she figured because he had told her so much about Ikemar—the subject he taught, the mission they shared and, after all, the brunch date they'd planned—that Harrison probably knew damn near everything about the man. He was not about to disabuse her of the notion.

"We'll check this person out, of course." She removed a gallon-size Ziploc bag from her leather pouch shoulder bag and delicately pinched the corner of the mysterious sheet between her latex-encased fingers.

Looked to Harrison like a page torn from a newspaper, now that she'd lifted it from the desk. "Something I might be able to help you with?"

"It speaks for itself," the woman said, carefully delivering the exhibit to the plastic bag and zipping it shut. "It's a notice in *The Tribune* announcing an upcoming talk hosted by London University. The subject is"—she read the lines through the clear plastic—"'the present status of African Studies in the UK and the US. Visiting Professor Ikemar Umar of Nigeria University and Professor Leslie James of Howard University will be the guest speakers.' You get the idea."

"Is there a particular relevance to…"

"There are hand-printed swastikas all over the page," she said bluntly. "The killer making his point," she added. "As if he hadn't made it clear with what he did to the flag, which I guess is Nigeria's."

"Yes."

"Son-of-a-bitch."

"Yes."

"You can go now. I have your card. You have mine."

The permission to leave made it imperative that he do so, or she'd question his idling. The horror of what had transpired, not as individual events occurring in time, one following the other, but as a composite, suddenly hit him like a bomb. He had to speak to Erika. Immediately. It didn't matter about what, strangely enough, only that he hear her voice.

He headed for the staircase on the run. Couldn't remember descending it, only that he was at its top, then its bottom. Once outside the building, he spotted a red telephone kiosk directly across the street. A rare sight these days, left there solely for his occupancy, it seemed. He made a beeline for it, hearing an angry car horn blast as he did so.

He shut himself inside the booth and took out his cell phone. "Erika?" he cried breathlessly, anticipating her voice before hearing it, only to experience the shock of hearing his call go straight to voicemail after only one ring. "Impossible. Call me now," he recorded. Thought this would alarm her. Called again. "Hi Erika, please call me. It's urgent. I'm okay, though."

He texted her. Knew she would text back. She *must*, after all.

She didn't.

He tried calling again; texting again; was suddenly cast back to the Palm Court, performing the same futile exercise. The similarity of his two attempts and the catastrophic outcome of his first sent him into a panic. Where was she? He punched in John's number.

"Thank God," he exhaled, hearing John's unrecorded "Hello" after the first ring. "Where is she, John?"

"You sound frantic. What the hell's up?"

He'd tell him after he knew Erika's whereabouts. "Where is she?"

"I don't know, pal. She skipped out on me. You know your wife, what she's capable of pulling. She's a sweetheart, but when she wants to set out on her own, she finds a way."

"Yes, but where did she *go?*"

"That's just the point. She didn't want me to know. You either, I guess."

"*Think*, John." The walls of the kiosk were closing in on him. "How about that address you got from the NCA—where the custodian was suspected of stalking a woman? I don't have it on me. I left my notepad at the hotel. You have the address, John?"

"Calm down, Harrison. Yes, I have it. Why are you in such a frenzy over this? There's something else on your mind, isn't there?" He waited for a reply.

Chapter Twenty

"Twenty-seven Margo Lane," Erika instructed the cab driver she'd managed to wave down, arms flailing, outside the Liverpool station, Lime Street. Gratefully, she hopped into the cab and swung the door shut. Almost there. Minutes away. One way or another, she was on the brink of finding out if her two-hour journey had been worth it.

Objectively, the trip couldn't have run more smoothly: right on schedule, excellent amenities, solicitous on-board crew. Subjectively, it had been a trial. Except for distracted glimpses of affirmation, the lovely countryside view from her window seat, compliments of Rail Ninja, had been lost on her. She'd spent the time obsessing over her reasons for booking the trip; trying to justify it when there was a good chance it would prove useless, one such sequence streaming: *So, I'm sure Tim Thorpe's murder was committed, or at least orchestrated, by a British Museum insider. Perfect timing. Must have known about the Zoom meeting, that Tim would be at his desk attending it at that very moment. Clicks off overhead light but leaves desk lamp on. Allows Zoom attendees to witness the act. Gets the job done, gets out. No one the wiser. Then there's Keith Ashton's murder. That, too, had to have been masterminded by a museum insider. Someone who knew about the unpublicized transaction involving Picasso's Demoiselle study and to what location the drawing had been transported.*

She mind-stalked the killer as he carried out his plans and asked herself, over and over, who else besides Clifford Dean is an insider who must be investigated? Dean may have access to information given his natural—or coerced—desire to nose around for it, but *more* than that? Brian Latham, John's preferred candidate based solely on bad vibes, was ruled out after her first go-round and never reconsidered. But why be so hasty? Maybe she was biased in favor of Latham because of the help he'd been to her and Harrison in a prior case. And when it came down to it, wasn't her knowledge of Dean's nosiness based solely on Brian's say-so? *Think about this!* Maybe John, as an objective observer, had a point. And after all, wasn't it Clifford Dean's curiously scant early history that had most aroused her interest—admittedly, as an end in itself?

"Here we are, Miss," the driver announced, pulling up in front of one of the generic two-story two-car garage homes lined up on both sides of the tidy tree-lined street in Rural Town, Anywhere. Erika felt lost. She paid the cab fare along with a generous tip and asked the driver to stick around until he saw her enter the house—"and wave you off," she added as a precaution. He promised he would, but his detached smile only made her feel more unsettled.

Standing in front of the painted white door, waiting for a response to her push on its loosely socketed little bell, the decision to not look up the phone number and call ahead suddenly felt like a foolish one. Her idea had been to avoid getting shut down right off the bat. She'd thought she'd stand a better chance of getting through to the woman in a face-to-face encounter. The trade-off, that the woman might be somewhere between out of town and deceased, seemed worth it at the time. Now, it did not.

She pressed the ineffective-looking bell once more. Knocking would be her next option.

There was the sound of a lock snapping open or shut. Erika held her breath as she waited to see which.

The door opened to its chain length. "Can I help you?"

A pleasant voice, Erika thought. Was it pushing it to think *welcoming* even? "Hi, are you Melody Williams?" she asked. What she could see of the woman's face, just about level with her own, seemed in keeping with the voice. "I'm Erika Shawn," she said, choosing to go with her professional name. "I'm with *Art News* magazine in New York, and you're under no obligation to talk to me." She smiled to underscore her good intentions.

"Good to hear," the woman replied, offering a smile of her own, only, as

Erika could not help but acknowledge, less calculated. "Yes, I'm Melody Williams. Are you here to interview my husband?"

"That could be an unexpected bonus," Erika declared, nonplussed. "I'm actually here to ask you a few questions about someone you may know on staff at the British Museum—Clifford Dean?"

"The name's not registering—but what are we doing, talking like this?" She unsnapped the door chain. "Come on in."

"Thanks!" This was going better than expected. Erika directed a grand wave at the cab driver, who took off mid-arc. "You don't know how lucky I feel," she said, stepping foot inside the house and coming face to face with Melody Williams. "I had no idea if you'd be at home, no less willing to see me." Melody reminded her of a photo she'd seen at a Woodstock Retrospective of a fine-featured woman with graying hair worn in a single braid draped over her shoulder and clad in a loose-fitting ankle-length dress. It was not the particulars that prompted the comparison, though. Melody was a handsome, but not a fine-featured woman. Her ash-blonde hair was worn in a thick ponytail and her loose-fitting clothing consisted of a white T-shirt and oversized baggy pants—her husband's?—cinched at the waist with an embroidered sash. It was the look of accessibility of the two women, the openness, that linked them in Erika's mind.

"It didn't require luck finding me at home; I almost always am," Melody said, leading Erika from the vestibule into the living room, a colorful eclectic of styles and patterns, pillows and throws. "I work from home. I illustrate children's books."

"So, you're an artist," Erika said, her attention distracted by the oil paintings adorning the walls.

"No. My husband's the artist. I'm the illustrator. Mesmerizing, aren't they?"

"Electrifying." The paintings were bold; vibrant colors blossoming from the shadows; life emerging from darkness. Even from a distance, without taking in the details, the point was made, the rewarded struggle seen. "I must have a closer look before I leave. Is your husband at home?" She sniffed the air; smiled. "Do I detect the scent of oil paint?"

"You do, yes. And my husband is in his lair, the basement. Working day and night to complete the paintings for his upcoming show at the Walker Gallery, here in Liverpool—oh!"

"What is it?"

"I was repressing the name. Clifford Dean." She backed away from Erika. "What *about* him? He hasn't been *looking* for me, has he?"

"No, no not at all," Erika assured her, inching toward one of the colorfully patterned side chairs flanking the equally inviting couch. "He doesn't know a thing about you—about my coming here. Do you think we can sit a while? I'll tell you everything." She had every intention of doing so. Anything to regain Melody's initial trust.

"I suppose so, fine. Sit down." She set herself down on the couch.

Erika took the chair.

Melody popped back up. "Can I get you anything, Erika? Tea? Coffee?"

"I'm fine, thanks." She was about to go for her pad and pen but thought better of it. She would rely on her memory; make this as non-threatening an exchange as possible. "Let me ask you a question. Have you heard about the recent murder that took place at the British Museum?"

Melody sat back down. "Do I live on planet Earth? Of course, I've heard."

Erika explained Harrison's and her connection to the tragic event through the Zoom meeting. "We're looking into the case, Harrison and I, not in any sort of official capacity, but because we've been called upon to do so by the group. We've had some experience in the area of crime-solving in the art world—we've sort of fallen into it, you see—so they're relying on us to pick up on things the professionals assigned to the case might overlook. That sounds kind of smug, doesn't it?"

"It does but go on." Her look had softened.

"Of course, we'll give the police any relevant information we come across," Erika said, wrapping up her preamble and bracing herself for the sensitive part. "For the crime to have been pulled off without a hitch, it looks like someone associated with the museum must have supplied the killer with insider information. Clifford Dean is one such person. There's not a shred of evidence against him, but his sketchy résumé is concerning, at least to me and my husband. Now, the news reports did not identify the Good Samaritan by name, but Mr. Dean, a member of the custodial staff, is the person who performed CPR on the victim. Still, I believe there's a possibility he might have been the source of inside information, either innocently or through coercion."

"Why should any of this concern *me?*" Melody asked, visibly perturbed.

"It doesn't concern you per se, Melody. It's just that Mr. Dean's official records seem to have begun in earnest, so to speak, in 2015. It's almost as if he'd been given a NIN number at that time. Or"—she hesitated—"counterfeited a new one. The few times the number comes up before 2015 it seems, well, *planted*. It feels that way, at least." She cracked a resigned smile. "He could probably sue me for slander if he overheard me talking like this."

"Include me in your allegations and you'll have a class-action suit on your hands," Melody retorted, only half in jest. "I think you're about to tell me my address is the only solid fact you can lay your hands on."

"Exactly."

"For all the good it'll do you. A person sat in a car in front of our house for an unusual length of time. I reported the problem, gave the police the license plate number, and they tracked the rental to a man named Clifford Dean. He had a half-baked excuse for sitting in front of my house, but I didn't want to take the matter further, so I dropped my charge—or complaint, or whatever they called it."

"'Half-baked'?"

"Something about not remembering his friend's address; waiting around until his friend answered his call and gave him directions."

Half-baked is right. "Would you recognize Mr. Dean if I showed you a photograph of him?" Erika asked, causing Melody to wince. *Getting too real for her?* Erika wondered.

"No, I wouldn't recognize him. I got the license plate number, but I didn't get close enough to get a good look at him. I didn't care to, really."

"How about taking a look now, no harm done," Erika gently suggested. She took her cell phone from her jacket pocket, turned it on, and went straight to her photo app, where she'd stored Clifford Dean's personnel file photo.

"Never saw the man in my life," Melody said, after studying the photo.

Erika turned off the device and slipped it back into her pocket. She slid forward in her chair and leaned toward Melody, hoping to draw her in. "Melody, if you had to name someone you were afraid might have been in that car, who would it have been?" She expected the question to be shot down and was prepared to rephrase it.

"My ex-husband," Melody answered without skipping a beat. "Except it couldn't have been."

Erika stifled her surprise. "Why couldn't it have been?" she asked, not moving an inch.

"Because he was dead."

Be still. Wait.

"He committed suicide two months before the incident."

"Are you sure?" Erika heard herself say, giving away the trajectory of her thoughts.

"Walked into the ocean," Melody said, her voice taking on an unexpected coldness. "Left his clothing in a neat pile in the sand, along with a few cloying lines of remorse—hah! A phony right up to the end."

Go ahead. Say what's on your mind. "Is there a possibility he faked his death? It's not an outlandish thought., Melody. It has been done."

Melody looked heavenward. "You sound like Charles."

"Charles?"

"My husband. The two of you, over-dramatic. Mark is dead,"

"Your ex-husband, Mark. Mark…"

"Mark Jason. Yes."

"You wouldn't mind having another look at…"

"I would mind, yes. The man in your photograph is not Mark." Melody abruptly rose from the couch. "Come, I'll show you a photograph of the real thing. I can see you won't take no for an answer."

Erika followed Melody through the living room to the kitchen, a cozy medley of styles and colors, perfectly in keeping with the character of the room they'd come from. The only surprising element was the imposing black wheelchair standing outside the circle of kitchen chairs of assorted vintage hugging the circular pine table. "We keep one on every floor," Melody said, catching Erika's glance. "That way there's no lugging up and down stairs." Very matter of fact. She might have been talking about a cat-litter box. "You okay down there, Charlie?" she called past the open door to the basement. "We have a visitor. We're coming down if it's okay with you. *Is* it?" To Erika, just above a whisper: "He's off-and-on about allowing people to see his work in progress." To Charles: "She seems like a good sort!"

A hearty laugh from below. "Bring her down, Mel. But only if she's got a tube of red magenta on her; I'm all out!"

Melody in the lead, the women trotted down the carpeted stairs, watching out for the chair lift hitched to its track at the bottom of the staircase.

Except for a boiler, a tiered washer-dryer unit, and a file cabinet at the far end of the basement, the space matched Erika's image of a stereotypical atelier: a general disarray of canvases, four or five deep propped against walls, one blank canvas supported by a paint-spattered easel standing in the wings, shelves cluttered with drawing pads, palettes, paint tubes, and brushes, some fanning out, bristles up, from what she chose to believe, for some oddly romantic reason, were empty jam jars.

In the center of his domain, the artist himself, Charles, a regal-looking Black man, sat tall in a wheelchair identical to the one upstairs in the kitchen. In his right hand, he held a long-handled brush. He lifted it from the canvas resting on an easel at arm's length from him as Melody and Erika stepped toward him. His working palette sat on a bridge table by his side. He laid the brush among a cluster of its companions in a flat pan alongside the palette and wiped his hands with a cloth draped over an arm of the wheelchair. "Excuse the attire," he announced, extending his hand to Erika. "I wasn't expecting guests. Charles Williams. And you're...?"

"Erika Shawn," Erika said, sticking with her professional name. Charles was wearing a light blue T-shirt and white shorts that ended just above his knees—both articles of clothing paint-stained impressionist canvases in themselves—and Erika could not help but notice the disparity between his muscular upper body and his frail-looking legs. Except for this peripheral

147

observation, her attention was focused on the oil painting in progress. At its center, in black and tones of gray, the stock images of war—rifles, tanks, grenades—were welded to contorted human bodies. Moving away from the cauldron-like interior, the imagery became less, and less brutal, metal and human flesh disentangled, colors became more and more saturated. At the outermost, incomplete portion of the painting, the colors were evolving bold and neon bright, the humans were intermingling in a carnival-like atmosphere: dancing, playing, joyous.

"You appear to be transfixed," Melody said. "You're not alone." She ran her fingers through her husband's untamed hair and bent to kiss his face, landing it on the side of his nose. "It's the usual reaction."

"Whatever the outcome of our meeting," Erika said, "I hope you'll allow me to do a profile on you, Charles—may I call you Charles?"

"You may. 'Profile'?"

"Erika is with the magazine *Art News*," Melody informed him. Smiling, she added, "I believe she's who she says she is."

"Let's hope. So, Erika, to what do we owe the pleasure?"

Erika gave him a rundown of what she'd told Melody.

"Charles, I'm going to show Erika a photograph of Mark. Do you mind very much? She has an idea, though she's being tactful, that Clifford Dean, the stalker who wasn't a stalker, is really my ex, Mark Jason, returned from the dead."

"From the never-dead, you mean," Charles said. "No need to be tactful, Erika. I believed that myself, until I realized it was my active imagination running away with itself, as it has a habit of doing."

Melody shook her head. "I'll get the photo. It's in the file cabinet." She headed towards it.

Erika turned on her cell phone to show Charles the photo on record of Clifford Dean. Turned off the device after his declarative "No way is this person Mark Jason."

"Here we are," Melody said, returning with a lidless box in hand. She carefully placed it on the table, steering clear of her husband's art materials. She rifled through whatever was in the box, came up with a color photograph of a man in a military uniform, and handed it to Erika. "This is Mark, about a year or so before he went to prison," she stated coolly.

"Prison? For what?"

"For fucking *this*!" Charles grunted, slapping a withered thigh.

Erika was speechless.

"I shouldn't have opened it up," Melody said ruefully. "The wound. I'll put this stuff away, Charlie." To Erika: "You, see? No resemblance. Give it here."

Erika returned the photo to her. From a passing review, she'd seen no resemblance to Clifford Dean. "My curiosity offends you. I mean it *must*. I'm sorry."

"Apologies definitely not in order," Melody countered. "How could you *not* want to know what happened?" She kissed Charles again, this time on his lips. "Enough. I think it's time I dispose of all this," she said, tossing the photo back into the box. "Maybe God sent you to me to have me do just that," she directed at Erika.

Charles stiffened. "You're not serious—about God choreographing all this, I mean."

"No, of course not. Erika, do you want this material? Maybe you have a scrapbook of curiosities?"

"No scrapbook, but yes, I'll take it." Good. She would not be needing to ask for a copy of Mark Jason's photograph, after all. And who knew what *else* she'd find in that box!

Melody made a move toward the steps. "I'll fetch a bag to put these things in. Who wants tea and sandwiches? Never mind. That's what you're getting, like it or not."

Chapter Twenty-One

There'd been no time for tea and sandwiches for Erika. She was determined to catch the 5:10 train back to London and end the day with a leisurely dinner with Harrison and John and, over a round of Bloody Marys or some equally effective tension diffuser, apologize for having given them the slip. Melody had insisted on driving her to the Lime Street Station and also packing a cucumber and egg salad sandwich and an orange—peeled!—for her trip back. She'd double-wrapped the food in aluminum foil and sealed it up in a plastic bag before allowing it to share company with her donated Mark Jason material in its newfound storage compartment: a lovely lined crocheted bag she herself had made. Erika had felt like she was being shipped off to grade school. As Melody waved to her from the car, she visualized her mother, already lonely, waving goodbye to her as the doors of the school bus sighed closed.

She was tucked against the windowed side of her compartment, her tote and crocheted bag beside her in the vacant seat. She planned to explore the Jason material with Harrison later that night. Until then it would remain untouched. She was also eager to tell him about her discovery of a brilliant artist, Charles Williams, and the virtual interview to be set up in preparation for the profile she'd try to get into *Art News* in the near future.

The immediate item on the agenda was to renew contact with Harrison. She pulled her cell phone out of her pocket and turned it on. It did not take long to see that she'd been inundated with emails, texts, and voice messages from Harrison. With a pang of guilt barbed with annoyance, she called him. It felt like he responded before she'd punched in all the digits.

"Erika—what the *hell*!"

"Hi to you, too, Harrison."

"Are you okay? We're on a train to Liverpool, on our way to get you! We're due in at five forty-five. Erika, are you okay?"

"I'm okay, I'm okay! What are you doing? How did you know I was—"

"We figured you'd gone off to see the woman who was stalked, where else? We tried calling but the number's unlisted. John had to track it down. Are you still there? Stay where you are!"

"Oh, Harrison, I'm on a train back to Euston Station. And *I'm* due in at seven-twenty! Did you speak to Melody?"

"No one answered. I didn't know what to think!"

"People go out or turn their phones off. It happens. I left word that I'd be back, that I was fine. I didn't want to be hampered or fussed over, so I went off the grid for a while."

"Off the grid? More like off the face of the earth!"

"Harrison, why are you so agitated? What are you keeping from me?"

"Is there a stop before Lime Street?" Harrison hooted. "Conductor?" A pause. "Damn!"

"Harrison, what's wrong? I mean aside from this passing-in-the-night craziness?"

"I don't think I can talk about it without your being beside me, Erika."

"Harrison, are you—"

"I'm fine. Looks like the next stop is Liverpool. We'll take the next train back. They run pretty often. We'll be in London I'm guessing around nine. You'll go straight to the hotel?"

"Yes, of course."

"You promise?"

"I do."

"Erika?"

"Yes?"

"I love you."

"I know. I love you, too."

"I mean very much."

151

"I know. Me, too. Very much."

"Be there. In the hotel room."

"Yes. Yes."

There'd be two more rounds of promises before he'd finally allow her to travel on, alone in the night, without him.

* * *

They fell into each other's arms some hours later. Neither looked at the time. He told her what had happened, from beginning to end, and she cried as if she'd known Ike forever, she hardly knew why, maybe because she imagined the all-embracing pain of his last moments, or because of the senselessness of his death, a man with such transformative hopes and with such boundless determination to fulfill them.

John understood that they wanted to be left alone, so he said he'd wander down to the bar and have himself a beer and burger, check in with them tomorrow.

Neither of them was hungry, but because they knew they *ought* to be, they split the egg salad sandwich and orange Melody had foisted on Erika and shared a bottle of sparkling water from the room bar. All they wanted, really, was to fill their senses with each other, quietly. A few hours of space, and they would be back in the thick of things. Promise.

Detective Hogarty was the first to remind them that there would be no such respite. They must have known, of course. Why else would they have made sure that both their cell phones were within reach and fully charged?

"You've heard about Professor Umar's murder," Hogarty started right in, overriding Erika's "Hello?" "Your husband reported it. It was all over the news, as well. Damn *waste* it was—what did you say, Erika?"

"Only 'hello,' Detective." She activated the speakerphone and rose to a sitting position on the fully made bed. She and Harrison had been holding each other, orbiting the earth with recuperative small talk about who cares what. She was still in her blouse and skirt. Harrison, also fully dressed except for his shoes, sat next to her. Already she was revving up to the task, pulse rate climbing. "Have you found out anything yet?"

"What about Bradan Yusef?" Harrison inserted. "You find him?—It's Harrison, Detective; how are you?"

"Yes, hello. About Yusef. We did find him. He's a student of Umar's—was. He did not privately meet with the professor on that or any other day. He was out of town that day, visiting his sick mother in Essex. Confirmation from all sides. The professor was obviously tricked into believing he had an appointment with Yusef. So far we have no leads on who this imposter might have been." With a rueful laugh, he added, "But I wouldn't be surprised if your wife could help us out there. She did tell you about our meeting earlier today, I take it?"

Harrison looked questioningly at Erika.

"We haven't gotten around to it," she said. "It was a rough day."

"What did I miss?" Harrison asked.

Hogarty summed it up in a nutshell, concluding with: "Impressive woman, your wife."

"Actually, I'd like to get back to you after we review some special material I've been given," Erika declared, in no mood for light-hearted kudos. "By the way, how did your interview with Jacob Tembe go after John and I spoke with you?"

"Ah, yes! Thanks again for picking up on those discrepancies in menswear! Tembe finally broke down and came out with a new statement which, I have to say, sounded too unbelievable not to be true. Only now, with our revised analysis of the visuals, not so unbelievable after all."

Erika scooted closer to Harrison, keeping him in the group, if not the discussion. After she hung up, she would tell him everything about her day on the lam from beginning to end. "How did Tembe explain himself?" she directed at Hogarty.

"He said he'd gotten a call from a fellow who wouldn't identify himself. Chap said he was a fan of his blog, admired his take on things, his passion. Asked Tembe if he'd be interested in pulling off a performance guaranteed to go viral, low risk, high gain. To take place right after closing time in the African Gallery, room twenty-five. 'It'll knock the socks off the Eurocentrics,' his exact words, Tembe said. The contact told him to wear a black suit, black T-shirt, black shoes, he'd supply the black ski masks. Had to be black because this was going to be a light show, and for it to work they had to be dressed in black, exactly like he said, no variations. Told Tembe to meet him in room twenty-five. Tembe said he waited there until he heard the commotion as us bobbies made our entrance, at which point he beat a hasty retreat."

"Did you let him go?" Erika asked.

"Yes, with the proviso he stay in town for further questioning, when we catch up to his alleged handler."

"I'm guessing his mystery look-alike," Erika said. "The person caught on camera on the administration floor, right near Thorpe's office."

"Our candidate for Thorpe's murderer," Hogarty added, the two of them exchanging remarks as naturally as a couple finishing each other's sentences.

"How did it go, Tembe's release?" she asked. "Was there a crowd waiting outside headquarters?"

"A mob scene. Some folks cheering, a lot more calling for his head. Hell, you whisper a half-sentence in the WC and next second, it's around the world. I don't know how social media does it. I'll ask my four-year-old granddaughter. She'll know."

"There's a vigil for Ikemar scheduled for tomorrow night at eight p.m.," Harrison said, his morose tone calling attention to the near buoyant drift of what had gone before. "It was organized by the student's 'London Classicists of Color' society and will be taking place at the Main Quad on Gower Street."

"Yes, Harrison, thank you, I know that," Hogarty said, a touch of resentment in his voice, as if he'd taken the notice as a form of chastisement, which indeed it had been. "There'll be a unit on patrol in the area in case there's a problem."

"Good to hear," Harrison said, "although I hope the event will be a peaceful one."

"Agreed. I'll call you if anything new comes up regarding Tembe or the anonymous man in black," Hogarty announced stiffly, as if unsure to whom he should be addressing this promise.

"Looking forward to hearing from you," Erika replied, her cordial tone intended to bolster Hogarty's commitment, nothing more.

Hers were the last words spoken before contact was terminated.

Harrison was unusually quiet, looking off into space in what Erika read as a kind of resigned passivity. She felt she might yield along with him into that helpless state, but resisted—for both of them. "Let's FaceTime with Lucas," she said, her spirits rising at the thought of it. "Afterwards, I'll tell you everything I did today, minute by minute until you beg me to stop."

He shrugged, forced a smile. "Sure." He fetched his laptop from the living room area and when he returned, Lucas had already been beamed up.

Lucas was wide awake and in high spirits, bouncing on Grace's lap this time, screeching with glee at the sight of his parents, especially his mommy, and his enthusiasm was returned in equal measure by Erika; Harrison and Grace, the more sober-minded costars.

Erika's elation spilled over into the moments after the call. "Let's get ready for bed," she said, rising from it. "We'll talk after. There's a lot to say and we have to plan what we're doing tomorrow, and for the few days we've got left of our trip. We can't stop, you know. We've got to go on. You want to take a shower with me? Save time?"

"Erika, am I losing you?"

The question was an explosion, yet delivered so softly, it was as if she knew she'd been shot, but not in what part of her body.

"*Am* I, Erika?"

She climbed back into bed and moved his laptop aside. "Where did *that* come from? How can you ask—how can you *think* that?"

"I don't know. You have it all. Your career, your child, your breakthrough ideas, your fawning detective, lapping up your every word. What do you need me for? An occasional roll in the hay?"

She could not help laughing. Higher pitched than her usual laugh. "First of all, where did you come up with that dated expression? Second, where do you come off calling it *occasional*?"

"I'm serious."

"So am I." She was giddy, on the verge of tears. "This is coming out of nowhere. You know I love you—*need* you, Harrison. You fulfill me." She snuggled up to his inert form. "And not only in the hay." She kissed his lips. "Although rolling in it is nothing to sneeze at." She held him close. "It must be the day, what it's done to you. Say that's it, Harrison. Please."

"That's it," he said, not moving. "The culmination of things. After what happened with Ike, my not being able to make contact with him. I was scared shitless when I couldn't reach you. And then you and Lucas, with that special thing you've got going for you, and that jolly conversation with Hogarty—not jolly, I'm sorry—in sync, that's what it was. You were in your element. I felt superfluous."

"But you do realize you were wrong?" Her voice was pleading. She hadn't meant it to be.

"I realize I was wrong."

"You don't sound convinced."

He turned to her. Looked into her eyes, finally. As if moved by a force stronger than reason—the survival instinct?—he embraced her, more tightly than he'd intended. "I'm an idiot. Don't hate me for it."

"I *love* you for it," she said.

"Let's not go overboard," he said, sounding more like himself.

They were cheek to cheek, but she heard the smile in his voice. They were home again.

Just in time to face the sequence of calls that came in rapid succession, each following at the termination of the one prior, as if adhering to a schedule.

Madame D. The gist of her call was to report that Pierre Jolet had been appeased. "At first, he was angry, hurt, and frightened, in no particular order, that his story about the near-theft of Mozambican artifacts was leaked without his say-so. I told him his cooperation in the matter had helped the police immensely in the Timothy Thorpe murder case."

"Did Jolet ask *how* it had helped?" Harrison asked.

"I told him it was complicated."

"And he bought it?"

"I said it with authority."

Greg Smith. The main item on his agenda, after expressing shock and regret about Ikemar Umar's murder, was to report his findings on Andrew

Barrett's auction-house receipts. He'd found two sales recorded in Christie's archives, three in Sotheby's and one each from a couple of lesser-known houses in Paris. "The artifacts were described in detail—mediums, markings, damage—so I had a good many key words with which to search the archives for future transactions involving the objects. Nothing came up. This doesn't mean that there were none, including under-the-table deals or downright theft. Nevertheless, this is a good sign. It doesn't prove that Barrett's cache is intact at some unknown site, but at least it doesn't prove that it *isn't!*"

Greg's subsidiary item was recognizing that his in with Detective Hogarty was no longer a valuable commodity: "My role as informant has been usurped by you, my dear Erika." Said all in good humor, although Harrison wasn't quite up for it.

Amilah Adamu. Devastated by the news of Ike's murder, she called to get a first-hand report from Harrison about whatever he had witnessed. Harrison felt it his duty to give her a full report. He was drained by the end of it, running on fumes. Erika took over the call to hear Amilah's reaction to Jacob Tembe's release from police custody. "At least the Brits didn't pin Thorpe's murder on him to bring the case to a quick resolution," Amilah said. "The police performed admirably outside headquarters, handling the protesters. Emery—the head of the UDC, as I've mentioned—was angry that one of you jumped the gun by reporting Tembe to the police before he'd had a chance to review the situation but was placated by how well the police handled the situation."

"Shall we turn off our phones?" Erika asked after the call from Amilah had concluded. Harrison looked beat. "No, we better not," she answered herself. "You never know…"

"No, you don't," he replied dolefully. "Not ever." He stroked her face. "Let's try to get some sleep."

"Shower?"

"In the morning."

"Sure."

Exhausted, they nevertheless went through their side-by-side ritual of brushing and flossing their teeth then washing up, Erika adding the step of moisturizing with the elegantly bottled cream provided by the hotel.

Their ablutions wearily out of the way, they called John to set up a meeting for early a.m., cleared the bed of phones and laptop and themselves of clothing, turned off the table lamps, and crawled into bed, burrowing deep under the covers. They held each other close. It was enough—more than enough. This is what it would be like in the end, past passion and the preening for it. Sex in its purest form, as memory.

Chapter Twenty-Two

Recovered, but just, from the day before, Erika and Harrison were still in their bathrobes at 6:10 a.m. when John knocked on their door, twenty minutes earlier than their scheduled meeting.

"So, what's the plan for today?" John asked, ready to get down to it. He was a man of action, especially in times when the temptation was to sit around licking one's, or anybody else's, wounds.

"Come in, John," Harrison said, widening the door space to allow him passage, now that Erika had done re-securing her robe. "We just finished breakfast and are about to get dressed. If you don't mind our dishabille, we can start right in."

"Dis- who? Whatever. I'm ready to go." He eyed the food cart sitting next to the doorway, ready to be discarded. "You mind?" He nodded toward the abandoned half of a croissant.

"Be my guest. Want us to order up for you?"

"Thanks, I've already eaten." He grabbed the croissant piece and scarfed it down. "Shall we sit?" He answered himself by taking the armchair catty-corner to the couch.

Erika and Harrison took their places on the couch, on either side of the lined crochet bag given to Erika by Melody Williams. "We'd like you to look over this material with us," Erika said, giving the bag a pat. "Before we do, is there anything you've got on your mind you'd like to tell us about? From the looks of it, I think you do."

"I'm that easy to read?"

"Not always."

John crossed his legs and casually grabbed his ankle, getting comfortable, or wanting to appear so. "I actually do have something on my mind, been bugging me for a while. Would you mind sharing your friend Greg Smith's email and cell phone number with me?"

"Not at all," Harrison said, sitting forward. "What's up?"

"Look, you're my pals, sure, but you're also my employers, so I don't feel comfortable going off on a hunch of my own, even if I think it's in your interest. Without your okay, that is. You understand?"

"Not any more than I did a minute ago."

"Okay, here's the thing. Ever since Erika and I had our powwow with Brian Latham, I've been stewing over it. I didn't like the guy straight off—you know that, Erika—and a couple of things sounded shady. I didn't like the way he ran on about his wife's charity. A small thing, you might say, but an attempt to distract, I think. Another piece of information we didn't need to know is that the nerdy research student has the hots for Cherry Ames, the chick who happens to work for Latham. Which is another diversionary tactic in my opinion—pawning off his own thing for the lady in question on somebody else. Worst of all, his stirring up suspicion for the custodial guy, Clifford Dean. Who says Latham didn't take it upon himself to review the staff members' personal files, pick out one that looked a little fishy, and plant the seed of doubt about him? Again, my humble opinion."

"Brian Latham?" Harrison asked. *Our* Brian Latham?" He looked to Erika for mirrored consternation and was surprised to find her pretty much unruffled by John's statement. "Erika?"

"I know," she said, appreciating his reaction. "I was shocked myself when John first expressed his suspicions about Brian. But after bumping into Clifford Dean right before John and I met with Detective Hogarty, I began to see his point. Dean was, if anything, disarming, and Brian, when he caught us talking together, seemed anxious to separate us." To Harrison's questioning look, she added, "You didn't know about this encounter. I'm sorry. We still haven't gotten around to my minute-by-minute rundown." She gave a helpless shrug. "But we're getting there."

Harrison reached out to rub her shoulder. "I get it, darling," he said, detecting the worry in her voice. If they'd been alone, he would have reassured her that last night's insecurity had been a momentary lapse on his part. *Nothing to worry about,* he tried to convey through his kneading. Did he feel her tension ease, or did he imagine it?

She laid her hand on his, and he knew. "Why do you want to contact Greg?" she directed at John, while her body sighed under her husband's touch—God, it took so little. "What are you planning on asking Greg to do?"

"From what you've told me, it looks like Greg is pretty tight with the British Museum's Board of Trustees. I'd like to ask him to pump the members with whom he's got the closest ties and ask them what they know about Timothy Thorpe's relationship with Brian Latham. Both associate curators, offices on the same floor, who knows what else they've got in common, like grudges? Also, I'd like to do some nosing around on my own, tail the guy for a spell. Basically, I need your permission to go rogue. Do I have it?"

Erika and Harrison exchanged nods. "Sure, John," Erika replied, speaking for both of them."

"Good, because I've already rented a car for the occasion."

Harrison grabbed his cell phone from the coffee table and pulled up Greg's email address and cell number. John recorded them on his cell phone, nostrils flaring like a racehorse at the starting gate. "Thanks!"

"No problem." He picked up the crocheted bag sitting between him and Erika. "Let's have a look."

"Whatever's in there," John said, "how the hell could you keep your hands off it?"

Erika smiled. "We have our traditions. We like to reveal things together." Her smile vanished. "We weren't up to it until now."

Harrison emptied the contents of the bag onto the coffee table and set the bag on the floor. Aside from the color photograph of Mark Jason in Royal Army uniform, the items exposed were all newspaper clippings. Harrison examined the photograph, sharing the view with Erika, then handed it to John. Neither Harrison nor John knew the why or wherefore of the exercise, so Erika gave them a rundown on what had transpired at the address in Liverpool that the NCA—National Crime Agency—had dug up at John's request. "Remember? It was the only concrete association with Clifford Dean the agency could come up with?" She told them she'd come to suspect that Mark Jason, the man in the photograph, and Clifford Dean were one and the same individual. "I asked Melody who she thought the person who stalked her might have been if it hadn't been Clifford Dean. Without a blink, she said her ex-husband, Mark Jason, except he was dead. I suggested people have been known to fake their own deaths." Erika appealed to Harrison and John, who were starting to look skeptical. "You know, to start new lives, disencumber themselves of their unsavory pasts?"

"I get you," John said, uncrossing his legs. "What else?"

"Dean evaded the stalking charge by telling the police that he couldn't find his friend's address and was waiting for him to return home to guide him, or some such. It seemed to me Melody bought into his weak excuse too readily, as if for her peace of mind, she *needed* to."

"Sorry-ass excuse, more like," John edited, tapping his foot impatiently, again the horse at the starting gate. He looked at his watch. "Guys, I hate to break up the party, but are you anticipating the need for my immediate service regarding this matter? I mean, I got some stalking to do on my own, you understand."

Harrison sat back. "John, we haven't checked out the news clippings yet. From what I saw at a glance, they may throw some light on the subject—on the *suspect*. Look at this". He picked up one of the clippings. "This is from *The London Gazette*, 2011. 'Lieutenant Mark Gregory Jason was found guilty of grievous bodily harm by an army tribunal yesterday, Thursday, 7 April, at 4:30 p.m.,'" he quoted. He looked up. "Aren't you interested, John?"

"I am, yes, but time is of the essence. I want to be within surveillance distance of the Latham residence, with any luck before there's any movement to and from. May I be dismissed?" he asked, on the rise.

"I guess so. Of course."

Erika had picked up another clipping and was absorbed.

"Leaving now, Erika," John said. "Any comments?"

"What? Oh yes." She tapped the clipping. "We'll be fine, John. We'll take it from here." She handed the clipping to Harrison and picked up another one.

"See you later, John—oh wow!" she exclaimed, in response to her reading matter. Before the door had shut behind John, she was clueing in Harrison. "This clipping is dated 1 September 2011, five months after the guilty verdict and sentencing," she reported. "It sums things up. Mark Jason was awarded the Victoria Cross medal in 2010, two years after his heroic action in Iraq, says here, 'for consistent bravery and inspirational leadership.' This article announces that the Queen has now formally, and I quote, 'cancelled and annulled the award.'"

"From the heights straight to hell," Harrison commented. "Must have done a job on the man's psyche. Does your article give details on the actual event that prompted this fall from grace? Mine just refers to, quote, 'an altercation between Jason and Charles Williams, outside Mr. Williams's art studio in the village of Withnell Fold.'"

"*Altercation?* How delicate. My journalist is more direct. 'Charles Williams was brutally attacked with the buttstock of a rifle,' he reports. He goes on to say that witnesses at the scene testified that Jason may have been on the verge of aiming his weapon at the victim but was subdued by one of the onlookers before they could tell for sure. Williams suffered a broken back resulting in his paraplegia; the onlooker, minor injuries." Erika laid the clipping on the coffee table.

"What a story. Do you really think Jason and Clifford are one and the same?"

"It goes against my impression of Dean, but not my reading of the circumstances."

"Look here," Harrison said, scanning another of the clippings. He stopped cold.

"What is it?"

"The Clifford Dean alleged stalking incident. I think I remember John saying it took place early May of 2015. That what you remember?"

"Yes, Harrison. Why?"

"'Mark Gregory Jason was released from prison today,'" he read aloud. "Can you guess the issue date?"

"You're kidding." She spent a moment calculating before taking a stab at it. "February 2015?"

"That's it!" He shook his head, waited for her to explain.

"I may have left the timeline out of my debriefing to you and John just now. Anyway, Melody said her ex-husband had committed suicide two months before the alleged stalking event, which we know took place in May. That would put the death, or faked death, in March, right? If faked, I figured it would take Jason about a month to get his ducks in order—procure a counterfeit insurance number, undergo some cosmetic tweaking, dream up his ideal demise—before having the gall to stalk his ex-wife virtually out in the open. Which puts his release from prison around February."

"It's coming together like a jigsaw puzzle," Harrison said.

"Yes, except sometimes you find yourself forcing the pieces together because you're so sure they *must* fit. You remember doing that ever?"

"Literally?"

"What do you think? Yes."

"I never put together a jigsaw puzzle. So, no, I don't remember."

"What else don't I know about you?" she wondered aloud.

"I don't like Brussel sprouts."

"I already knew that."

"That does it then. You know everything. Let's get dressed and get out of here. I'd like to drive to Brentford, do some hunting about for goldsmith L. P. Sutton's hypothetical vault. We can't let our search for Andrew Barrett's cache of African artworks go by the wayside. You want to come with me?"

"I do, but first let's make a couple of calls. I want to get in touch with Melody and Charles Williams. I rushed off so I wouldn't miss my train back to London, and there were issues left unresolved. I also want to call Hogarty about the latest development regarding Clifford Dean. You don't mind, do you?"

"Of course not. What's my hurry, anyway? The drive from London to Brentford is less than twenty minutes and it's still too early to call these people. I'd also like to touch base with the director of the Brentford and Chiswick Local Historical Society before we set out. We're going to need some guidance." He popped up from the couch. "I'm feeling manic this morning. I want to get out there, but I want to be back in time for Ikemar's vigil. At the same time, I feel like Ike is breathing down my neck, demanding that I get things done."

A hot shower was in order. A long one.

* * *

"I never fully thanked you," Erika said, addressing FaceTime's dual headshot of Melody and Charles Williams.

"For what?" Melody asked.

"For talking to me, a perfect stranger. For your hospitality, for driving me to the train station. Shall I go on?"

"Please don't," Charles laughed.

"I told my husband all about you. He'd like to meet you. Harrison's an art history professor, so that makes all four us in the art world, in one capacity or another."

Harrison was sitting beside Erika on the couch, the two of them in all-purpose ensembles of pants, white shirts, blazers, the pairing unplanned. At the mention of his name, Harrison leaned into the frame, temple-to-temple with Erika. "Hello, there. Thanks for taking in my wife."

"Lord, you'd think we adopted her," Charles replied good-humoredly. "Enough."

"Understood," Harrison conceded with a grin. "Erika tells me she's doing a profile of you for *Art News*."

"Which is another reason for this call," Erika pitched in. "We didn't have a chance to set up a virtual interview. Will you be free for about an hour or so, say, two weeks from today, four p.m. your time?"

"Be happy to talk to you then."

"Melody, would you join us? I'd like to have your input."

"Glad to," Melody said, "but why you need me in on it, I don't know."

"Never mind," Charles said. "*I* need you in on it."

"Good," Erika said. "By the way, will you be able to email me a few—well, at least six—high-res photos of your paintings?"

"The Walker Gallery will supply them. They're putting together a brochure to accompany their exhibit of my work, so they've got what you need. They'll require published credits for the images. Can you manage that?"

"Absolutely."

"Done," Charles declared.

There was a pause while Erika shifted gears. "I wanted to apologize for prying into your personal lives," she said.

"As I recall, you already did," Melody said. "And as I told you, there was no need to. I assume you went over the material we pawned off on you?"

"Yes, and what an ordeal you went through, Charles. I feel bad bringing it up, but I—*we*—had to say how sorry we are you had to suffer so." The words were inadequate, cloying almost.

"It's great that you two found each other after that terrible encounter," Harrison commented, trying to brighten the mood.

"What?" Charles exclaimed, totally surprised. "You don't know what provoked Jason's attack?"

"Darling," Melody said, "I didn't save the scandal sheets. These two don't know the backstory."

"Ah, so I'll tell them," Charles declared forcefully, as if someone was objecting to his doing so. "Without mincing words, Melody and I met fifteen years ago at an art exhibition at the Walker Gallery. We got to talking. Had lunch. Fell in love by dessert. By chance, I had never dated a white woman. She had never gone out with a Black man. I know that saying you're colorblind these days is decidedly un-woke, but be that as it may, we didn't give a shit. I was Charlie, she was Mel. I was divorced. She was still married to Mark. After Mark returned home from Iraq, he discovered we were having an affair and that Mel planned to divorce him. He didn't take it well. I'm in this wheelchair for life, but it was worth it." He smiled slyly at Melody. "And we've learned how to make it...*work*."

"TMI, my love," Melody pretended to scold. "And on that note," she said, addressing Erika and Harrison, I propose we call it a day. Speak to you in two weeks, unless—"

"—something comes up sooner," Charles wickedly finished, taking pleasure in embarrassing his wife.

"Well, *that* went better than expected," Harrison remarked after the call had ended. "Interesting couple. I'm looking forward to seeing Charles's work."

"It'll amaze you," Erika said. Returning to her cell phone's keypad, she proposed, "How about we make a call to Detective Hogarty, then reach out to the historical society, get a head start on our quest?"

"Let's do it."

"I've got a theory I've been mulling over. You'll think it's crazy at first. It's not. You want to hear it now or while we're on the call?"

"On the call. It'll save time." He stroked her ear with his thumb. "Surprise me."

She did. Practically the first thing out of her mouth. "I've got a theory," she announced on speakerphone, after verifying it was Hogarty on the line. She was more confident about her theory, now that it did not seem as outlandish as when she'd finger-printed its logo in the mist on her bathroom mirror. "I think there's a good chance that the perpetrators, or at least the masterminds behind Timothy Thorpe's, Keith Ashton's, and Ikemar Umar's murders are one and the same person."

Erika imagined Hogarty's visible reaction pretty much matched Harrison's: the classic mix of surprise and disbelief.

Hogarty was the first to put it into words. "For starters, the motivation behind the Thorpe and Ashton murders is just about the reverse of Umar's," he said to the accompaniment of Harrison's drawn-out nod of agreement.

"The *expressed* motivation," Erika corrected. "Yes, the person who called *The Guardian* did confess to having murdered Thorpe in revenge for the West's dragging its heels in the matter of repatriation and incidentally as a call to arms to its proponents. And yes, the person who murdered Ikemar professed his hatred of Africa's culture as anathema to Western education. But what if these divergent statements of outrage are unified by another motive—the killer's *real* motive? What if the killer's got a grudge against *both* factions?"

"'A plague on both your houses'?" Harrison rephrased, quoting Shakespeare.

"Exactly! *Think* about it." The photograph of Mark Jason, Melody's allegedly deceased husband, was lying on the coffee table. "Harrison's going to take a picture of a man's photograph and send it to you, Detective, okay?" Harrison nodded his consent.

Hogarty dictated his email address and within two minutes acknowledged receiving the copy of the photograph.

"I assume you have a face-matching expert on call?" Erika asked.

"Not on call, on file. Why? What challenge have you got for us now? Looks like a chap in Her Majesty's Royal Army. To what do I owe the honor?"

"I'd like your expert to compare this man's face to Clifford Dean's."

"The custodian who tried to save Timothy Thorpe's life?"

"Yes."

"You plan to keep me in the dark here?"

"We'll tell you everything after you've come back with the expert's finding. That way you'll approach it objectively. My hypothesis hangs on those digital algorithms, or whatever. Will you trust me?"

"Do I have a choice?"

"Do I have to answer that? Oh, I've just got one more…"

"*Assignment*, but you hate to use the word? It's okay. What is it?"

"First, did you take possession of the Picasso study displayed by Mick Ross on his 'No Holds Barred' vlog site?"

"With the 'Picasso The Pimp' et cetera printed over it? Yes, of course."

"And do you also have custody of the desecrated Nigerian flag found draped over Ikemar Umar's body?"

"No, I gave it to my aunt to upholster her chair. What do you think, of *course*, I have it in custody!"

"This will call for another expert. Can you have the black paint used in each case analyzed to determine if they could possibly have come from the same source?"

"Absolutely."

What? No accompanying dig? "Thanks for putting up with me, Detective."

"My pleasure, Erika. Now may I be dismissed?"

CHAPTER TWENTY-TWO

She obliged.

Harrison's call to the Director of the Brentford and Chiswick Local Historical Society was cut and dry. He stated his case, only slightly shy of the truth, and Winifred Crabb, head of the Brentford Library, expressed her willingness to meet the couple at her office any time after noon; give her time to put together her notes. A quarter past was the agreed-upon time.

* * *

The Wheatleys' taxi pulled up opposite the entrance to the Brentford Library at 12:10, twenty minutes after they'd hailed it outside the hotel.

The library was framed by ancient trees, dense and welcoming, and along with its warm terracotta facing and white-grilled windows, its initial aura was residential. The institutional component appeared only on their approach, when the raised letters in the arched section above the doorway came into focus: "The Gift of Andrew Carnegie 1903."

Winifred Crabb's office was on the ground floor. There were visitors milling about, but directions were unnecessary. A modest name plaque on her door identified the room's occupant.

For Erika, the name Winifred Crabb conjured up images of ample bosoms and orthopedic shoes. In this case, decidedly misleading. Winifred—"call me Winnie"—was a lithesome woman around fifty-five, dressed to the nines in a designer suit, the herringbone pattern matching perfectly at the seams; definitely not a knock-off. She was standing in front of a wooden file cabinet as they entered her domain, and her gold bangle bracelets clinked slightly as she shut its open drawer. Her smile, as she greeted them—radiant, contagious— reminded Erika of Amilah's, only Amilah's shone without the aid of makeup. Winifred's was highlighted by ruby-red lipstick, complemented by the hint of blush on the apples of her cheeks and a subtle smudge of umber shadowing her light blue eyes. Her gray-streaked brown hair was pulled back in a serviceable bun, her only concession to type.

"I composed a summary for you," Winifred said after Erika and Harrison had taken their seats across the desk from her, "so you needn't commit all of what I have to say to memory or take copious notes."

"That was kind of you, Winifred," Harrison replied, finding 'Winnie' too familiar an address for comfort.

Winifred did not correct him. Getting straight to the point, she said, "I decided to give you some background on L.P. Sutton's establishment—that's Lawrence Peter Sutton, incidentally—before I escort you to its present iteration. It will make your interaction with the owner of the shop that much easier and besides"—she smiled—"I know a history junky when I see one."

"Being one yourself," Erika suggested.

"Indeed. The research your husband hinted at"—she wagged her finger at Harrison—"only served to whet my appetite. I want to hear more. The reference to Sutton's vault, as I understand it, was found in the rough draft of a letter dated 1897, unearthed but a month ago."

"You explain, darling," Erika charitably yielded to the man who'd invented the story.

"Sure. Well, as I've told you, Winifred, Erika, and I, through no intentions of our own, have managed to acquire a reputation for art-sleuthing—or -snooping—and our latest request for help has come from the woman who quite by chance discovered the letter in question. She's the great-grandniece of the individual who penned it, as a matter of fact."

"Tantalizing," Winifred commented. "Where did she find it? Between the pages of an old book? In the secret compartment of a desk?"

"You're good; she found it tucked between the pages of the family Bible," he said, revising his story on the fly. "The writer mentions his purchase of a chain-link necklace from L.P. Sutton Goldsmith and goes on to say that during his and his wife's extended period abroad he means to store their valuables, including his wife's jewelry and their collection of art works, in Sutton's vault. 'Commodious' is the word he uses to describe the vault."

"I presume the man's descendants have seen neither hide nor hair of his treasures," Winifred said.

"Right."

"Should you find a vault somewhere in the dank underground recesses of the building—à la 'The Cask of Amontillado'—what *then*, Mr. Poe? If there are treasures to be found, do you have proof of ownership?"

"We do, but we're not at liberty to present them until we have good reason to. Our client is a very private person. May we leave it at that? The proof, in the form of a partial inventory, is found in the pages of a journal contemporaneous with the letter."

Winifred nodded. "Fair enough. Now, let me tell you the history of the Suttons so you have an idea of what you're dealing with. The original owners of the establishment, Lawrence Peters and his wife, Clara, lost their two sons, their only children, at the Battle of the Somme, at Deville Wood, August 1916. Clara took her own life that same year, and Lawrence walked out of Brentford early 1917, without notice and leaving all that he owned or had an interest in behind. His shop was left unattended for some time, and no relatives came forward to claim rights over it. And then—it happened spontaneously, with one or two people acting on their own at the start—the townspeople began caring for the grounds: planting flowers, pruning shrubs, mowing the lawn. Maintaining the site as a shrine, you might say."

"The light in the window," Erika mused. "Did Sutton ever return?"

"No. After five years—that brings us to 1922—the governing body of Brentford offered the property up for sale for its assessed value. The contents of the shop were sold at auction and both the proceeds from the auction and the sale of the building were put in escrow for a period of ten years, to be transferred to Mr. Sutton, should he reappear."

"The contents sold at auction?" Harrison asked. "Did this include the contents of the vault?"

"I would assume its contents would have been put on the block along with the rest of the unclaimed merchandise."

Erika prepared herself for an unkind reply. "Winifred, is it possible that any of this deal, say the sale of the vault's contents, may have been transacted off the books?"

Winifred predictably balked. "Under the table is what you're saying. Let's not beat around the bush." With a roll of her eyes, she appealed heavenward.

"This is exactly why I'm talking to you in advance. We must tread lightly with the present owner, or we will alienate him right off the bat, as your colorful expression goes." She suddenly blanched. "I'm sorry! I haven't told you that the present owner of the property is the grandson of the individual who purchased the property in 1922, and that you would be insulting his grandfather if you made such allegations! Forgive me."

"That's okay," Erika said, embarrassed for having caused embarrassment. "It was a cynical remark on my part."

"May we put this behind us?" Harrison suggested, growing impatient. He had already begun worrying he and Erika would be late for Ikemar's vigil, never mind that it would not be starting for at least another five hours. Anyway, his gut was telling him that this exercise was a lost cause. Only thing left to do was prove it. He rose to his feet.

His companions took the hint.

* * *

They walked the short distance to the business center of town, Winifred regaling Erika and Harrison with anecdotes about, of all things, the Brentford Football Club, established in 1889, and the stir that surrounded the replacement of its crest, some years back, to one featuring a more prominent bee. Winifred had become more solicitous, and at the same time, frenetic, since her minor outburst over the suggestion of foul play at the sale of Sutton's property, and Erika figured she hadn't yet forgiven herself for it.

"Here we are," Winifred said, coming to a halt before one of the many storefronts on Nettles Road, her charges drawing up beside her. Raised lettering across the lintel above the store's wide glass door read: *Finley Electrical Ltd.* Through the glass they could see a number of aisles running from the front of the store to the back, offering unidentifiable items presumably related to matters electric. Appliances were lined up at the far end of the store, partly visible between the aisles. One customer was standing mid-aisle behind a shopping cart and plucking what looked like a pack of light bulbs from a shelf.

"I told Ryan Finley we'd like to visit sometime this afternoon, and he was most gracious," Winifred said. "He's got a yen for history himself, so I don't doubt he'll be forthcoming." She stepped forward. "Shall we?"

* * *

Ryan listened attentively as the Wheatleys told their story, Erika alternating with Harrison as narrator, confident in the role, now that she'd heard his edited version. Ryan had bid an employee to "watch over things" while he saw to his guests, and he and they were now installed in his small windowless office towards the rear of the store, fighting off varying degrees of claustrophobia.

"You wondered what had become of the contents of the putative vault at the time of the sale in 1922," Ryan said, addressing Erika and Harrison, his Parliamentary manner of speech unexpectedly paired with his physical presentation. Ryan was a burly man perhaps in his early sixties, with a salt-and-pepper scruffy beard and mop of hair, and wearing a red and black Scotch plaid flannel shirt, blue jeans, and lace-up boots. Though Erika had never seen one in the flesh, the words "forest ranger" had instantly come to mind.

"As a matter of fact, we do indeed have a vault on the premises," Ryan went on. "It's where I keep, among other things, all the original papers of that sale. The sale was an unusual one, as you've learned, with legal ramifications that may yet be called into question. You yourselves are dealing with an issue that has remained dormant for over a century, so you will certainly understand. This was originally a goldsmith's shop. My grandfather converted it to a furniture store. My father added footage to the rear of the building and added electrical appliances to the inventory. When I took over, I dedicated the entire space to electrical goods. Every alteration has been documented in the event we're one day asked to give an accounting." He rose from the metal folding chair behind his table desk and gestured toward the wall of shelving abutting his guests' seating arrangement. "Excuse me, I'll have to ask you to stand."

They complied, and Ryan pushed their chairs out of the way. As they watched, crammed at the other side of the room, Ryan slid the shelved structure along the wall, exposing a steel door behind it. The door was painted black with a gold border. Its lintel bore the name "L. P. Sutton" in raised gold letters. The portrait of a dour-looking royal graced the door's central panel.

"Queen Victoria," Winifred announced, in case anyone doubted her knowledge.

"None other," Ryan confirmed. "The vault dates back to the goldsmith's proprietorship." He repositioned himself in order to block his guests' view of his hands as he worked the combination lock, then disengaged the steel rod bolts of the antique's hinged door. "Quite a laborious exercise," Ryan said, swinging open the door to reveal another, less massive door behind it, requiring a little less effort to unlatch. He reached into the compartment and drew forth a metal container. "Come have a look at the vault's interior," he said, stepping aside. He placed the container on his table desk. "See if you can envision this space containing all that you believe it once did—or might have."

Winifred stood back, allowing the Wheatleys to monopolize the viewing area.

Harrison's negative outlook hadn't changed. Nevertheless, if only for appearance's sake, he poked his head in and had a look around. The cement-lined space looked more or less impregnable, but it was much too narrow and shallow to have accommodated all the items Andrew Barrett had alluded to in his journal.

Erika was more hopeful than Harrison, therefore more disappointed than he after having a look of her own. She shook her head to Ryan's questioning look.

"I suspected as much," Ryan said, with surprising warmth. "I'm really sorry. Let's have a look at the documents, anyway. I guard them with my life, but I've never taken a proper look at them myself in all these years. Afraid to, I suppose." He opened the lid of the metal container and began shuffling through its contents.

"We shouldn't take up any more of your time," Harrison said, aware of the plaintive tone of his voice. Couldn't be helped. He was feeling more and more trapped in these tight quarters.

"Perfectly okay," Ryan said. "I'm curious myself." He waved a letter-sized white envelope in the air. "Here we are. It says 'Twelve February, year nineteen hundred and twenty-two, L. P. Sutton Goldsmith, assessment, property interior.'" He untucked the envelope's flap and pulled out the folded sheets. Postponing his obvious curiosity, he handed them to Harrison.

Harrison shared the view with Erika.

The streamer *"Contents of L. P. S. Vault: 0"* appeared on the sheet after the title page. The line below read *"Contents of Strongroom: 0."*

Harrison looked up. "Strongroom?"

Ryan nodded. "In the basement. I know you'll want to see it."

"Sure, thanks," Erika said, overshadowing Harrison's muttered decline.

Ryan was searching through the container, removing items one by one and setting them aside on his desktop. "I'm looking for further reference to either the vault or the strongroom, something to give us a clue to what, if anything, they contained prior to my grandfather's purchase. I'm finding documents—here's a liability waiver...signed deed...ah, interesting photo of the grounds...surveyor's papers—no, nothing explaining the empty compartments. Whatever information I've got on inventory is what you're holding in your hands." More to Harrison than Erika: "But don't despair. The municipality has files of its own. I'm sure Winifred will help me search the archives for anything that may prove useful to you. Who knows, it's always possible that before the sale of the property took place, the contents of either or both the spaces in question may have been shipped to points unknown—as *yet* unknown!"

Ryan seemed to be taking on the project as his own. Erika understood firsthand what it meant to have a participatory role turn into an obsession, so she empathized. Harrison understood, too, but his discomfort outweighed his empathy. He handed the inventory papers to Ryan and braced himself for the useless trip down to the basement, which he would tolerate only because Erika wished him to.

Ryan returned his office to its original state and led his guests down the staircase just outside the room. The basement, unlike the creepy crypts in the "The Cask of Amontillado," referenced by Winifred Crabb, was a well-lit open expanse evoking not a whit of spookiness. The space was dedicated to boxed in-stock merchandise arranged in neat and, to the untrained eye, indeterminate groupings.

The strongroom formed a classification of its own. Its metal door was located on the basement's west wall. After unlocking the door by pressing a series of numbers on a keypad—hand cupped over the pad for security—Ryan ushered his guests into the enclosure, unique, his guests at once discovered, for both its structure and contents.

Erika estimated the windowless room to be about eight by twelve feet. Its wood-paneled walls and ceiling were reinforced with cross-braced steel beams. Metal shelving covered the far wall, floor to ceiling, and appeared to be welded to the beams. While the basement's main expanse had been furnished with boxes of all sizes containing scores of hidden objects, the strongroom was an eye-catching smorgasbord of vintage bits and parts and devices and gizmos all vying for attention on the shelves and scattered about the floor or perched on tables—look at me, no me!—with plugs and buttons, switches and pull cords ready to be inserted, pressed, tugged, toggled.

"Everyone has his definition of treasure trove," Ryan declared. "This is mine. My father started the collection and I've expanded it. He amassed appliances and devices he liked the looks of; didn't care how old or new. That decorative nineteen-forties Philco radio—second shelf, third from the left—is one of his picks, as are the Victorian toggle switch plates right beside them. My interest is more about function and antiquity. For instance, those Morse receivers on the first table over there"—pointing to his left—"that was my purchase; the first radio receivers producing continuous wave transmissions. Take a look around if you like. One of my favorites, the US 1947 Farnsworth TV, ten-inch screen, is also back there, on the floor near the shelving."

"Quite a museum you have here," Harrison commented with an uptick of interest. Unless Andrew Barrett had accumulated a massive amount of items between 1897 and his death during the pandemic of 1918, this room may very well have been big enough to house his treasures, he thought—dared hope. "I won't try to hide my preoccupation with our project," he confessed. "I believe this space would have been able to accommodate the belongings that we're trying to locate, Ryan. You will be taking a look at those municipal archives you mentioned, yes?"

Ryan smiled. "You can count on it, Harrison. I'm fast becoming as immersed in your quest as you are."

"I told you Mr. Finley has a yen for history, didn't I?" Winifred amiably chided. "For one thing, he's an active member in the Friends of Gunnersbury Park and Museum." To Ryan: "Forgive me for tooting your horn." To the Wheatleys: "In fact, you two should visit the Park before you head back to town. It's an idyllic place with a lovely nature walk. It's only ten minutes away. I'll take you there, if you like."

Erika and Harrison declined the offer. Although they used their limited spare time as an excuse, neither was up for a nature walk, or any other kind of amble, with Winifred Crabb. Especially not Harrison. Especially not today.

* * *

"Was I being a drama queen back there or were you being a Panglossian?" Harrison asked Erika on the cab ride back to the hotel.

"Are the two mutually exclusive?" Erika gibed, arching a brow at the fancy allusion to Voltaire's incurable optimist.

Harrison uttered a laugh; his first in a while. "Seriously. Was I rude? I think I was rude."

"Good observation." She grabbed his hand. "No, not really. You were tense and impatient, and after what you went through, almost impossible not to be."

"Thanks." He intertwined his fingers with hers; hung on for dear life.

Chapter Twenty-Three

John's text read: "Where are you?" Harrison answered: "In our room. Why?" As he showed the texts on his cell phone screen to Erika, the words "Coming now," appeared below them. Harrison's "Okay" was answered seconds later by a rap on the hotel room door.

"Who is it?" Erika asked, on the other side of it.

"You decent?" John responded.

"*Now* you ask?" Erika came back, opening the door. "What's going on?"

"How was the trip to Brentford? Any success?" John eyed the food cart.

"Not very promising, but a chance it'll lead to something. Go ahead, help yourself."

Harrison emerged from the bathroom. "What's up, John?"

John waited until he'd polished off one of the two remaining tea sandwiches. "I've got to notify the police."

"About the food?"

John grimaced. "What the hell is this, cucumber? No wonder the English have bad teeth."

"What are you talking about, John?" Harrison sat back down on the couch, where he and Erika had been trying to unwind after their meeting with Ryan Finley and in preparation for the vigil for Ikemar Umar later that evening. "Take a seat. What's on your mind?"

Erika reclaimed her spot beside Harrison, and John, after consuming the last of the tea sandwiches, took the seat he'd sat in earlier in the day, completing the déjà vu.

John was holding his cell phone. He fiddled with it, then looked up. "This is about Brian Latham. We've got a problem." He pointed the screen in their direction, extending his arm to give them a good look at the photograph he'd retrieved from his app.

Erika leaned forward to get an even better look. "Wait, that's Cherry Ames!" The officious young projects assistant was frozen in the act of, honing in for a kiss from Brian, similarly angled across the table from her. Her hand was unequivocally encased in his, dispelling any doubt about the nature of their engagement. Erika sat back, squelching the urge to pass judgment. "I get it, John, but what's the point?"

"There must be more to this," Harrison said. "Otherwise, I'm embarrassed."

"I thought you knew me better than that," John balked. "I'm not some lowlife snoop."

"Sorry, John," Erika said. "We're a little on edge right now, looking for a time out. Don't take it personally."

"I'll try not to."

"What's the pitch, already?" Harrison grumbled, instantly waving off the remark. "Sorry."

"I get it. I'll get out of your way in a minute, but this is critical."

"Would you like a cup of tea?" Harrison formally offered, in an attempt to make up for his impatience. Along with John and Erika, even he had to laugh at his oafishness.

"Here's what happened," John began, after turning down the beverage offer. "After I left you this morning I drove straight over to Latham's place, hoping to beat his departure. While I was parked, I gave Greg Smith a call, asked for his help getting the scoop on Thorpe's relationship with Latham, talk to his board member chum to check if there was any bad blood between them, anything off about their working relationship. Good guy, Greg. Got back to me two hours later, while I was still warming the car seat waiting for Latham to make his move, hoping he hadn't gone AWOL or slept in. Hold up, I'll get to Greg's call in a sec.

"Lucky break, three minutes after I hear from Greg, here comes my man Latham strutting out to the curb. He hops into a Ford Fiesta and drives off. I pull out and follow a reasonable distance behind. I admit it, after waiting around for so long I'm hoping the guy will lead the way to a Mafia conference or the like, but the only stop he makes is at a Dunkin' Donuts-type establishment and all I'm thinking is, here's a man after my own heart.

"After that stop, Latham drove straight to the museum. I idled near his parking spot, waited until he got out, and saw him heading for the building. He looked cheerful as a schoolboy, clutching his box of scones or whatever. I would have chalked the whole thing off to my screwed-up instincts and been done with it—had I not gotten that call from Greg." He waited a beat for dramatic effect before continuing.

"From Greg, I learned that before the tragedy Thorpe and Latham were both in the running for the position of head curator and that the board's general mindset was heavily weighted in Thorpe's favor. Right now, the board's set to announce Latham's appointment."

Erika felt obligated to serve as Brian's advocate. "Workplace competition is the general rule, John."

"A fact of life," Harrison added.

"Hold it," John said, raising his hand like a school crossing guard. "Don't you think I know this? Wait until I'm done."

The order was greeted with respectful silence.

"Greg went on to inform me that although this board member chum of his had not attended Latham's wife's charity event, 'Literacy United,' he did put him onto a couple that had. I took a chance that Latham was going to stick around the museum this morning, at least until he'd demolished his bakery supply, so then and there I contacted the couple and set up a time to meet them. Great how my FBI deputy status gets me where I want to go.

"Anyway, this nice elderly couple—rolling in it, from the looks of their apartment—ask me in for a spot of tea—so, what else is new? They end up being very cooperative. Especially the wife, who revealed herself to be a bit of a gossip, high-class, mind you. I won't tell you how we got there, because it'll include a long story about the couple's lousy relationship with their daughter-in-law, but the bottom line is—and this is crucial—Brian Latham was missing in action for about an hour from the charity event—'four-ish to five-ish,' my lady said. She remembers looking for him, wanting to ask him a question about the value of one of her paintings, I forget which, and it wasn't until five-fifteen or so that he finally reappeared—looking rather flushed, she observed.

"So now listen, the charity event took place at the British Library, which is, I checked it out, an eighteen-minute walk or seven-minute drive, from the British Museum. Does the timing jibe with Timothy Thorpe's murder, or what?"

"The murder took place at four twenty-four," Erika recited, her voice just above a whisper. "What about the photo you got of Brian with Cherry Ames?" she deflected.

"That came later. After the chat with my informants, I checked back at the museum, thought I'd hang around the entrance, wait for Latham to exit come the end of the workday. To be honest, I thought I'd seen all the action I was going to see for one day, but I was wrong. Early afternoon, Latham and Cherry left the building, climbed into a taxi, and the rest is history. The photo was taken at a pub, a ten-minute drive from the museum. I sat at the bar. It was a dark place, and they were sitting at a corner table staring at each other's eyeballs. Neither looked my way."

"And this relates to Tim's murder, how?" Harrison asked.

John served him a tight-lipped grin. "Well, unless he and Latham were competing for the same woman as well as the same job, I guess it doesn't relate. It only reveals another aspect of the man's shady character." Dead serious: "You understand I'm going to have to report what allegedly occurred the day of the charity event-slash-murder, right?"

"I do."

"John, do you think you can hold off for one day?" Erika delicately posed. "I know this information is relevant to the case, absolutely, but would you let us talk to Brian before he's hauled in for questioning? Assuming he's innocent, his having been under suspicion and all the public exposure that comes with it—I think it would break him. If he has an airtight alibi, wouldn't it be kinder for one of *us* to draw it out of him, avoid a scandal?"

John shook his head. "This is sounding a lot like the day you ordered me not to spill the beans on Jacob Tembe and look where *that* got me."

"I see your point, of course, I do, but I'm asking you to give us a chance to speak to Brian within the next twenty-four hours—*less* than." She looked to Harrison for support.

"I agree with you John," Harrison said, "but on the other hand, I trust Erika's instincts. How about it?"

John rolled his eyes. "You guys are just like my wife. I can never say no to any of you. You have until noon tomorrow. If I don't hear from you by then, I blow the whistle." He rose from the chair. "Which reminds me, I'm due to call my wife. I'll get the hell out of here now. Meet you in the lobby at 6:30. We can drive over to the campus together."

"There's no reason for you to attend the vigil, John," Harrison said. "You never met Ikemar."

"You think I'm going to leave you two to wander about alone at an event held out in the open that may possibly turn ugly? No way." Despite John's claim to the contrary, there were some decisions about which he was unshakeable. "Stay where you are. I'll see myself out."

Erika's text, transmitted to Brian Latham moments later, read: "Urgent. Meet us tomorrow, 8 a.m. at our hotel, the Kimpton Fitzroy." She received his reply almost instantly: "Will do." No questions, no reservations.

Chapter Twenty-Four

T he vigil was to be held on the Main Quad, an impressive expanse between the formidable King's Building and Somerset House, East Wing. The organizers had advised that if it was raining that morning or if an evening rain was predicted, the event would take place below the Quad, on basement level 1.

When Erika, Harrison, and John entered the Quad via its Main Gate on Gower Street, a tickling drizzle, light as mist, had already made its gentle presence known. It had been unpredicted, and so far, there had been no decision to move the proceedings below ground.

It was only ten minutes past the event's scheduled start, yet it appeared to be well underway. A crowd of about a hundred, mostly students, judging from the general age range, were focused on a wiry young white man whose unenhanced voice was deep and powerful, pounding the air like a bass drum, urgent and foreboding. Atop a small podium in the center of the quad, he was speaking of Ikemar more as a symbol than a man, creating an analogy between his having had his throat cut and the study of African history being "slashed from the archives of human enterprise."

"Heady stuff," John commented, meaning no harm, but receiving a killer look from a flaxen-haired debutant half his size.

The ambience, even discounting the speaker's well-intentioned bombast, was that of a rally more than a vigil. It was daylight, and sunset would not be mellowing the mood for another two hours. There were no choir-like candles flickering thoughts heavenward. The memorial flowers and cards arranged in a dedicated area some distance from the podium might elsewhere have seemed abundant; here their presence was dwarfed by the sheer breadth of the place. Though the twenty or so police officers stood apart from the crowd, mute and motionless as palace guards, their presence was felt all the more keenly for their conditioned aloofness.

A round picnic table fitted with an umbrella stood alongside the grouping of memorial gifts. A young Black woman sat at the table, nodding and gesturing instructions—*yes, sign the guestbook, help yourself to a pamphlet*—and as the orator was bearing down on his closing lines, John and the Wheatleys wandered over to the table.

"Thank you for coming," the young woman said aloud, now that the speech was over and before another began. "Were you friends or associates of Professor Umar's?"

"Both," Harrison replied, keeping it simple. "Thank you for arranging all this. Shall we sign in?"

"Please. Are you familiar with the London Classicists of Color society?"

"Only superficially," Erika answered, as Harrison signed the guest book for them both. "But we'd like to learn more." She picked up a pamphlet describing their mission. "May I?"

The woman smiled. "That's what they're there for."

Erika dropped the pamphlet into her tote bag. "Thank you—and good luck."

"You, too."

"This is a good photo of the professor," John commented, referring to the framed photograph of Ikemar in full Doctoral regalia set behind the pamphlets.

"Doesn't do him justice," Harrison muttered.

"Okay, man," John appeased. He dashed off his name and email in the guest book. Laying down the pen, he remarked to the woman in charge of the table, "Smart move." He nodded at the open umbrella.

"Pure luck," she answered. Noticing the next speaker stepping up to the podium, she sat forward and in a hushed voice, informed her small audience, "That's Noah Brown, one of the officers—Treasurer, I believe. Let's listen."

The young Black man who rose to the podium credited himself simply as being a member of the society, and after only a brief statement of the society's goal to "decolonize the Classics and provide moral support for those who suffer in the struggle to achieve it," he proceeded to extol his "teacher and mentor" at length, describing Ikemar in the most personal and loving terms, bringing him to a kind of holographic life with personal stories and anecdotes. "Think of it," he said. "When I answered a question in class—when *any* of us did—we knew if the professor tilted his head, just a little, like this"—he demonstrated—"and pinched the tip of his chin"—again, mimed—"we knew the answer we'd given was wrong. I don't know about anybody else, but I felt bad for him; I could tell he was not happy disappointing me. It was weird, you know? Turned around."

Noah's observations were greeted with the murmur of agreement combined with the nostalgic, slightly nervous lilt of subdued laughter. By the end of his address, the atmosphere had become more in keeping with a memorial service. The more reverent mood continued when a white-haired older woman approached the podium and was warmly embraced by Noah, who'd just descended from it. The woman was holding several sheets of paper in her hand, and when she put her arms around Noah and pressed her hands against his back, the sheets crumbled. After she and Noah drew apart, he took the sheets from her and, in another form of embrace, smoothed them out against his chest.

"That's Rachel Stein," Harrison whispered hoarsely against Erika's cheek. "The woman who was with me when..." No need to finish. He'd spared her none of the details of that day. She'd insisted on living it through with him.

Erika nodded and slipped her hand around his waist.

Rachel mounted the podium with Noah's assistance. She glanced down at her papers and then into the crowd. "I'm not the stentorian, unlike these lads. Hello, can you hear me?"

"Yes, Professor!" and "We hear you, Rach!" rang out simultaneously from two individuals farthest away; both voices taking her in, urging her on.

"I'm Rachel Stein," she began. "I teach English Literature and I reside at the Virginia Woolf Building. I was a housemate of Ike's and, now that I'm called upon to define our relationship rather than continuing to enjoy it, a *friend* of his as well. I remember remarking to Ike, over a tuna fish sandwich, I believe it was, that I wished he weren't leaving us after only a year. How cruel—how *grotesque* an irony that wish appears now." She paused—to catch her breath, to reflect on what she'd just said, to recall her father's last words, it could have been anything—and in that unmarked wink of time, an object was tearing through space, heading her way. Maybe she saw it coming, maybe not. In any event, she was unprepared for its contact with her forehead, and when it came, her arms flew in the air, the notes she had not yet referred to flew out of her hand, and she tipped back and fell from the podium, shoulder or skull striking the ground first, hard to tell which.

Noah dropped to his knees beside her. Onlookers uttered sounds of alarm and outrage while recording the tableau on their cell phones. Someone shouted, "Who did it, who saw?" Someone followed with "Served the bitch right!" and the people standing close by threw the responder to the ground and began kicking him, the question if he'd hurled the missile or merely—*merely?*—approved of the act, too fine a point for them to consider, the bastard deserved to be beaten. Two police officers, broke ranks to rush to the bastard's rescue. Another had already leapt to the aid of Rachel Stein.

Erika and Harrison had made a beeline for the fallen professor, almost colliding with the oncoming police officer. "How is she?" Harrison asked.

"My head hurts, but I think I'm okay," Rachel answered. "What happened?"

"I told her to lie still and wait for the medics," Noah said.

John's concern for the victim was peripheral. His aim was to watch out for Erika and Harrison, who had in a flash become his charges. He had a hand on each of their shoulders as his head slowly swiveled right to left like a searchlight in a prison yard. He was ready for anything.

Noah pulled an object out of his jacket pocket and handed it to the officer. "This is what hit her. I didn't think about fingerprints. Sorry."

The officer looked from one to the other. "A rubber hamburger?"

"It's a dog toy," Noah said. "Son-of-a-bitch probably didn't mean to knock her off her feet. Shouldn't you cordon off the place or something, find out who did this?"

A chorused roar, barely human, erupted from the direction of the quadrangle's arched gateway, drawing attention from all else. From the inarticulate howl arose individual voices. "Back where you belong!" "Go home!" "Destroyers!" Until someone in the crowd or the crowd as a single organism decided on a single set of syllables, "GET OUT, GET OUT, GET OUT," chanting them as it strode through the gateway, an army of some fifty strong, eight or more wielding cricket bats, the others weaponed only with bare fists and adrenaline-enriched rage.

The memorial attendees were suddenly trapped between the imposing walls of academia, King's and Somerset. Some froze, others scattered for routes out of the area other than the main gate, while still others swarmed like bees around each of the police officers as they headed into the fray. Noah refused to leave his post beside Rachel Stein. "Help is on the way," he assured her, his voice trembling. "We'll be fine."

John was as adamant about his guardianship as Noah was of his. "We're leaving by the main gate—now!" he commanded his charges, gripping each of them by a wrist. The marauders had already inundated the quad's central area and were grappling with the small band of police and indiscriminately bat-whacking and punching body parts of whoever entered their space or failed to exit it quickly enough. "The gate is free—see? Someone just escaped through it! Let's go before it's too late!"

They had no choice but to obey, but Harrison insisted they switch positions so that Erika would be walking between John and him. No way was he going to march out of here without Erika being in his grasp. Erika was determined to be in contact with Harrison herself, and John realized that timing took precedence over debate and relented.

Sticking to the area outside the hub of the melee, they were almost to the gate, when one of the thugs on the action's periphery was jostled into their vicinity and unleashing blame for his misstep on the nearest warm body, was about to come down on Erika's skull with his cricket bat. Simultaneously, Harrison and John let go of Erika and caught the bat at the top of its arc, Harrison mid-bat, John higher up, and as a unit torqued the bat out of the assailant's grip, hearing the crack of his wrist bone a millisecond before his shriek of pain.

"Go!" John barked, grabbing Erika's forearm as she reached out for Harrison with her free hand. "It's okay, he's right behind us!"

"Go!" Harrison echoed, wanting her to forget him, beat him to the gate. Clinging to her now would hamper her movement.

But she resisted John's tugging and both of their urgings—even Lucas, calling her from across the ocean, failed to change her mind—and there was nothing Harrison could do but grab onto her hand and slow her down.

Sirens were blaring as police cars and ambulances converged on the area, and what seemed like a battalion of officers on foot were nearing the archway as the threesome passed through it. John pulled them off to the side just before the troop began pouring into the passage, choking it off to all other access.

"Just what he wanted," Erika said gravely, slumping against Harrison, her voice barely audible beneath the sirens' blare.

Harrison understood.

John passed. Right now, the only thing he needed to occupy his mind was overwhelming relief.

Chapter Twenty-Five

"Terrible incident," Brian said, crossing his legs one way, then another. "*Terrible*," he repeated, stressing the first syllable as if this would convey his concern more adequately, when it was clear from the moment he'd stepped into the Wheatleys' hotel room, his focus darting about like a nervous cat's, that it was his own situation, not those of the poor bastards who'd been attacked the day before, that monopolized his concern. "I can only imagine what it must have been like for you chaps." He tugged at his tie as if it were a boa constrictor. "Damn thing; mind if I take it off?"

"Of course not," Erika said, kind enough not to point out that she and Harrison, in sweatpants and T-shirts, were hardly in a position to object. "Have some eggs and crumpets—I *think* they're crumpets—and tea or coffee." She and Harrison had ordered up an array of breakfast fare especially for Brian.

"No thanks," Brian said, eying the meal as if they meant it to be his last. He shoved his tie into his suit jacket pocket. "You're not recording our conversation, are you?"

"Brian!" Harrison objected. "What kind of people do you think we are?"

"I couldn't say. You tell me."

"We don't record people behind their backs, for one thing!" *This is my own fault*, Harrison thought. Brian had called asking for a heads-up before driving over to the hotel. He had told Brian that there was "incriminating evidence against you out there," but that as a team they might be able to nip it in the bud. Any less ominous an alert and Brian might have ditched the meeting, he'd worried. He should have taken the risk, been more tactful.

189

Brian re-crossed his legs. "Well, are you going to tell me what's on your collective mind, or are you taking delight seeing me sweat?" He uncrossed his legs. "I'm not sweating, by the way."

"Sorry, Brian," Erika said, "but there's no delicate way to talk about this. I hope you understand we're not passing judgment; nothing like that."

"What are you playing here, good diplomat, bad diplomat? Get on with it."

They were sitting in what had become their general meeting formation, Erika and Harrison on the couch, their guest, or in this case, the defendant, catty-corner on the chair. Harrison gestured for Erika to take the lead.

"The afternoon of Timothy Thorpe's murder you were at your wife's charity event," she began. "Our source tells us—"

"Wait," Brian interrupted. "Where are your cell phones? I'd like to see them, please."

Harrison opened his mouth, by his facial expression to say something combative, but Erika held up her hand to forestall him. "That's fine, Brian." She removed her device from the pocket of her sweatpants and laid it on the coffee table.

"My sweats don't have pockets," Harrison said, rising from the couch. "My phone's in the bedroom area recording the conversation next door. I'll be right back." When he returned, he tossed the phone on the table and sat back down.

Brian checked both their devices. They'd both been turned off. "Go on," he cued Erika. "About your *source*," he added. "I'm guessing it's that private eye of yours. I got the feeling I just wasn't his type. No point in covering up for him."

"We're not covering up, Brian. Yes, it was John Mitchell who took it upon himself to check you out. What can I say, he follows his instincts, but never bases his conclusions solely on them, not by a long shot. He's a keen observer and there was something about your tone and demeanor that rubbed him the wrong way. But set that aside. In the end, the facts are the facts, no matter what the motivation behind the search for them. And here they are." She relayed John's stalking itinerary and findings from start to finish, from the stop at the pastry shop to the pub rendezvous, while Brian's changing emotions—surprise, fear, anger, shame—flashed across his face like a fast-motion film.

"Why?" Brian asked at the end of it. His look was unfocused. It was unclear what he was asking about, or to whom.

"Why did we put John up to this?" Harrison filled in, taking a stab at it. "We didn't. We just didn't stop him. We respect his hunches. It doesn't mean we accept them on faith. We respect you, too, Brian."

Brian cracked a cynical smile. "Remember I helped you with your project? I gave up my time for you, and gladly. And you were kind enough to recognize my contribution, gave me credit for it. Don't think I don't appreciate that. We had a good relationship, I thought. Why now this *vendetta* against me?"

"There is no vendetta, Brian. And we do have a good relationship."

"We're wasting time," Erika declared, suddenly restless. "The quality of our relationship is not at issue. We've got until noon to get back to John with solid proof that you, Brian, could not have been at the British Museum at the time of Timothy Thorpe's murder. If we don't, John will turn over whatever information he has that suggests otherwise. And well he should. It's as simple as that. What'll it be, Brian? Where were you during your absence from the charity event, and are you able to come up with proof of this in any shape or form by noon today?" She checked her watch. "You've got three and a half hours. Take it or leave it."

"No character judgments up for grabs here," Harrison assured him. "How you conduct your personal life is not our concern, nor should it be. We believe you're innocent. All we want to see is that you're spared the unpleasant effects of negative publicity."

Brian was stone-faced, impossible to read. Sooner or later, he had to move his lips. They waited.

"Okay," he said at last, returning to life. "I guess I have no choice. I was with Cherry, that's it. I slipped away, couldn't have been for more than an hour, to be with her. Her apartment's a five-minute walk from the British Library, where the event was held. I know there's a surveillance camera in the lobby of her building, we joked about it once, so there must be a recording of me walking in and out of the place, what was it, May fifteenth?"

"Fourteenth," Erika corrected, with a sigh of relief. "Thank you, Brian. Let's get this information to John. He's the only one among us who'll have the clout to get the building manager to show him the records."

"The man who wants to see my fry? I'm supposed to trust *him*?"

"John does not want to see you fry, Brian! He's giving you the opportunity to clear yourself under the radar, don't you get it? Who else would you have approach the building manager, me? Harrison? *You*?"

"No. I don't know. Your detective friend will let on why he wants to have a look at the surveillance video. Word will get around I'm a suspect in a murder case, one way or another."

"No mention of the murder will be made," Harrison offered.

"How's *that* going to work?"

"John will say he's been hired by a woman checking up on her husband," Erika said, supplying an answer while Harrison was trying to come up with one. "A fictitious woman, of course. Suspects her husband has a mistress in the building and was with her sometime between say, three and six. John will look at the video, see you coming and going, mentally record the times. and inform the manager, sorry, seems my client was mistaken. Her husband never showed up."

"What if the manager wants to help out, asks to see a photo of the mystery man? What then?"

After a beat: "Well, then, he'll show him a photo of Harrison!"

Harrison wasn't sure he approved of this idea, but he couldn't put his finger on a concrete reason why. "Guess I'm okay with it."

"So am I," Brian said. It looked like a smile was on the horizon, but then his face fell. "Oh Lord, what if the hour I spent at Cherry's fails to coincide with the time of Thorpe's murder?"

We'll cross that bridge when we come to it seemed too flip an answer. "Positive thoughts, Brian, positive thoughts," Harrison replied instead, cringing at his impersonation of a motivational speaker.

"I'll give it a try," Brian said—gratefully, to Harrison's surprise. He dictated Cherry Ames's address, then rose from the chair—with difficulty it seemed, as if in the last half hour, he'd aged ten years.

* * *

John was jogging on one of the treadmills in the hotel's fitness center when Harrison's call came in on his cell phone. "How's it going, Harrison?"

"We've been texting you. You haven't responded. You okay?"

"I'm fine. I'm at the gym. On a treadmill."

"You sound out of breath."

"Thanks for the pep talk. I'm on a six percent incline. Give me a break."

"We just saw Brian Latham. He's got a potential alibi. Come see us, we'll tell you the plan."

"Tell me over the phone. I'll be out of here in five minutes. Ready to go in twenty."

"You've got to see us first, pick up a photo."

"A photo? Of who?"

"Of me."

"The oxygen must be going to my head. I thought you said a photo of you. I'll be right there. Cooling down now."

He arrived at their hotel room for his briefing in less than thirty minutes.

John thought his people were a bit mad, but clever, too, he had to admit. "Pretty hot," he commented, before pocketing the two-by-three photo of Harrison Erika had taken from her wallet. "Hope the manager doesn't fall for you right off the bat."

* * *

While they were waiting to hear back from John, Harrison received an email from Ryan Finley. The couple read it together.

Dear Harrison and Erika:

It was a pleasure spending time with you yesterday. After you left, Winifred and I drove to the municipal office to search its archives for the file on the 1922 sale of L. P. Sutton's property, including the disposal of the building's contents. The good news is that it was remarkably easy to unearth the documents, thanks to the meticulous record-keeping of that institution. The bad news is that our findings resulted in a dead end for you and your client's search for a lost cache of valuables. The contents of the vault consisted of jewelry items in need of repair and tagged with their owners' names as well as a number of pieces fashioned by the goldsmith himself. Where possible, the tagged items were returned to their owners. The unclaimed items were sold at auction along with Sutton's handiwork. As for the contents of the so-called strongroom, it appears that this nomenclature is misleading. The room was actually refitted as a bomb shelter in 1915 by the Suttons, who had it lined in concrete, finished with wood paneling, and bolstered with steel beams. It contained canned goods and other items appropriate for its intended use, and as such, were either donated or scrapped. Winifred and I wish you the best of luck with your project, and anytime we may be of further assistance, please let us know.

   Sincerely yours,

   Ryan

"Disappointing, but hardly unexpected," Harrison said.

"I'm pretty confident we got the math right, anyway, thanks to John. Bottom line, we estimated that the approximate number of miles Packard's moving company transported Andrew's start-up collection from the Barrett home in Hertfordshire to its place of safekeeping was about twenty-eight miles, right?"

"Twenty-seven point eight one eight one eight one to be exact, according to our math whiz."

She smiled. "Oh, right."

"Anyway, when you came across that chit from the goldsmith dated—what, one day before Barrett's entry in his journal saying that he'd found a safe place for his treasures? On top of that, finding out the goldsmith's place was twenty-eight and a half miles from Barrett Farms? How could we *not* jump to conclusions?"

"There was no way," she agreed. "So, now we have to use our compass, real or digital, stick its point into Hertfordshire, and draw a circle whose radius is twenty-eight miles. It's understood we don't think of the twenty-eight-mile radius as an absolute, especially considering that new roadways have been built which may slightly skew the travel-miles data. We look inside and outside the circumference of our circle. We'll come up with something." She hesitated. "Am I being too hopeful?"

"Hope is our only option. We'll look for banks, storehouses, dungeons, you name it. As long as the facility was extant in 1897."

"I'm with you. Now let's email our thanks to Ryan. A separate one to Winifred."

"Yes. Then let's check the news. Maybe there'll be an update." Early morning broadcasts had added nothing to last night's sketchy coverage of the Quad attack. "If no luck, we'll call the Virginia Woolf Building, at least try to find out how Rachel Stein is doing."

"Do you suppose Detective Hogarty might give us an update?" she suggested.

"You mean before it's released to the public?" He gave a dismissive shrug. "I suppose the man would do just about *anything* for you."

"Let's hope," Erika replied, choosing not to acknowledge his wry tone of delivery, figuring he was already regretting it. "The more assistance we get from Hogarty the better."

* * *

The BBC News Channel was still reporting the incident in generic terms. Statistics were given, but names were withheld. There had been twenty-three persons injured; five critically. Eighteen arrests had been made. To what association, if any, did the rioters owe their loyalty? How had the majority of them avoided capture? These were questions not yet answered.

Harrison called the general number for the Virginia Woolf Building. The line was busy and remained so for fifteen minutes. When he was at last able to get through, a virtual assistant advised that the message center was full.

While they were debating whether to run right over to Virginia Woolf or first try to contact Detective Hogarty, they received a call from John on Harrison's cell phone. "So soon?" Harrison opened, recognizing the incoming number. He activated the speakerphone.

"No dice," John replied. "Building Manager's away for the weekend, and the second in command, the senior-ranking concierge, will not give me access to the surveillance camera's digital record."

"The manager can't be reached?"

"Oh, he can, but the concierge says the manager will want to check me out in person. Forget it. The guy won't budge."

"You showed him your FBI Deputy ID?"

"Sure. He was impressed, but not enough to break the rules. Which I think he made up on the spot to cover his ass, by the way."

"The manager will be back Monday?" Erika asked.

"Officially, yeah, but unofficially back in town tomorrow—Sunday—night. There's a chance I can catch him then. We'll see."

"John, will you wait until you're able to view the video before you contact the police?"

It took a while for John to reply. "Deal. Just remember, it's on you if Latham skips town."

* * *

Erika debated between updating Brian with a cryptic text or giving him a call. She decided on the latter. The call went straight to voicemail. "Hey Brian, it's Erika. Research on our project postponed to Monday. Have a great rest of your weekend! Harrison says hi. Bye!" She assumed Brian would get the gist, and that no snoop, spy, or spouse would.

Focus returned to the assault that had occurred the day before; how they were going to obtain detailed information about it, most importantly the names of its victims and the seriousness of their injuries. Run over to Virginia Woolf Building or give Hogarty a call?

The question became immaterial when Erika received a call from the detective himself. For Harrison's sake, Erika punched on the speakerphone before a word was transmitted. "Hello, Detective," she greeted, somewhat coldly, for Harrison's benefit.

"Hello there," Harrison announced, making his presence known.

"Are you two, okay?" Hogarty asked. "I know you were going to Professor Umar's service. You weren't on the list of casualties, but that's not a guarantee."

"We were lucky," Erika said. "We were only shaken up. Thanks for calling to check up on us."

"Not my only reason for calling."

"I wonder if you might let us in on some of the details of yesterday's incident," Harrison requested, not ready to change the subject. "Rest assured we'll keep the information to ourselves."

"No problem. In any event, the facts are about to be released to the public. I'm at my desk. I have the data right in front of me. First off, the thugs responsible for the attack are members of a ragtag group of neo-fascists who've just come onto the market; a start-up company you might say. We've got the ringleader in custody. The casualty list has changed since earlier in the day. The number of injured has risen to twenty-five, four are listed as critical, and as of the latest notice from the hospital, there has been one death."

"Who died?" Harrison bluntly asked.

"A nineteen-year-old student of Professor Umar's. Samuel Dowd. It was touch and go for a while."

Harrison felt like he was going to throw up. Had he thought he'd feel relieved, hearing a name other than Rachel Stein's? The very question was a profound insult to the memory of Samuel Dowd—no, to the boy himself. "Shit," he cursed himself.

"Did you know Mr. Dowd?" the detective asked.

"No. I didn't."

Erika's look asked *are you okay, my love*? It was one of the rare times she couldn't read his mind.

He nodded *yes*, but she would not know that it was her embracing concern that made it so. To Hogarty, he said aloud. "I do know Professor Rachel

Stein, Detective. I hardly know her, but we did share that horrific experience and..."

"You discovered Ikemar Umar's body with Professor Stein. There's a special bond between people who've shared a tragic experience. It's not the first time I've seen it in action."

"She was injured. Is she alright?"

"Here she is," Hogarty said, apparently reviewing his list. "She was admitted to the hospital with a concussion, under observation overnight, and released this morning."

"Oh, good. Noah Brown? Mr. Brown was watching over her when all hell broke loose. He wouldn't leave her side. Is he okay, too?"

"Let me see. Not on the list. Must have escaped injury. By the way, three of the injuries were sustained by the perpetrators themselves. Two in the course of resisting arrest. One from an unknown assailant. Suffered a broken wrist."

"That'd be me," Harrison confessed, omitting John's participation to save him the trouble of a possible Q&A session. "It was either the thug's wrist or my wife's skull. It wasn't a difficult decision."

"Lost you for a second, I didn't hear that," Hogarty fired off before Harrison could add another word on the subject. "But no worries, let's move on to other matters," he stated emphatically, in case Harrison lagged on the uptake. "I'm talking about those jobs laid on me by my taskmaster." With a little chuckle, adding, "You haven't forgotten, have you, Erika?"

"I didn't imagine you'd get back to us so quickly regarding the Clifford Dean vis-à-vis Mark Jason issue," Erika answered, overly formal for Harrison's sake.

"Time is of the essence here," Hogarty responded, taking his chumminess down a notch. "I told our experts they were to get me the results within twenty-four hours, and they did. In truth, the results were not difficult to come by. As for the face-comparison issue, a high threshold value was placed on the exercise, and even with a high degree of accuracy demanded, the confidence score turned out to be quite high. There's a greater than ninety-eight percent chance that Mark Jason and Clifford Dean are one and the same individual."

"Amazing," Erika commented. "Jason's wife was positive the photo of Clifford Dean could not have been that of her ex-husband."

"Understandable. The bold differences in facial features that highly prejudice our perception will distract from those Euclidean distances that reveal the more essential likenesses. In this case, for example, Mark Jason has markedly protruding ears. Clifford Dean's are flat against his head. However, the distances from their ear canal openings to the corners of their lips are identical. In fact, the slight asymmetries in the right-ear and left-ear distances are exact matches. Same goes for the difference in nose shapes. Jason has a bump in his. Dean does not. But the dimensions of the medial depression between the nose and upper lip are exactly the same. The conclusion: Mark Jason has undergone both ear and nose cosmetic surgery. Probably acquired dental veneers as well, judging from what little can be seen of the upper teeth in both photographs."

"Thanks for the explanation," Erika said, already anticipating the second set of test results to be discussed. What Hogarty was about to reveal would either tend to favor or refute her hunch that the individuals behind the murders of Timothy Thorpe, Keith Ashton, and Ikemar Umar were one and the same. "The black paint," she couldn't resist prompting. "What was the consensus?"

"Looks like you were right on the mark, Erika. Close to a one-hundred percent chance the acrylic black paint lifted from the desecrated Picasso drawing and Nigerian flag came from the same source. Both samples are categorized as 'bone black,' both are carbon-based and have a distinctive yellow undertone. The fillers, additives, antifoaming agents, opacifiers match up exactly, as do their surfactants, a new word for me. I'm told they're used to disperse pigments, not that that adds to my understanding. My expert gave me the name of the manufacturer—not a widely distributed brand—but I don't have it right in front of me. So, there you have it, Erika. Your bragging rights."

Harrison was aching to dispute Hogarty's characterization of Erika but figured she would rather speak up for herself.

199

"I'm not gloating, Detective," she objected on cue.

"Well, you should be. Egos aside, I'm interested to get your take on this, see if we agree." He whistled. "Look at me. Seeking approval from a rank amateur. What's the world come to?" Again, that distinctive chuckle, as he eased back into chum-dom. "So, what's your take, Ricky?"

Harrison bristled.

"As we previously discussed," Erika declared, again countering familiarity with formality, "I believe the aim of the individual who committed the murders, or at least masterminded them, was to provoke racial unrest—no, that's too weak a term. Conflagration. This person is thinking big. Think of the violence, the daring. If he didn't commit them himself, he must have chosen a surrogate with a lust for it."

"In prison, perhaps," Harrison suggested. "It's where Mark Jason had ample opportunity to find a suitable candidate, or recommendation for one, someone he could contact on the outside after his release."

"Yes," Erika agreed, though not wholeheartedly. Although she had become more confident about her thoughts on the killer's intentions, she was reluctant, as ever, maybe more so than ever, to point an accusing finger at a particular individual. In fact, the more likely it appeared that Jason/Dean was the guilty party, the greater the burden of proof she put on herself to condemn him. Still, the focus was now on him, and every observation must be taken into account. "Here's something else to consider," she offered. "Mark Jason lost his army pension after he was found guilty of a serious crime. Now he has a custodial job. Let's assume he was the individual who choreographed those murders. Why would he have desecrated—or directed someone to desecrate—Picasso's study of *Les Demoiselles d'Avignon* when he could have made a fortune ransoming it? There's only one reasonable answer."

"Because his *mission* was more important to him than accumulating wealth," Harrison answered. "More important than *anything*, as you would have us believe, Erika, and quite convincingly. I'm wondering, though, if his driving force would have evolved into a definitive plan whatever his circumstances after he'd served his prison term, or did his employment by the British Museum provide the catalyst?"

Erika shook her head. "My problem is, I don't want to make a leap to judgment, not quite yet. Yes, Jason fits the profile perfectly. He faked his identity, got himself a counterfeit National Insurance Number, has a grudge against the Black man who robbed him of his wife and the white man who robbed him of his freedom. Still, there's something not sitting right with me." *Something about that meeting in the hall. What was it?*

Hogarty cleared his throat. "If I may be so bold as to join in?" he said, waxing sardonic in his push-pull approach to the Wheatleys, more especially to Erika. "I do agree with your reasoning, Erika, but let's review Keith Ashton's murder, see if our thoughts gibe on this one. I didn't think so at first, not when I was examining the Ashton residence, but I've since concluded that the individual who broke into the home had one thing in mind, and that was taking possession of the Picasso. Mr. Ashton interfered, and the intruder eliminated him, though with none of the bravado with which he graced his other two murders."

"Exactly my thought," Erika said. "But what's key here is that the black portion of the paint desecrating the Picasso drawing almost certainly came from the same source as the black paint desecrating the Nigerian flag, indicating both crimes were either committed or choreographed by the same person. The first act was vehemently *anti*-Eurocentric, the second, brutally *pro*. Both conceived to stir up opposition, I believe. The attack on Ikemar's memorial was a direct result of this cycle."

"Agreed," Hogarty said. "Meanwhile, I find it ironic that after presenting a convincing case for the prosecution, you come back as a hung jury. Well, while you dangle there, I'm going full speed ahead."

"Of course," Erika replied, even as she was thinking of ways to approach the suspect in question. Her only meeting with him had been cut short by Brian Latham. Their next must remain uninterrupted.

Chapter Twenty-Six

After several false starts, Erika realized if she waited for the opportune moment, she'd be waiting forever. She gave herself ten seconds more, allowing Harrison to finish pouring his morning coffee without mishap. "I'm planning on having a chat with the custodial worker," she said, aiming for the easy grace of a country music singer and failing miserably.

"Uh, what?" Harrison said, doing no better.

"I'll need to get Dean's—I'm going to continue to call him Dean, that's how I think of him—I'm going to need to get Dean's phone number," she barreled on. "I'm sure John hasn't yet deleted the museum's personnel list. I can get the number from him."

"No," Harrison objected, at the other end of the word-count spectrum. He studied the breakfast cart with all its steamy offerings—eggs, bacon, sausages, muffins—and then back at Erika, sitting beside him on the couch in her cotton gym shorts and his old T-shirt. "The morning was going so well," he sighed, recovering his voice, at least. "Why do you want to scare me?" He rubbed her thigh. "Come on, sweetheart."

"We'll meet in a public place. John could be watching out for me, not so very far off."

"I don't understand why you feel you have to talk to this man."

"There's something nagging at me about our last encounter, the way Brian broke it up. He didn't want me to talk to him. I want to find out why, or at least try to."

Harrison waved aside her explanation. "Let me ask you a question. Do you think Dean committed the three murders?"

"He does check all the boxes. Opportunity being one of them, even in the Thorpe murder case, the most puzzling one. I can see him slipping into Thorpe's office in black-suit disguise and after strangling him to death, quick-changing into his standard uniform in the custodial supplies closet just down the hall. For his closing act, returning to scene one to perform CPR on his murder victim."

"You're dodging the question, Erika. The answer is a simple yes or no."

"Yes, probably, but his profile seems almost too perfect, you know? I think of Jacob Tembe, how *his* profile seemed to fit the bill, and how close *he* came to being indicted for Thorpe's murder."

"He wasn't, thanks to you."

"Maybe. In part. The point is, there are alternative scenarios battling it out in my head. If Dean's the guilty party, then surely, he set up Tembe to be his scapegoat. But what if someone played puppet master to *Dean*? Someone who knew his real identity and deep-seated resentments and used him to play a role, even a red herring, in his *own* twisted plot? What if Dean has atoned for his crime of passion, egregious though it was? Wasn't he once a decorated hero of the highest order? Isn't it possible that a fragment of that man survived? Isn't it possible that his faked death was an attempt to bury his past, to reinvent—to *regenerate* himself?"

Harrison took her face in his hands. "Listen to me. I'm moved by your obsession with getting it right—with not getting it wrong, with not *doing* wrong is what it is, really. But in the end, it comes down to this. Dean is most likely the person who committed these barbaric crimes, you've said so yourself. Do you really want to chance it at such close range? Say something that gets his hackles up, or with a gesture, a glance, cause him to suspect your intentions? You don't know how his mind works."

"Darling, he might not even agree to see me."

"If he does, and if you're determined to go through with it, I'm going to be right by your side." His eyes were locked on hers. "Unless you can be dissuaded. How about it?"

She held his gaze. "I'm determined." She covered his hands with hers.

"And I'm sorry, but I think it'll go better if we're one-on-one. I'll be saying uncomfortable things, and I don't want him to feel outnumbered."

He sat back, unintentionally causing them to break contact. "Do you even want me in the wings with John?"

"If you feel you must be, but not close. Dean might recognize you from the Zoom meeting."

"*What* uncomfortable things?" he asked on the double-take.

"What?—oh. I haven't made up my mind." She took a swig of her coffee before reaching for her cell phone on the lamp table. "It might be best if I wing it."

* * *

Francis Russell, 9th Duke of Bedford, looked out over the land that was once his family's backyard, now in name only: Russell Square Gardens. Erika, attempting to trick herself into believing she was completely at ease, rested her weight on one hip and studied the bronze nobleman atop his pedestal as if he were the only subject of interest to her on this lovely spring day. Somewhere in the vicinity—perhaps one of them on a park bench, one on the grass at the foot of a tall tree, she would not allow herself to look for fear of giving them away—John and Harrison were also simulating interest in something other than what was on their minds.

"Kind of a mixed metaphor, don't you think?" came a voice from behind.

She turned abruptly, startled. Already he had the upper hand. "Hello, Clifford," she said deliberately, thinking she must not slip up on the name. "'Mixed metaphor.' That's a good one." The Duke of Bedford was in Roman attire, leaning on a plow and surrounded by sheep and angels. She assumed this is what he was referring to.

"I'm a big fan of Wikipedia," he said. "The Duke was a great pioneer in scientific farming." He was wearing sunglasses. He took them off and tucked them inside the pocket of his white button shirt. "Did you know that?" Without waiting for her answer, he asked, "Would you like to sit by the fountain or right here?" He gestured toward an empty bench by the side of the path.

"Right here."

"You were pretty vague about why you wanted to talk to me, especially in person," he said, as they headed for the bench. "I mean, who does that these days?"

She forced a smile. "I do. I like to see who I'm talking to. In three-dimension."

"You have a point."

"And it's such a lovely day."

"That it is."

She wondered what he would think if he knew she was trying to picture him pre-surgery, with protruding ears. "To be honest, I felt awkward when we bumped into each other in the hall the other day."

"How so?" He pigeon-toed one sneakered foot on top of the other and clamped his knees together, like a schoolboy needing a pass for the restroom.

The appearance of discomfort heightened her own. The shoulder strap of her bag was pulling at the shoulder of her pantsuit jacket, and she was suddenly sure, without daring to check, that the edge of her bra was showing in the vee-opening of her blouse. "Mr. Latham seemed very anxious to break up our conversation," she said, casually slipping the strap from her shoulder and letting it drop into her lap along with the bag. "Didn't you get that impression?"

"Maybe," he said, avoiding her eyes.

"I think you know why," she braved. "When you were questioned by the police, along with the rest of us witnesses, I bet you held something back. I'd like to know what."

"You just curious, or are you working with the police?" he asked, focusing on the woman coming down the path pushing a baby carriage. A small girl in a pink jacket was hanging onto the handlebar with one hand and barely keeping pace. As the unit passed in front of them, he gave a little wave to the girl. She frowned back. He gave a good-natured shrug. "Oh, well." He appeared to have forgotten he'd asked Erika a question, or no longer cared.

Assuming neither was true, she answered it. "I'm not working with the police," she underplayed. "Nor am I involved purely out of curiosity. If you knew the reason for the Zoom meeting the day of—"

"I do know."

"Oh?"

"People don't drop their voices when they see me coming down the hall," he said sharply, clearly miffed.

"I didn't mean to imply otherwise."

He studied his feet. "I may not be a board member, but I'm a respected member of the staff. I hear things. I *know* things."

"You're not making eye contact with me and you're not giving me straight answers."

"If I didn't let on to the police, why do you think I'd bare my soul to you?"

"Precisely because I'm *not* the police. Because I thought you'd empathize with my desire to know why two colleagues of mine were murdered." She let that brew for a minute, then, trying a new angle, broke the silence with a pointed question. "You're a smart man, Clifford, what do *you* think could have motivated someone to murder these men?"

"Sorry, my brain doesn't function along those lines," he said flatly. "Try asking Mr. Latham."

Tactic failed. "What have you got on him, Clifford?" she asked, back to the direct approach. "Get it off your chest."

"What does it matter? You'd go straight to the police with whatever I'd tell you in confidence. What's the expression, rob Peter to pay Paul?" He shook his head. "It's no use," he sighed, his brow knitting in anguish. "I just...*can't.*"

Erika was conflicted. The more out of reach his knowledge became, the more significance it acquired. In order to shatter his reserve, she needed to bombard him with questions. Yet all the questions she needed to ask were out of bounds. She considered crossing the line, addressing him by his given name. Imagined Harrison's reaction to the idea and reconsidered. Without thinking, she scanned the grounds, looking for him. She had promised herself she wouldn't, and here she was, catching herself in the act, unable to tear herself away, because there he was, sitting under a tree, just as she'd pictured him. A dog was straining on his leash trying to get at him, but

Harrison was hanging tough, not budging, pretending to read his magazine.

When her focus returned to the custodian—her lapse couldn't have been more than three or four seconds—she saw his tortured look had morphed into a sardonic smirk. An unnatural transformation, she thought, unless his anguish had been faked, and she had just caught him off guard enjoying a private joke.

The disparaging curl of his lips vanished the instant he saw that her eyes were on him. The mean squint took a nanosecond more to default to neutral. "You *do* understand my quandary, don't you?" he entreated, as if a beat had not followed his last plaintive remark.

"I do, but I wish I didn't," Erika said regretfully, responding in kind. "I think you've got something you'd like to get off your chest, and I think it might be to your benefit if you did so. Even if it *did* get passed on to the police." It pained her to realize she'd been the gullible fool; worse to continue acting like one. "Well," she said, rising from the bench, "I won't keep you any longer. If you change your mind, you know where to reach me."

He stood beside her. "Sorry," he said, in a boyish tone that reminded her of his sneakered-foot-over-sneakered-foot pose. He slipped his sunglasses back on and extended his hand. "We still friends?"

"Were we *ever?*" she replied, giving his hand a most genial shake and returning his innocent smile in equal measure. For safety's sake, she couldn't very well have shouted "The jig's up, Jason!" but it was impossible to let him off scot-free.

Anxious for him to be out of earshot, she purposely lagged behind as they started down the path toward the square's Woburn Place exit. Even before making eye contact with Harrison, she was rummaging in her bag to retrieve her cell phone. She could have texted Hogarty, but she needed to vocalize her pent-up emotion.

The call went straight to voicemail. "The jury's returned with a verdict," she snapped. "Sorry Detective, that sounded angry. It's not. Oh, it's Erika. Thanks for giving me—*us*—a call back."

She looked for Harrison. Where had he gone? She saw he was still under the tree. Of course. He was waiting for the coast to be absolutely clear before moving from his post. She doubled back to meet him halfway. She had no idea where John was lurking. Better concealed than Harrison, no doubt. After all, he was the pro.

Harrison rose to his feet, and Erika started running toward him, helplessly, like the fabled girl in the red shoes.

* * *

Twenty minutes later, "I was royally played," Erika informed John, as he settled into what had become his reserved spot in the group's usual meeting area.

"You? Played? No way. What happened? You run into Meryl Streep?"

She explained. Harrison, hearing the story for the second time, marveled at it again.

"Wait," John said, after she'd completed the account. "You're basing your opinion of a man's guilt on a *facial* expression? I better watch myself. My ulcer acts up, I tend to grimace."

Erika smiled. "It was a dead giveaway, John. The man had just expressed real consternation; it was written all over his face. Seconds later that face was twisted into a self-satisfied smirk. Erased the instant his eyes met mine. It was sinister, unnatural. You would understand if you had experienced it. The point is, it's not as if this revelation came from out of the blue. There's a good chance there's already enough circumstantial evidence to bring a murder charge against him. At least in Timothy Thorpe's case."

"What about the problem you had with Brian Latham breaking up your chat with the guy? What was *that* all about?"

"I can't say. Maybe Dean had caught him in a compromising position with Cherry Ames and he was worried Dean would rat on him. Maybe Brian thought Dean was an unsavory character and wanted to keep me away from him. It's irrelevant, now that I'm onto Dean's—Jason's!—goody two-shoes act."

"What worries me is that he's onto *you*," Harrison said.

"Words out of my mouth," John agreed. "Here on in I'm sticking to you like glue, Erika. Like it or not."

"Words out of *my* mouth," Harrison shot back.

"Two alphas for the price of one," Erika retorted. "Lucky me."

John grinned. "You got that right. By the way, Harrison's on sentry duty this afternoon while I drop by Cherry Ames's apartment building. From what you've told me, there's little point in my going, since it looks like your case against Dean-slash-Jason is pretty much sewn up. However, I don't see any harm in checking out Latham, especially since I got the green light on it. I'd been told the building manager wouldn't be back until later today, but when I called the concierge before our *operation* this morning—mainly to remind him I was still interested—he told me the manager's back early from his trip to wherever and that he'd let me know if and when I could come by today."

"I take it he responded," Harrison said.

"About five minutes before I knocked on your door."

"When's your appointment?"

"Open-ended. I figure I'll grab a bite to eat at the coffee shop around the corner and head out."

"You've got Harrison's photo to show to the building manager?" Erika asked.

"Close to my heart," John said, patting his jacket's breast pocket. He rose from the chair. "I'll let you know how it goes down. Meanwhile, don't let our charge out of your sight, Harrison." He winked. "I got a pair of cuffs in my room she gives you any trouble."

"Good to know," Harrison said, feigning dominance, giving Erika a glance that refuted any notion of it. He rose from the couch to show John out.

"Say, John," Erika said, rising as well, "I've been meaning to ask, where were you concealing yourself at Russell Square?"

"No way," John replied, heading to the door. "You think I'm giving away my trade secrets?" Arriving at the door, he turned and added, with a grin, "I was the guy with the dog. You know, the nipper?"

* * *

Detective Hogarty returned Erika's call ten minutes after John walked out the door. "From your message, looks like you've come around," he said, after their hellos and Erika had put him on speakerphone. "You want to tell me about it?"

For the third time, she related her story.

Hogarty's reaction was much the same as John's, minus the descriptive reference to ulcers. "With all the prosecutorial skill you brought to this case, it took a *smirk* to bring you around?"

Again, she tried to convey the nature of the experience and how it had not been the determining factor in her decision-making process, only the last push.

"The kick in the pants, as it were."

"Yes. Detective?"

"I'm listening. What is it?"

She hesitated. "I'm thinking you should do a search of the custodial closet for, like, evidence that could possibly be associated with the Thorpe murder. Am I meddling?"

"I wouldn't say meddling, no," Hogarty said dryly. "Insulting, maybe, but not meddling."

"I knew it." *I've finally gone too far.*

"Don't fret about it, but did you really think I'd be sitting on my hands, waiting for directives from you?"

"I'm sorry."

"Go easy, Mr. Hogarty," Harrison interjected. "I think you'll agree Erika's been a big help."

"What, am I in court now? I'm being admonished?"

"Please, let's not go there," Erika entreated. "My fault."

"Good observation," Hogarty agreed, the two of them leaving Harrison dangling. "Let's move on. Yes, of course, we've gone through the custodial closet—with a fine-tooth comb in fact. We're actually analyzing the composition of several hair fibers found on one of the shelves. Got the DNA on Dean and the fellow that comes in on Dean's off days. Let's see where it leads. Maybe nowhere. Hair could be Dean's coworker's. Murder took place on a Saturday. The chap was off that day, airtight alibi."

Erika had high hopes of where those fibers had come, but she kept her mouth shut.

"I know what you're thinking," Hogarty said, with a snicker, more friendly than snide. "You're thinking *wig*. The wig we're counting on Dean's having worn to impersonate-slash-implicate Jacob Tembe. We'll see."

"You plan on getting a search warrant for Dean's—*Jason's*—apartment?" Harrison asked, refusing to tread lightly.

"Absolutely," Hogarty replied politely, refusing to take offense, maybe wanting to come off the bigger man. "All in good time, Professor. If the hair's acrylic, no time at all."

"Let's not keep you any longer," Erika jumped in, interested in wrapping up before any more ego-fraying could take place.

"Sure thing. I should be getting back the lab test results shortly. I'll give you the news. I'm not obligated to, but I know you'll be expecting me to. Adiós amigos."

* * *

After Hogarty's call, the couple was faced with an unallocated time span, which they were determined to use constructively. Compiling a list of potential storage venues for Andrew Barrett's putative treasure trove was the activity decided on. Their initial plan was to run over to the British Library and pore through Baedekers of Victorian London and supplemental reading matter to check if there were any sites that met their mileage requirement and were extant. After a moment's reflection, they decided it might be more efficient to see what they could tease out of the internet before rushing off, unprepared, to the more challenging rummage in the stacks.

"We have plenty of time," Harrison assured Erika, booting up his laptop. The library closes at five on Sundays, and it's only a few minutes away."

Erika was perched lotus-style on the couch, cell phone at the ready. Legal pad and pen on the cushion beside her; Harrison prepared with his own writing materials. "Good. I'll start with banks and gold and silver reserves.

You want to take storage facilities and churches—the ones with underground vaults?"

"Will do."

"Let me know when you want to trade ideas," she said. Harrison was sitting at the other end of the couch, hunched over his laptop, fingertips already skating over the keyboard. *We in a race?* "Someone hear a starting gun?"

"Huh?"

She smiled. "Never mind." A moment later, with her slender, nimbler fingers she was lapping him on the track.

"Say, I've come across a couple of catacombs I've never heard of," he commented, after they'd been working a while in silence. "The Clerkenwell catacombs, a system of tunnels built under a prison; the prison demolished in 1893 and replaced by a school. Twenty-six miles from Hertfordshire, by the way. Then there are the Camden catacombs, built in the nineteenth century under what was to become the Camden markets. Twenty-three miles from Hertfordshire. Pushing our mileage limit a bit, but we should consider researching these sites' construction and accessibility, then and now."

"What about the famous London Catacombs?" Erika asked. "Vaults installed below the churches that contain a couple of thousand coffins. When were they opened?"

"In 1837," Harrison answered, double-checking his notes. "Do you suppose Barrett could have found a way to store his collection in what would surely have had to have been more than several coffins? This idea's a stretch, to say the least."

"Maybe he could have ostensibly reserved a few chambers or niches for Barrett family members and instead used the space to harbor his art objects." She cracked a wan smile. "Or maybe our imagination's running away with us?"

"I think maybe the latter—hold it! Your suggestion about Barrett reserving burial space. It reminds me of something." His fingers began skimming over the keyboard as if of their own accord. "Here we are—yes!" he looked over at Erika, as if expecting a high-five acknowledgment.

"What, Harrison?"

"There are catacombs under a number of private cemeteries in London. And, of course, family mausoleums and below-ground crypts have been available for centuries."

Erika uttered a drawn-out "Ohh."

"I see you remember."

"Yes. At the Zoom meeting. Olivia mentioning the Barrett family's burial grounds."

"Trouble is, I don't remember the name of the cemetery. Do you?"

"No, but if you show me a list of names, I might be able to pick it out." She sidled closer to him to view his screen. The title displayed: "Magnificent Seven Cemeteries."

"There are over a hundred cemeteries in London," Harrison supplied. "I thought we should start with these, all opened in the nineteenth century."

The list began with Kensal Green Cemetery, built in 1833. It was followed by West Norwood, built in 1837. "That's it," she declared. "West Norwood."

"You sure?"

"I'm positive. Olivia's story was fascinating, but I found it hard to follow the family lineage. I must have been concentrating really intently. My memory needed jogging is all."

Harrison realigned the laptop and typed in a prompt. "Thirty-one miles from Hertfordshire. Pretty good fit. Let's contact Olivia, see if members of the Barrett family are entombed in a mausoleum or below-ground crypt, rather than buried in the more traditional manner." After a reflective pause, he added, "If we're planning on disrupting the contents of a family mausoleum—or a below-ground crypt, even worse—we better be prepared for some resistance."

"Legal resistance."

He nodded.

"We need to reach Olivia. I think we should hold off going to the library until we do."

Harrison agreed, and an email was sent to her at once.

As one matter was put on hold, another hastened to take its place. Informing Melody that her ex-husband was still alive would not be an easy task, but it was one that had to be performed. Erika supposed that someone other than herself might be the more conventional bearer of such news, but the immediate attachment she'd made with the Williams as well as the circumstances under which it had been formed, seemed to make her the most—the *only*—suitable candidate.

"Stay by me, Harrison," she said, reaching for her cell phone.

Chapter Twenty-Seven

He was a person of interest now, no getting around it. He suspected as much when the ballsy bitch confronted him outside the custodial closet, pretending to run into him but only looking to feel him out before her powwow with the detective. Yesterday, though, he knew for sure the authorities had him in their sights, when he'd come back from his rounds and saw the spare Lysol container facing sideways like it never does, nozzle pointing at him like a pistol. A simple thing like that was all it took to know they'd been pawing around, looking for evidence to use against him. Not that he was worried they might actually have found some useful bits to stick in their Ziplocs, only that they'd gotten off on the prospect of *trying* to. It meant they had something on him or thought they did. Big enough to get their juices going, but not big enough to swing a jury.

He did a quick recap of his tactics, starting with his basic no-frills hacking of emails and official files. It was how he'd learned of the Zoom meeting, Ashton's Picasso-Braque exchange, Umar's student list. If any of the injured parties had picked up his scent, he would have heard about it by now. Jacob Tembe he'd found mouthing off on the dark web, dying to put some skin in the game. He'd contacted him on a Stealth Phone, so no way that eager beaver would have been able to track him down. As for the maneuver of his two selves, man in black and custodial worker passing in the hallway, he'd made sure the latter had stuck to the surveillance camera's blind spot, so that the act of their crossing paths was never seen, merely *inferred*. All clear on all counts.

He planted himself in his old easy chair, its leather dry and cracked like he remembered his grandmother's face, and pondered the minor characters in his orbit, such as it was. Latham, for one. Latham had caught him going through his trash that one time, but if nothing had come of it then, why should it now? Especially now he'd caught Lothario in a naughty act himself, off-hours with Cherry Ames. Again, there was that smartass Erika Shawn or Wheatley or whoever cropping up in his mind ever since he'd spotted her in the museum lobby, thinking right then and there she was up to no good, whispering sweet nothings in the ear of her sidekick, whoever the hell *he* was.

The woman kept him on his toes, he had to admit, a smart mouse in their cat and mouse game. That is, until her gaze inadvertently froze on her husband playing undercover cop in Russell Garden. Little squeaker couldn't help herself.

Who was he kidding? He couldn't get her out of his mind, worrying she knew more than he was allowing himself to *think* she knew. Which brought him right around to the elephant in the room, *his identity*, the beast that may have kick-started the focus on him as a person of interest. Had this woman, or any-the-hell-body else, for that matter, discovered that he was in truth the convicted felon, Mark Jason, resurrected from the dead?

It was a definite possibility. To be sure, he'd learned the ins and outs of the identity-change business from the experts, but these gurus were behind bars themselves, how unerring could they be? He believed his credentials would hold up—they *had* held up—under routine conditions. But if the authorities had decided to scrutinize the personnel file of each and every museum staffer who'd been on the premises the day of Mr. Thorpe's murder, well that was another story.

The more he thought about it, the more certain he was that his identity had been exposed. He shrugged. What could he do? Even if this was not the case, *something* had prompted the clue hunters to poke around in the custodial closet. If nothing else, he was a realist. This was the endgame. There were decisions to be made.

He would like to have had more time. He'd made a list of future actions to consider. Causing havoc at the opening of the museum going up in Benin

City, at the top of it. He'd begun outlining a manifesto, although he wasn't sure for what purpose, who he had in mind for an audience. Surprisingly, he was not particularly agitated about the turn of events. Had he had enough of it? Was he just in general *fatigued*? He stared idly at the wall opposite, with its scratches and gouges of renters before him, him at the end of the line. It felt almost nostalgic, looking at those cheap reproductions of his, works of Picasso and Braque, Matisse, Modigliani, each clinging to the wall by a single tack, a tired lot, now they'd done their job of feeding the fire in him. He had needed some grand cause to universalize his loathing for those self-righteous white bastards who had destroyed his life, and these images had provided it. His stoked-up rage had resonated with repatriation sympathizers and hangers-on with grudges of their own against the white man, and their rallying cry had in turn produced, with his help, a tide of glorious retaliation against the Black population, that hardy conglomerate that had spawned Charles Williams, the cause of his misery, the Big Bang of his destiny.

It's not that he hated one race more than another or that he felt superior to the Black man or a superior specimen of his own sallow race. He was not a Charles Manson, that scrawny narcissist racist pig, who thought he'd come out of his hole and rule the world after the apocalypse he'd slash-started had shat into a new age and population profile. No way was he that man. He was a shit like all the rest. "Thy enemy is thyself," he thought aloud, pulling the phrase out of a hat. *From the Bible?* he wondered. *If it isn't, it should be.*

How to choreograph the end? Since under no circumstances would he risk the possibility of incarceration, the only creative element would be choosing the manner of death. Self-immolation would evoke the image of a phoenix rising from the ashes, which would suit the occasion philosophically, but in Iraq he'd seen men, women, children howling in pain as flames engulfed them, and he was neither brave nor crazy enough to condemn himself to such torture.

He supposed he could find some poetic justification for jumping off the Westminster Bridge into the River Thames, but there was always the chance he might be saved by some naïve soul, fancied himself the Good Samaritan.

After all, not *all* rescues are shams, as in the case of Mr. Thorpe's. He was just starting to contemplate the pros and cons of ingesting a large quantity of pills as a viable option, when he heard a sharp knock at the door.

He could not remember the last time anyone had paid him a visit. He rose from the chair and walked slowly to the door, savoring the newness of the experience. He half-expected it to be the Erika woman, his lovely nemesis.

"Who is it?" he asked tentatively, wondering if it had been a mistake to have answered the summons.

"Police," came the response, firm but not alarmingly so. "We're here to execute a search warrant for the property of Mark Gregory Jason alias Clifford Dean. Open the door."

Mark stood stock still, as if the situation would cease to exist if he remained silent.

"Open the door, sir. You can take a look at our IDs and the document issued by the Magistrate's court. We will not enter your domicile until you've checked us out. Okay?"

When he'd been discharged from the armed services, Mark had been required to hand over his gear, but a year after he'd been released from prison, he'd purchased a Sig Sauer P226 pistol, same model he'd been issued when he'd served in Iraq. He wasn't sure at the time why he needed to possess this particular weapon or why he'd decided to keep it in the kitchen cabinet, near at hand and loaded. Now he knew.

The police, having received no response to their repeated order for the occupant to open the door, had no choice but to break it open. The loud thud as it gave way was synchronous to the shot fired from Mark's Sig Sauer. He was already dead when they found him lying face down on the kitchen floor.

Chapter Twenty-Eight

Olivia was all aflutter as she ushered her guests into her "spare" room, as she called it. "Spare in the true sense of the word, meaning no excess," she hastened to add, waving at them to take their places on the rather petite settee, from which Erika believed they might later need help dislodging. The three imperial items Olivia had salvaged from the sale of Barrett Farms, the grandfather clock, the secretary desk, and the high-back chair on which she'd sat during the fateful Zoom meeting, took up almost all of the remaining floor space.

When her guests had docilely crammed themselves onto the settee, Harrison in the middle, Olivia sank into the high-back chair. Although she'd been introduced to John at the door, her unabashed perusal of him indicated she was still troubled by his presence. "I'm not sure you'll be allowed," she directed at him. "Do you have sufficient proof of identity? At least two?"

"I do, Ma'am," John answered. "May I ask why they're required?"

"I'll get to that," Olivia replied, giving a tug at the cuff of her jacket, same way Erika remembered her doing at the Zoom meeting.

"You're keeping us in suspense, Olivia," Harrison gently prodded. "You called, we came at once. Still, we don't know the nature of the emergency. Might it have something to do with the Andrew Barrett matter? We did want to ask you a question about the Barrett family accommodations at the West Norwood Cemetery, but if you'd rather—"

"What? Heavens no. I mean yes, this is about Andrew Barrett, but no, the nature of his burial is totally irrelevant. Oh dear." She closed her eyes.

"Let me reboot." She took a few deep breaths and opened her eyes. "Alright then. Forgive me, all of you. As you've heard me mention, Erika, Harrison, I'm a woman set in my ways. Cemented would be more accurate. I have my poached egg every morning, I deal with students and mathematical equations that know their place, and if I'm wrenched out of my little sphere of activity or called upon to make a decision that might have far-reaching effects, I become quite insecure." She gave a dainty shrug while looking from one Wheatley to another. "Which is why, for example, I placed Andrew's documents in your hands. Which is why I was more than distraught on hearing of Ikemar's death and why my nightmares over it have not abated."

There followed a moment of silence, as if mutually agreed upon. Ruined, for Erika, by the news, still bloody raw, of Ike's killer's suicide the day before; even in death, Jason slicing into Ike's allotted time.

Olivia heaved a sigh. "Which is why, finally, I must have you people come along with me today. They have made the necessary preparations for the event this very morning. Have you heard of the London Silver Vaults?"

Erika and Harrison blanched simultaneously.

"Goodness, what have I said?"

"The word 'vaults,'" Erika replied.

Harrison whipped his cell phone from his blazer's breast pocket.

"Well, have you?" Olivia repeated. "Heard of the London Silver Vaults?"

"No," Erika admitted, embarrassed somehow. *Should* she have heard?

"Twenty-six point three!" Harrison declared, staring down at his cell phone screen.

Erika and John guessed the cause of Harrison's excitement. Olivia was at sea. "Miles between Hertfordshire and the London Silver Vaults on Chancery Lane, Midtown," Harrison explained. "A great match." Responding to Olivia's puzzled look, he elaborated. As a math teacher, she got the point at once, including the finer calculations foot-noted by John.

"I think my friends may be jumping the gun," John suggested, more confident in speaking up, now that he'd shown himself to be fluent in math and Olivia was starting to warm up to him. "Are you saying the treasure trove they've been on the hunt for has turned up at the London Silver Vaults, whatever the heck that is?"

"I don't know!" Olivia cried, throwing up her hands. "That's what I'm hoping we'll find out today!"

"Please, Olivia," Harrison implored, can we start from square one? What is this place and why have you brought it to our attention?"

Erika felt a little less sheepish, now her ignorance was shared.

"First," Olivia began, the London Silver Vaults might well be the most secure marketplace on earth. A large subterranean space below Chancery Lane, it was opened in 1885 as 'The Chancery Lane Safe Deposit' and its twenty-nine vaults were originally rented out to store family valuables. A few years later the strongrooms became the domain of silver dealers and remain so to this day. A number of the vaults have been rented by individual families for generations. The structure above the vaults was bombed during World War II and destroyed, but the below-ground vaults level remained intact. The above-ground structure was rebuilt and opened in 1953. It's the building we'll be visiting later this morning."

"But just *why* are we visiting this building?" John asked, the only one who dared risk offending Olivia by voicing the question.

"Well, you see, John—may I call you John?" Olivia began, totally unperturbed, "a few days ago I received a call from the contracts manager of the Vaults. Apparently, an agreement my great-granduncle Andrew Barrett negotiated with the company in August of 1897 is about to expire. The manager had been looking for a Barrett family member—in all the wrong places, as it were—and had finally come around to me. I'm to either renew the contract, for a lesser term, of course, or clear out the space to allow one of the retailers on their waiting list to take occupancy. I was told Andrew had set up a trust in the company's name to cover a specific vault's rent for one hundred twenty-five years, taking inflation into account. It seems there's a modest sum remaining in the trust, which I can use towards the upcoming calendar year's rent. Otherwise, they'll issue me a check for the balance remaining."

John, bucking his companions' gasps, grinningly addressed the hostess. "Yes."

"Yes, what?"

"Yes, you may call me John."

Chapter Twenty-Nine

The unassuming stone building, with its two little conical-shaped bushes bracketing its modest wood door, did not look like the front for a subterranean storage space that had withstood the Blitzkrieg of World War II. To Erika, it looked more like a building providing office space for accountants and dentists.

The lobby offered a hint of its real function. At one end, a sleek L-shaped seating arrangement in royal blue looked fit for formal conversation, no smoking or slouching allowed. Along the wall leading away from the arrangement, a series of glass showcases displayed a sampling of vintage and modern silver items to be found in the vaults below.

A slender gentleman in a pin-striped suit and bow tie was waiting for the Chatham party in the lobby. Several days prior he had put Olivia through a rigorous authentication process. "I've been notarized, authorized, certified and who knows why, finger-printed!" Olivia had told John and the Wheatleys on their cab ride to the Vaults.

The gentleman greeted Olivia as if she were an old friend and introduced himself to her companions. "Alvin Greer, contracts manager. Shall we get started?" He escorted the group to a conference room off the lobby, where they were introduced to a tall, athletic-looking woman as "our corporate lawyer, Jan Newcomb. Jan will answer any legal questions that you and I haven't already covered, Olivia, and she'll also be overseeing our transaction today. To make sure we're proceeding up to snuff," he added with a discreet chuckle.

After they'd all taken seats at the conference table, Newcomb addressed

Olivia's escorts. "Am I correct in understanding that the three of you wish to accompany Ms. Chatham on her visit to the Barrett-designated vault today?" They answered in the affirmative, and she informed all present that she would be tape-recording the proceedings. There were no objections and the device in the center of the conference table was turned on. "Thank you." After noting the date and time, the names of those present in the room, and the purpose of the meeting, Newcomb asked Olivia if she had decided, on her own and under no duress, to allow the three guests to visit the site. Olivia said, "Of course. We are all beyond excited. Can we get on with it?"

Greer pointed to a stack of documents sitting beside the tape recorder and reminded Olivia that both the company's and her great-granduncle's written orders must be followed down to the letter. Olivia was chastened.

"I don't know whether this is following protocol," Harrison unexpectedly announced, "but would it be possible for my wife and I to have a look at the agreement?"

"The purpose of which is…?" Newcomb inquired.

"To check the signatories. We've done some research on Mr. Barrett, and it would be helpful in completing the picture."

Newcomb looked around the table. "I don't have any objections, that is, if no one else has."

None had. Newcomb removed a dauntingly thick clip-bound document from the pile and flipped to the last page. She slid the document in front of Erika and Harrison, sitting catty-corner to her, but did not remove her hand from it.

The names of the company's executives, lawyer, and notary public were, as expected, unfamiliar to the couple. Andrew James Dexter Barrett's signature was, of course, no surprise. Spotting the signature neatly penned directly below Barrett's, while not exactly a surprise, was gratifying proof of one of their theories. "Here he is!" Harrison declared, as if the man had just materialized. "Michael Henry Ewing, the solicitor Andrew and Lily discovered the day they were searching the *London Gazette* for promising bankruptcies." Responding to the puzzled looks from all but Erika, he explained the reference in Barrett's journal to his purchase of Daniel

Edgerton's African art and the part Ewing had played in it.

"We were going to do some probing into the solicitor's records," Erika submitted, after Harrison had finished. "We wanted to see if we could find a connection between him and Barrett after the Edgerton sale. If he had drawn up Barrett's will, for instance. Now that appears more likely to have occurred."

Newcomb and Greer began speaking simultaneously, Newcomb ceding the floor to her colleague. "We know for a fact that Mr. Ewing did indeed draw up Mr. Barrett's will," Greer advised, brushing an invisible speck of matter from his lapel. "Reference to it is right here in this document. Alas, there is no mention of the will's specifications and I'm afraid your research would duplicate ours, including its dead end. You see, Mr. Ewing's law office was vandalized and burned to the ground in 1919, when his associate defended a white seaman who'd killed a Black man during a race riot in Liverpool. Perhaps you're familiar with this period in our history. The riots occurred after World War I amid the competition for cheap labor. At any rate, apropos of this case, Ewing kept all his records in wood file cabinets, hence all were destroyed."

"Which is why I, by default, seem to be the sole heir of my great-granduncle's estate," Olivia reported, wrapping up the story.

"Exactly," Newcomb said, removing the Vaults contract from the Wheatleys' perusal and setting it aside. Addressing Erika, Harrison, and John, she requested, "Before we set about opening the Barrett vault, may we check your credentials, please? We prefer two identifying documents, but since Olivia has vouched for you, one will do, so long as it's a good one."

Enhanced ID divers' licenses sufficed for all three.

"Let's begin," Newcomb recited, suddenly looking tense. "Let it be noted that on this day the envelope containing the combination to the lock on the door to the Andrew Barrett vault has been removed from the executive safe of The London Silver Vaults and Chancery Lane Safe Deposit Company Limited, and furthermore, that on this day the envelope's wax seal has been examined and authenticated by sigillography experts of Fox and Associates and determined to have never been broken." From the bottom of the pile of documents, she drew forth a letter-sized envelope encased in a plastic zip bag and, hands shaking, showed it to Olivia, sitting to her left, opposite the Wheatleys.

Olivia, looking unsure of herself, nodded her approval. "Will that do?" she asked. "You want to open the envelope?"

Newcomb, followed by Greer, rose to their feet. "Mrs. Chatham will open the envelope at the door to the vault," the lawyer formally stated. "At that time, *only* she will be permitted to view the combination number contained within, and the *only* one permitted to open the lock." Focusing solely on Olivia, she said, "I understand that you've chosen to relinquish occupancy of the vault at the termination of Mr. Barrett's contract. Am I correct?"

"You are."

"In that case, you have a little over two months, until August the sixteenth, to catalogue and disperse the contents any way you choose. Speaking for the administration, I'm sure you'll get all the logistical help you need with the process." She looked to Greer for confirmation.

"You must never feel overwhelmed," Greer said. "We will not permit it." He made a grand 'all rise' gesture as if to a choir. "Come."

Those still seated rose on cue, and they were led, like ducklings, down a hall to a security checkpoint and afterward, to the world below.

Chapter Thirty

A massive door—the word 'door' hardly sufficed, Erika thought—led to the subterranean chamber that housed the individual vaults. When the door swung shut behind them, the corridor that lay ahead seemed at once endless, as in a dream, and yet contained, sealed off from the rest of the known world. The shiny waxed floor, the overhead fluorescent lights, the evenly spaced glass cabinets mounted along the wall, created, in Erika's mind, the sterile atmosphere of a hospital or a laboratory. She knew the glass cabinets were filled with silver objects, but her imagination toyed with the idea that they contained biological specimens of some kind. The few people wandering through the corridor, peering with interest at the contents of the cases, added to the effect.

"A little eerie," she whispered to Harrison, taking his hand.

She was smiling, so no harm in his saying, "You think we'll be allowed to leave?"

She gave him a hip-bump as they proceeded down the corridor, Alvin Greer leading the way.

Close to the end of the corridor, Greer halted in front of a glass case, the only empty one they'd encountered. He raised his hand like a tour group leader to indicate they stand in place. "Here we are," he said, tilting his head toward the vault door beside the mounted case.

John pointed to the empty case. "Hope this isn't a sign of what lies ahead," he said in jest.

"Don't laugh," Greer retorted, grinning himself. "I hear tell a gentleman rented one of our spaces for many years—granted, not one hundred twenty-five—to store but one farthing!"

This exchange was not sitting well with Olivia and the Wheatleys. "May I have the envelope, Ms. Newcomb, if you please?" Olivia primly stated.

"Of course." The lawyer handed the envelope to Olivia. "Before you open it, the rest of us must step away from the area to allow you privacy."

All but Olivia moved several yards away and turned their backs to the action about to take place.

After a few minutes of listening to Olivia's heavy breathing and an occasional exasperated grunt, presumably when a lock rotation had gone too far or not far enough, her entourage at last heard the Eureka! utterance: "Wheatleys, come here at once! I can't go in alone!" When they turned to her, she was standing by the closed door and stuffing the envelope into her purse. "Just the two of you, at least at first. No one minds, I hope. I'm very nervous and I don't want to feel crowded."

No one minded.

Erika and Harrison silently approached. "Open the door, one of you," Olivia said softly, as if she were divulging a secret. "I'm a little frightened. I don't know why."

"Of course," Harrison said, grabbing hold of the thick door lever and pressing down on it. Slowly he pulled open the door, as impressive a construction as the one at the entrance to the below-ground space at large.

"Oh." It was the first word uttered. Olivia's.

"This is…" Erika followed.

"I know," Harrison agreed.

It was a trite thought, Erika knew, but she had to express it. "It's as if this room has been frozen in time. Not preserved. Frozen." Dare they enter this space and break the spell? Contaminate it with the dust on their clothing, the dirt on the soles of their shoes, their *breath*?

From the doorway, the room, about as large as a typical dining room, could be seen in its entirety. The wall space was almost completely occupied by glass-encased shelving and vitrines, all filled with artifacts and objects of art that Andrew Barrett had without doubt collected over the years. There, in the crowded gallery case closest to the viewers, was his first purchase:

the half-man-half-shark and its companion hybrids from the West African Kingdom of Dahomey, along with the altarpieces included in Edgerton's collection—made of iron and strips of wood, as Andrew had reported in his journal. In front of the ceiling-high display cases on one wall stood two table-high cases. They, too, were neatly cluttered with treasures, among them altarpieces and statuary, bowls, flasks, helmets, horns, crowns, busts carved of wood, others cast in metal. There appeared to be just enough space between the rows of display cases for an average-sized adult to walk through.

But the arrangement that had been the primary cause of Erika's heart-stopping frozen-in-time effect had been the home-office furnishings and the look of its having just been occupied, as if Andrew had stepped out on an errand and would be back momentarily, when time resumed.

On his carved wood Pedestal desk, an open book had been placed face-down, to be taken up, Erika imagined, after the non-existent interval of a century had passed, and Andrew was once again seated at his desk in his maroon, brass-studded leather chair that seemed to have been just pushed back, allowing him room to rise.

Curiously, on the wall opposite the desk, a space had been left free of shelving for a wall- hanging of some sort. Whatever it was—and Erika hoped her suspicions were correct—Andrew had chosen to drape it with a large cutting of blue velvet, either to hide it from view or merely protect it from light and air.

"Come with me," Olivia urged, hooking her arm through Erika's. "You too, Harrison," she added. "Please leave the door slightly ajar, thank you." She stepped inside, Erika tiptoeing beside her in an instinctive but vain attempt to preserve the room's pristine state.

It took a moment, once Erika was inside, for the sanctity of the place to dip to a mood more history-oriented; its contents, more approachable. She gently broke from Olivia to step cautiously over to the desk. "May I?" she asked, holding her hand just above the desktop. "Touch, I mean?"

"Well, of course, you may. This isn't a crime scene, my dear. There'll be no forensics coming by. This is"—Olivia threw her arms open—"all mine!"

Tipsy almost, she spun about like a child at play.

Harrison jumped to her side to catch hold of her elbow. "Yes, it is, Olivia. I know how you feel. I'm a bit giddy myself." He ushered her over to the desk chair. "Have a seat. Take it all in."

She did as she was told. "You see? This is why I wanted you people with me. In an extraordinary situation, I'm not to be trusted. Yes, everything in this room is lawfully mine, apparently, but I know in the eyes of a higher justice"—she pointed heavenward—"*none* of it's mine!" She grinned. "Well, maybe the chair I'm sitting in. Don't make me get out of it."

Erika ran her fingers over the desktop. Its first touch in over a century, she thought. *Every act in this room is significant today.* The cover of the book lying face down was made of leather dyed the same shade of brown as the Barrett journal she and Harrison had read. Maybe this was another of them.

Olivia could see Erika was hesitating. "Go ahead, take a look," she encouraged. "In fact, I want you and Harrison to gather together any journals and letters and what-have-you and bring the items back to the states with you. I trust you will handle it all with great care, because after you're done studying the material, I plan to donate it to the museum presently under construction in Benin City." She raised a hand. "Unless, of course, you find any of it to be of a scurrilous nature. *That* material we'll keep to ourselves!"

"We'd be honored to examine the material," Harrison said, smiling at her zinger. "But you should think about this decision at your leisure, when you're more...*yourself.*"

"Nonsense. I'm sure one of the officials hovering about will be able to supply you with a briefcase or container of some kind, whatever you need for its transport. I'm quite myself now. Your presence has calmed me."

"This *is* one of Andrew's journals!" Erika declared. "Book three, in fact. Andrew had it open to the page where he was describing his marriage to Lily. He must have been reminiscing. It may have been the anniversary of their wedding...or of Lily's death." She looked up, her gaze locking on Harrison's. "Who knows?"

Harrison shook his head. "No one."

"Even *then*, only Andrew."

"Yes." He put his arm around her waist. "So, let's see what's behind the drape. I know you're hoping what I'm hoping."

"I am." She placed the journal back on the desk. "Olivia? Do you want to perform the unveiling?"

"No, dear. The honor should go to you two. I've been an onlooker up to now, and that's how things will remain. Go ahead."

A metal ring had been sewn to each of the upper corners of the velvet sheath; the rings slipped onto wall hooks placed above whatever Andrew had chosen to hide from view. Erika could not quite reach the rings, so it was up to Harrison to do the honors. There was just enough room between the back of the desk and the wall for him to stand. "Here goes," he said, preparing to remove the first ring.

Harrison unhooked the ring and carefully drew the fabric away from what lay beneath. "Oh God."

Erika was silent. He'd spoken for them both.

"Splendid," Olivia commented, rounding out the reaction.

Harrison unhooked the second ring, freeing the fabric from its mooring, and side-stepped out from behind the desk.

"Give it here," Olivia said, referring to the velvet curtain Harrison was cradling in his arms. Distractedly, he dropped it into her hands. She folded it into a neat square and laid it on her lap. "Well, then."

There they were, beyond a reasonable doubt, the objects that Andrew had obliquely alluded to in his journal's 'vision' entry. The plaques were protectively encased in a glass cabinet mounted to the wall. It was a mystery why they had also been shrouded. Perhaps the answer would be found in a journal. As a matter of human interest, it would be revelatory, but for now, this moment, all that mattered was that they had been found.

"Benin Bronzes," Erika said, uttering her first words since they'd been uncovered. "I think they may be a little larger than the ones on public display. You think I'm exaggerating the size because they're the only ones in the room or am I just goggle-eyed?"

"No," Harrison said. "I think they *are* larger. The ones on public display are about fifteen inches in width, twenty in height. I'm betting these add maybe one to two inches each way. Can't tell about the depth, though. They're typically a little over four inches deep."

"Also, they do seem *newer,* somehow, than any of the Benin Bronzes I've seen," Erika submitted. "As though they've just come out of the shop, never been exposed to the elements. Amazing." She stepped closer to them. "But what's most amazing about them is the subject matter," she marveled. "I've never seen anything like this. There are none like it."

"Yes. We've been talking size and condition, but that was my first thought. Subject matter."

"Mine, too." To Olivia, Erika said, "Would you mind if our friend, John joined us? I know he'd appreciate seeing these plaques."

"Bring him in, though without the officials, if you can finesse it."

John was relieved to join them. "Never knew how many topics bore me," he confided to Erika as she led him into the vault. "Starting with the recipe for kidney pie."

"Funny. Take a look at these plaques."

First, John's jaw dropped when he beheld the sheer number of objects inhabiting the space. "Wow! Busy fellow!"

"Look at the plaques, John. Stand up close, by the back of the desk."

His examination elicited another "Wow!"

The central figure in each of the plaques was a beautiful Black woman. In one she is in warrior's garb and flanked by male soldiers of lesser stature. She carries a sword in one hand, arrows in another. Around her waist, she wears a belt of bells from which a packet of amulets is slung. In the other, she wears a crown, yet is clothed as a commoner and surrounded by a woman, a man and a child, each holding one or two farmed products, including a papaya, an onion, a yam, a handful of beans. A sheep and a goat stand poised in the background, partially obscured by the group.

"So, would your wife approve?" Erika asked brightly, referring to his 'woke' comment at the British Museum's exhibit of Benin Bronzes.

John laughed. "She would. These are unique. Women and children aren't represented on the plaques displayed at the Brit Museum. Or at any other, I take it."

"Right."

"This woman looks like the Queen Mother Idia, depicted on that famous hip pendant," John opined, stroking his chin. "The pendant was commissioned by her son, Oba Esigie, early fifteen hundreds. I bet he commissioned these plaques in her honor, too. After all, he did owe her. Big time."

All eyes locked in various stages of disbelief on John.

"What? Didn't I mention I was boning up?"

"You did, actually," Erika replied, slightly shamefaced. "Sorry."

"Apology accepted. Go easy. I'm just recovering from my wild goose chase. Latham enters building at three fifty-eight, exits four forty-four. Tight alibi. Overblown hunch."

"Wait a minute," Olivia interjected. "Who owed *what* big time?"

The trio exchanged looks, deciding who should answer. Out of remorse, John was elected.

"Oba Esigie's step-brother was actually the fellow in line for the throne," he said. "But his mother went to war for him. I mean literally—you know, raised armies, was in the line of duty? The step-son was defeated."

"I see," Olivia said. "Thank you."

"The Queen Mother was quite a woman," John continued, on a roll. "Not only brave. She was also known for her medicinal knowledge and mystical powers. Like those bells on her waist. I'm pretty sure the jingling was meant to scare off the enemies."

"Fascinating," Olivia acknowledged. "I'm inspired to do some boning up myself!"

Harrison had slipped behind the desk to examine the mounted cabinet set-up more closely. "Say, there's a small square of paper sitting at the base of each of the plaques. One marked with the number one, the other, number two. What do you think, number one and two of Barrett's collection?"

"Let's see," Erika said, approaching the display case with the Edgerton purchase. Very cautiously she opened the door to the case and picked up one of the hybrid figures. Below it was a square marked with the number four. She carefully replaced the piece and looked under its neighbor, another of the hybrids. "Number three," she reported. "As these statues were among the next additions to Andrew's collection, I think you must be right, Harrison." She randomly checked under a few of the other items in the display case—a figurative urn, a scepter with a carved handle, a beaded crown—and discovered that each had been numerically designated. She closed the glass door and returned to the desk area.

"If we're right," Harrison said, "then there must be an inventory somewhere about that lists each individual object in this room."

Erika nodded. "From the way the numbered squares have been cut so uniformly, a pretty meticulous list, I'm guessing. "

"Good deduction," Olivia said, rising from the chair. She placed the folded fabric on the seat and went straight for the desk's center drawer, coming up with two more journals. Without so much as a curious peek within, she placed the books on top of the journal already sitting on the desktop. "These the Wheatleys will take with them," she announced to herself. Another ten seconds, and she'd removed all papers from the two side drawers. "Let's look these over"—again, to herself. For the next minute, she followed her directive. "All this has to do directly with the collection: an inventory—aha! with allocation instructions included— related receipts, photographs, and the like." She returned the material to the two drawers. "They will remain on site for whomever I appoint to catalogue the items and manage their swift repatriation." She brushed her hands together to indicate the day's business had concluded and swept up the small stack of journals from the desktop. She looked from Erika to Harrison. "Who?"

Harrison took the books from her. "Thank you. We'll get these back to you as quickly as you like."

"We must ask Mr. Greer for a suitable carrying case for them." She started for the door.

"Wait!" Harrison issued sharply, taking the others by surprise.

"What is it?" Olivia cried, turning back.

"Sorry to have alarmed you, but we've got to agree on something before we part company."

"What's troubling you, Harrison?"

"You might find it pretty forward of me, even offensive. Please don't. It's a practical matter that will affect the outcome of your project. You used the word 'swift,' as in 'swift repatriation.' I suddenly realized all that will entail."

"And?"

"Olivia, do you have a plan? This project, especially if it is to be carried out in the most secure way possible, will be a costly affair. To *insure* the collection alone, especially in transit, will be quite a hefty sum. Then there's the transportation fee—fees, I should say, since this will involve multiple locations, not only Benin City in Nigeria, but Cameroon, Mozambique, the country of Benin, others. You see where I'm going with this?"

"No worries," Olivia fairly scoffed. "The government will be happy to underwrite the project, if only for the publicity."

"That may be, but have you considered the fact that once this is under the aegis of the government, or the British Museum, or *any* organization with obligations and motives of its own, you lose control of both the trajectory and speed of the process? Don't you remember the primary mission of our Zoom meeting?"

"To get our governments and museums to move their collective ass," Olivia replied, crestfallen. "I see where you're going. Investigations into provenance, authenticity, even the character of my great-granduncle, which I don't think I could bear."

"Don't worry. It will be my honor—my *pleasure—our* pleasure, Erika's and mine—to underwrite this project. Start to finish."

"*What?*" Olivia gasped.

Harrison went on as if he had not heard Olivia's cry of disbelief or objection. No matter. "I suggest you have our friend Greg Smith manage the cataloguing and act as a kind of general contractor in lining up insurers and means of transportation—private plane would be my suggestion. Yes, Greg is himself associated with Art Loss Register, a major organization, but on a number of occasions he's acted as an independent agent on our behalf." He consulted Erika: "You agree with all this?"

"Every word. Also, Amilah Adamu would be of great assistance. And I think her being tied in with a major organization, the Federal Ministry of Information and Culture in Benin City, would, in this case, be a help, not a hindrance."

"Good thought."

"How can I possibly accept your generous offer?" Olivia asked, her emotions clearly in turmoil.

"Without objection and without publicizing our participation," Harrison answered coolly.

"But I don't think I can…"

"Don't even bother," Erika cut her off, grinning. "Harrison has made up his mind. Save your energy for lunch."

"*Now* you're talking," John declared, perking up.

Chapter Thirty-One

J ohn and Olivia set off for Olivia's favorite fish and chips shop. Erika and Harrison were not about to go tramping about town with Barrett's journals—dumped in a paper shopping bag from Harrods, best Newcomb could do; what if it *rained*!

Harrison removed the journals from the bag the minute the door closed behind them. "You want to order room service?"

"I want to dig into these books."

"Me, too." He laid them out on the coffee table. "Divvy them up or read one together?"

"Together." Erika sat down on the couch; reached for one of them. The first page read:

Andrew James Dexter Barrett

Book Two: 14 September 1897 – 4 January 1898

"Lucky hit," she said. "This is where we begin. Just about a month after the last entry in book one. Hurry up, I'm not turning the page without you."

Harrison threw his jacket over the armchair and sat down beside her. "Turn."

They read through the first entry without saying a word.

14 September 1897, ensconced, yet unsettled

My desk and chair have just been delivered. Lily would not allow me to order a second chair for her. "The vault is to be your sanctuary," she said. "We all need our private space, my darling. Do you think there'll be a chair for you in my boudoir?" The argument is flawed, but its proponent, relentless.

Anticipating my collection's substantial growth, I have had installed as many display cases as the vault can accommodate, while still permitting me to move about, and also a glass cabinet, custom-made to contain the plaques (model sailboats, I told the craftsman), is scheduled to arrive tomorrow. Until I have all the furnishings in place, my treasures will remain in the cartons they were transported in. After they have been brought out of hiding, no one will be allowed into the room except myself, and Lily, of course, if she can be persuaded.

As for the disposition of property under my provisional care, it remains a source of worry. I have added what I thought was a perfectly nuanced codicil to my will, and I have drawn up a contract with the London Silver Vaults that I thought took into account every possible contingency in both the natural world and sphere of human relations. Yet I fear all circumstances have not been considered.

The problem stems from my initial dilemma. I wanted to reveal the contents of the vault to no one, yet I also wanted to ensure repatriation as soon as it was feasible to do so. (There will be no problem, of course, if the African nations regain their independence in my lifetime or Lily's. Either of us would simply arrange its transport as expeditiously as possible.) In my codicil, I stipulate that when the African nations have regained their independence, our heir or heirs are to proceed to the London Silver Vaults with proofs of identity where they will be given the combination to my assigned vault. The disposition of the vault's contents will have been attached to the inventory therein. I request that the process be held in abeyance until independence has been secured and predict it will occur within fifty years.

What if I'm wrong? What if independence is never regained? What if no one cares to come forward? What if there is no one to come forward? What then? In my contract with the London Silver Vaults, I stipulate as the contract is nearing its termination date, they make every effort to find our nearest descendent. If one is found and the nations are still under colonial rule, the contents must still be dispersed. If no one is found, the company itself must disperse the contents. For when all is said and done, these treasures must not be hidden forever. They must be seen and appreciated. Most optimally by the nations that created them and to which they rightfully belong. If by the year 2022, the African nations are still under colonial rule, my contract requires that the administrators act in the best interest of those beleaguered nations by conferring with representatives from them as well as sympathetic organizations and individuals to determine the most favorable resolution. As if I could hold them to it! "Build a museum in Benin City!" I cry from my grave. "Another in Maputo while you're at it!"

"Fifty years," Harrison mused. "Not a bad prediction. Off by thirteen years. Nigeria gained its independence in 1960."

"Well, his cry from the grave was right on," Erika came back. "Let's read on."

The entries made during the next few months dealt primarily with three subjects: wedding plans, moving plans, and the accrual of art works and artifacts bought at auction and from dealers and individual collectors. Much of the sales narration was anecdotal in nature, and the Wheatleys assumed that the actual data—dealers, dates, provenance—would be found in Barrett's inventory.

Book Three began with the wedding gala in mid-January 1898, held on the grounds of the Worthington estate, bride and groom embarrassed by its over-the-top lavishness. "We could have been feeding the poor instead of stuffing our faces with cake," Lily at one point chided her father, who seems to have taken the scolding in good spirits—"as he takes all of his beloved daughter's reprimands," Andrew amusedly observed. *Book Three's* last entry, made in mid-1899, was an ode to Lily and the announcement of her pregnancy. "We are more in love than ever," Andrew wrote. "We are overflowing with joy." The first and last entries were the only lengthy ones in the journal. The rest were succinct, rather technical accounts of medical problems Andrew encountered on a daily basis.

"The journals serve different purposes at different times," Erika commented when they'd come to the end of *Book Three*. "I'm curious to see what use he makes of *Book Four*. You hungry, or shall we go on?"

"Both," he said. "Let's go on."

Book Four's title page indicated the start date, "10 July 1899," but omitted the end date. The journal began with coverage of significant or offbeat activities distilled from the daily routine, from the description of a perplexing medical case to the ingesting of a particularly cinnamon-y mincemeat pie. Running through the text, like a recurring musical theme, were phrases of wondrous anticipation as the day of their baby's birth drew near.

Erika and Harrison knew how that story had ended, but they were not expecting it to come without warning. In the entry dated "18 November 1899," the highlight was a dinner party celebrating Andrew's father's sixtieth birthday—"a big one!" Andrew hailed at the close of the day's report. Coming right up, the Wheatleys thought, would be Andrew's accounts, first, of how his family had celebrated Christmas, and next, how they'd rung in the new century. It was not to be. The title of Andrew's next entry was *26 February 1900, forever mourning,* and it began…

I know that it is possible to love more than one person deeply. Love is not a fund, and therefore the love bestowed on one does not leave less for another. I know that my affection for our son will grow in time, but in this moment my love defies nature. It is indivisible. It cannot be apportioned.

Not so my grief. My grief has no shape. It is boundless. I express it only to contain it, and yet I cannot but feel there is vanity in doing so.

"There's a subtle change in his handwriting," Harrison said. "More slanted, it seems. As if the letters are bearing the weight of his grief. I'm being maudlin, aren't I?"

"No, observant."

Further along in the entry, they learned that Lily had died ten days earlier. The circumstances of her death were limited to the word "hemorrhage," but his regret—"guilt" as he more starkly accused—at his not having been by her side was expressed more fully. Lily had gone into labor at least a week before she was expected to, and although the midwife was on hand that day, Andrew was out on an emergency call. "To mock my truancy," the fates had seen to it that he was delayed by a snowstorm on his way home, arriving ten minutes after Lily had drawn her last breath.

There was a six-month lapse between the entry of February 26, 1900, and the one that followed. It resolved one of the Wheatleys' unanswered questions.

16 August 1900, the plaques

A portrait of Lily hangs in our bedroom. It was painted just after we'd learned she was with child. She is wearing the dress she had on the day we met—"so that you will never forget that day!" her reason. "There were two barrettes pinning up your hair on that remarkable day," I said then. "I was sitting across from you at the dinner table imagining they would snap open, and your beautiful hair would come cascading down over your shoulders. Would you fasten them to your hair for the portrait, my dear?" She did so, but as ornaments only. In the portrait her hair is loose, as I loved it most.

Around her neck, she wears a locket. In it my sentimental darling kept a lock of our intertwined hair. For the portrait, the artist took it upon himself to paint the locket open. He reproduced our lock of hair quite accurately, but I have to step right up to the painting to make it out.

Lily is holding a book in her left hand. We told the artist to paint its title so that it was legible, but not boldly so. The title, Great Expectations. An excellent novel by Charles Dickens, but we did not choose it for its literary merit. We chose it to represent my wife's pregnancy.

How would I feel if when I returned home, I discovered the painting was missing? Would it matter if the abductor's intentions were, in his mind, honorable? That he thought he would keep my beloved portrait of Lily from falling into the wrong hands while I was serving time in prison or the equivalent? I imagine now, at this very moment, the stranger sitting at his desk, as I now sit at mine. He is studying the portrait of my wife on the wall opposite him, just as I now study the plaques, captives in their showcase opposite me. Both of us analyzing, but not understanding, not in the pits of our stomachs. The lock of hair, the title of the book. The belt of bells, the packet of amulets. Interested, respectful, both of us, but neither feeling the fathomless longing for union.

You have studied the portrait of my wife long enough. Cover it. Only by removing your gaze from her likeness can I conceive of it in a space shared with me alone.

Tomorrow I will have a covering made for the plaques. It will be a reminder that they do not belong to me.

The entries as subjective commentary virtually ended on August 16th, 1900, the Wheatleys discovered. After that, the book had been used as a catchall for miscellaneous data requiring blank pages on which they might be retained. To-do lists, rough drafts of letters, medical questions often accompanied by anatomical drawings, were among the jottings.

"Do you suppose Andrew ever considered returning the plaques and other Benin works in his collection to the exiled Oba Ovonramwen?" Erika asked. "After all, from 1902 on he was, if not king, a chief working with the colonial government."

"Maybe he did consider it," Harrison said, "but I think in the end he would have rejected the idea. Remember, Ovonramwen was acting in that favored capacity under the governance of the Royals, and by their leave. Andrew would probably have believed repatriation would have come with strings attached. If not ropes."

"I guess you're right. Besides, his experience during the punitive expedition in 1897 must have created an indelible mistrust of those in power. I imagine even when the once-exiled Oba died in 1914 and his son was actually enthroned as Oba of Benin, the mistrust prevailed."

"Yes. The nation's status hadn't changed. The title of Oba was conferred on Eweka ll not by his countrymen, but by the British. The man had his enemies, too. There was a group, lasted for a while, called the 'Anti-Eweka political coalition.' Accused him of killing a woman and petitioned to dethrone him. When the woman was found alive and well, the British courts vindicated him, but *still*. Dicey days."

"Let's not forget, despite what may have been his cynicism about the abuse of power, Andrew did have enough faith in humanity to believe African independence would eventually be regained."

"Amen," Harrison pronounced, underlining her statement. Andrew's journal, his final one, lay open on his lap. He closed the book with an air of solemnity, marking the occasion—the end of a chapter, as he saw it, for Andrew and Lily; for himself and Erika. "Amazing, isn't it," he said, placing the book on the coffee table, "how one man does good for so many, while another aspires to achieve the polar opposite." He sat back, put his arm around Erika's shoulders.

She nodded. "Andrew Barrett. Mark Jason."

He rubbed her shoulder. "Yes."

"It was a wonderful thing you did, Harrison, you know?"

"Wash my socks?"

"Really, sweetheart. You made it happen." She adjusted her position on the couch to face him more directly. "Andrew reminds me of you."

"My penmanship that good?"

"My God, your modesty is relentless. Your generosity—your humanity. That's what I'm talking about."

"You're describing yourself."

She cupped her hand to her ear. "I hear them."

"What?"

"The violins."

He smiled. "If you're going to compare me to Andrew, don't leave out his great love for his wife, Lily."

"The raven-haired beauty." She stroked her chin. "You asking me to dye my hair black?"

"Imp." He took her in his arms, then suddenly pulled away.

"What?"

He rose from the couch. "I'll be right back. Got to get something from my suitcase."

He returned a moment later with his Swiss Army knife.

"You're kidding me," she said. "You planning to file your nails"—she grinned—"or tighten a loose screw?"

He strode to the desk, grabbed a letter envelope embossed with the hotel's address from the desktop, and returned to the couch. He placed the envelope on the coffee table and sat back down. "Okay." He retracted the scissors from his multi-tooled pocketknife.

"Uh-oh."

He pinched a tuft of hair at the top of his head and snipped it off with the tiny pair of scissors. "There." He assessed the clipping. "Two inches. More than enough." He tucked it into the envelope.

"Aha, you clever beast!" She separated a tress from her own hair mass and held it out for him to harvest. "Such a good idea, darling," she said, tears welling up, as he united her clipping with his.

"I think so, yes," he agreed, finally showing a bit of pride. "Now all we need is a locket."

Chapter Thirty-Two

J uly 7. One month had passed since the Wheatleys had returned from London. Erika had begun working on her magazine profiles on collector-philanthropist Keith Ashton and painter Charles Williams; Harrison was outlining chapters for a book on two lesser-known artists of the High Renaissance, Mariotto Albertinelli and Fra Bartolomeo; and Lucas had spoken his first three-word sentence, "Come to Lucah [sic]!" as he dangled a sliver of meat at Jake from his highchair, making the poor dog jump for it repeatedly before releasing it, the beleaguered Lab unable to vocalize what was surely on his mind: "I'm too old for this."

It was 11:10 a.m., New York time. Erika and Harrison were pressed thigh-to-thigh at Harrison's desk, focusing on his computer screen as Amilah Adamu, third thumbnail from the right, top row, was in the middle of her opening remarks. Amilah had organized the Zoom meeting, but she'd asked the Wheatleys for names they'd like to add to the list. Greg Smith, John Mitchell, Joanna Ashton, Melody and Charles Williams, and Madame Denise Fontaine had been their additions. Madame D was as yet nowhere in sight.

"Ikemar's mission was to expedite the return of Africa's heritage," Amilah was saying. "He would have been thrilled to have witnessed what has just been accomplished—the return of so staggering a number of artworks to, among other nations, Mozambique and Cameroon and, most comprehensively, to Benin City in Nigeria. Olivia Chatham, by direction of her great-granduncle, Andrew Barrett, has returned his magnificent collection to the nations of origin—not on loan, as many of our well-intentioned but reluctant museum administrators have on occasion done, but as outright, irreversible *returns*! Thank you, Olivia! Thank you, too, Gregory Smith, of Art Loss Register—where are you, oh there you are, hi!—for managing to accomplish this feat as expeditiously as possible. It was such a pleasure working with both of you!"

"Same here," Greg called out from the bottom row of the grid. "Although I have to say, Mr. Barrett's inventory was the most meticulous example of cataloguing I've ever come across. Literally made our job a snap."

Olivia, enthroned in her high-back leather chair in the top row, waved her hand, as if in a classroom. "I wish to thank our generous benefactor who, to put it bluntly, foot the bill for this entire endeavor."

Harrison grit his teeth beneath his best poker face.

"I wish I could tell you his name, but unfortunately he wishes to remain anonymous."

Harrison unlocked his jaw.

"Bravo!" called out Kurt Reinhardt of the Humbolt Forum in Berlin, one of the nine guests on the grid who had attended the May Zoom meeting.

"Hello out there," a young Black man sang out with equal enthusiasm from the thumbnail next to Robert Labeque of the Quai Branly Museum in Paris, another of the May attendees. His caption read "Nasha Musa." He was new to the group. "You must allow me to thank all of you for your efforts. Most especially Olivia Chatham and her anonymous benefactor. Our organization has also received a generous gift from an individual who wishes to remain anonymous. Could it be the same person, I wonder?" He smiled. "We must have a private chat, Ms. Chatham."

Erika felt Harrison tense up once again at the thought of being tossed into the limelight.

The threat was off the table, at least for the moment, as Amilah, after bestowing her dazzling smile on the group, reminded Mr. Musa that she might be the only one present other than himself who knew what organization he was talking about!

"Ah, yes!" Mr. Musa replied, with a little chuckle of self-reproach. "I'm a bit ahead of myself with excitement. I mean, have you people seen the two plaques—the Benin Bronzes—included in the Barrett collection? They are magnificent!" He smoothed the front of his suit jacket. "Yes. Well, I'm here to represent the Legacy Restoration Trust based in Nigeria. It is a non-profit organization dedicated to backing projects centered in cultural heritage, in general focusing on art and archeology. Our main project at this time is the Edo Museum of West African Art under development in Benin City in Edo State. The architect is Sir David Adjaye. It will be a cultural center which will encompass contemporary art research and projects as well as provide a home for the world's largest collection of Benin Bronzes, to which has just been added a pair that will be the highlight of the collection. On behalf of His Royal Highness, Crown Prince Ezelekhae Ewuare—Oba Ewuare ll—a member of LRT's board of trustees and the personage I am representing as a working intern, thank you!"

A spontaneous burst of applause sounded from across the grid.

Where is Madame D? Erika wondered. She was starting to worry about her.

"I never thanked you for your letter, Erika, Harrison," Olivia said, after the applause had ended.

"Letter?" Erika asked. "Oh, the one we inserted with the journals? Thanks so much for letting us look through them." The Wheatleys had tried to return the books before they'd left for home, but their schedules had been at odds with Olivia's. Afraid to send the books through the mail, they had waited for Greg's upcoming trip to New York and had entrusted him with their delivery on his return to London.

"I think you were right about which of the journals is the appropriate one to donate to the museum going up in Benin City," Olivia said.

"Book One."

"Yes. It shows his character best, who he was as a man—his goodness, his charitable nature, his devastation at the outcome of the Punitive Expedition. And of course, his tolerance. To see that is healing—proof that ignorance was never universal. Seeing evidence of it in a personal journal has more of an impact than *hearing* about it."

Erika and Olivia's exchange had the effect of freeing up the conversation in general. Thoughts concerning the actual acts of murder—Tim Thorpe's,

Ike Umar's, Keith Ashton's—were released, curiosity openly mingling with sadness. John was asked questions about the cases after his identity as private detective had become known, and he answered them as best he could. Melody spoke of her shock when she'd learned that her ex-husband, Mark, had been alive all those years, and Joanna shared her grief over her husband's death, how in her dreams she experienced the event as his surrogate.

The communal catharsis gradually turned—or returned—to one more upbeat in character. Talk of the new museum's design and function was initiated by Nasha Musa and taken up by several of the attendees who'd not yet spoken—Pierre Jolet, Robert Labeque, Helena Simpson. Erika and Harrison answered questions about their experiences in London but were distracted by their concern over Madame D's absence.

"Why haven't we called her?" Harrison asked Erika.

"Because we're afraid to."

"I'm calling her."

"Yes. Now."

"Don't be so bossy, Gretchen! Just turn the thing on and let me be!"

The stentorian voice had come from the row below the Wheatleys, the grid having expanded to accommodate its source: the indomitable Madame Denise Fontaine.

"It *is* on," responded Gretchen, although one couldn't be sure from the headless image that it was she. "And the audio is on. You can be heard."

"Ah well, so the world has discovered what an irritable creature I am. You're dismissed for now. I'll bark when I need you to come turn me off." She waited for Gretchen to leave the room before addressing her rapt audience. "Apologies for the interruption, and for my late appearance. There was a bit of a mix-up about the time. It happens." To the Wheatleys, she lilted, "There you are, my dears. I've missed you! And how is my great-godson, the little angel?"

"Doing well, Denise," Harrison replied.

"We're so happy you're okay!" Erika chimed in.

"You must stop worrying about my kicking the bucket whenever there's a lapse in time. When it happens, it happens. And when it does, why worry?

There's nothing you can do about it."

Not a word from the grid.

"Pierre, *mon chéri*, you decided to put your trepidations aside and come, after all. I'm proud of you!"

"Good to see you, too," Monsieur Jolet muttered. "But it is time for me to leave the meeting. Good day, all."

Jolet's abrupt departure served as notice of adjournment. Plans were made to set up another meeting for the following month to discuss the progress of repatriation. Robert Labeque and Kurt Reinhardt arranged a one-on-one FaceTime meeting in the interim to exchange ideas on the subject, learn from each other. By the time they'd decided on a date and time, half the attendees had exited the site.

"How are things going in London?" Madame D asked whoever was left. "Has the turmoil abated since its agitator had the good sense to end it all?"

"Yes, I believe it has," Greg replied. "I wish I could stay longer to talk with you, Mum, but alas, I am being paged by a woman higher in command."

"Your wife."

"Yes. Next meeting, come on time. We'll talk more."

After Greg had left the meeting, there were only four attendees remaining, the Wheatleys, Madame D, and Amilah.

"I believe it's time to adjourn," Amilah gently proposed.

"One moment, dear. I just have to ask the Wheatleys...Are we all set for July twenty-eighth then? Is it truly going to happen?"

"Yes, truly," Harrison replied, beaming at her excitement.

"We'll send you all the details in a day or two," Erika said, stroking Harrison's neck. How important this woman was to him, so like his grandmother. And now she felt his hand on her knee. As Andrew Barrett knew to be true, but in his time of grief could not acknowledge, "love bestowed on one does not leave less for another."

"It's time to end this meeting," Amilah reminded the stragglers.

"Okay," Erika said. "Thanks, Amilah. Bye, Denise."

"Yes, thanks," Harrison repeated. "See you next time, Amilah. Bye-bye Denise. Details to come!"

"Au revoir, my dears. Amilah, thank you for your patience—*Gretchen!"*

The Beginning

Kingdom of Benin

West Africa

year 1530

J omi's father was dying, and his voice was weak. "Every man can name his one defining task in life," he said, as Jomi leaned closer to catch every word. "And this has been mine." As Jomi bent over his father, his hand pressed down on the pallet where his father lay. His father lifted his own hand from his chest and placed it on his son's.

Jomi looked down at his father's hand and tried not to cry. His father's hands were the only parts of his body that had retained their vigor, deceiving Jomi into believing he would live forever.

"You will know what your defining task is when it lies before you," his father said, "but first it is your obligation to aid me in completing mine." He nodded toward the corner of the room, where a large satchel containing the plaques, along with a substantial quantity of beans to mask their shape, had been propped. "Crafting these works was only the first part of my commission. Delivering them to Oba Esigie is the second. This *you* must do."

"I understand," Jomi said, still focused on his father's beautifully sculpted, deceitful hand. The tears in his eyes were blurring his image of it, and he prayed the tears would not spill from his eyes and embarrass him. He was fourteen years old. Too old to cry.

"You are not permitted to grieve until you have completed the assignment," his father said, noticing the watery eyes. "Soon I will be joining your mother in the spirit world, and together we will talk of your accomplishment. You are a strong boy, stronger even than Arhuanran, who, it is said, could pull a tree out of the ground by its roots. I have every faith in you."

Jomi knew that was an exaggeration. Not Arhuanran's feat, but his own ability to match it. He knew his father meant only to build his confidence, but he needn't have bothered. Jomi knew he was as strong as an ox. Just not as strong as Arhuanran.

Once again, his father nodded toward the satchel. "You do understand the significance of the plaques, do you not?"

"Tell me again," Jomi said. He knew the story, but he wanted to hear his father speak the words, as many as possible before he would hear the voice no more. He worried that he was asking too much of him, but his need to be lulled by the voice overrode his kind thoughts.

Jomi's father told him again how Oba Esigie's mother, the Queen Mother Idia, had gone into battle against his rival, step-brother Arhuanran. "Dressed as a man!" he added, as always, his voice rising a little with the disclosure, then softening as he continued. "The Oba's step-brother retained the title of Duke of Udo, a town twenty miles northwest of the kingdom. Still, the bitterness felt by those who supported Arhuanran's claim to the crown persists, and some will forever contest the Oba's ascendance. Be tolerant, son, but never let down your guard."

Jomi could not help but smile. Whatever the nature of his father's stories, he would find a way of embedding a word of advice.

"To honor the Queen Mother," his father went on, "the Oba commissioned me to create two plaques whose subject matter would be like none before. When I was told exactly what he wanted me to depict, I was hard put to keep my face from revealing my shock, but as I worked on the project, I was transformed by it, educated. These works are innovative, but I believe they ought not be."

252

His father's voice was growing weaker with each word uttered; his breathing, more labored with each breath drawn. Jomi felt guilty for urging him to use up his strength just to please his selfish boy. He lay his head on his father's chest, partly out of affection, partly to check the regularity of his heartbeat.

His father pushed him away. "Go now, while it's still daylight."

"It's not far to go. I'll stay with you a while longer."

"No. The longer you wait, the less likely I'll be here in this world to celebrate your return. Go. Stop to talk to no one. Do not lay down your burden until you deliver it to the palace grounds and only to one of the Oba's personal representatives."

There was no choice. Delay would only increase his father's distress. He kissed him on the forehead, fetched the satchel from the corner and slung it over his shoulder. It felt heavier than yesterday's trial heft, but that was probably because it now carried the additional weight of imminent responsibility.

It was not a long walk to the palace compound, but trying to make it look as if he was carrying nothing more valuable than a sack of beans was difficult, if only because it required him to draw on his acting ability, which was just about non-existent. As luck would have it, he encountered no one en route, for he imagined the expression on his face was that of a frightened rabbit.

His difficulties began only after he'd entered the compound and was headed to the palace. He sensed the commotion even before he heard it, perhaps as a warning from the spirits of his ancestors, or from his mother's alone, calling to him from the village beyond. For his father's sake, he set his fears aside, half-convinced himself that his imagination was toying with him or testing his manhood.

Standing motionless, on the brink of action, he suddenly heard shouting coming from inside the palace. He could not make out the words, only that they were hostile. He wondered if someone seeking an audience with the Oba had been denied it and had gotten into a harangue with the guards. Perhaps it was nothing more than a clash between individuals normally on good terms.

What he heard next demanded an immediate response, for all at once a group of about a dozen armed men came sprawling out of the palace. It was impossible to make out who had been the intruders, who was the Oba's faction, but from somewhere within the melee arose a series of vile curses directed at the Oba himself. Glued to the spot, Jomi was lucky that the men had been too involved in their skirmish to look his way. Before his luck ran out, he must remove himself from their line of vision.

So as not to draw attention to himself, he walked off slowly, knowing not to where only that it must be *else*where. As he did so, he heard a howl of pain and could not help but turn. One of the men had fallen and another was standing over him, sword raised.

He picked up his pace, though still without destination. He could not return home with his parcel and disappoint his father on what would probably be the last day of his life. The only reasonable option was to find a hiding place near at hand. He spotted a small building—on the compound, but off on its own, like an orphan. Sent to him, it seemed. His spirits lifted.

The building was deserted. The space was being used as a kind of storage or disposal area, he thought. The palace had been undergoing renovations for some time, so maybe that was the reason for the hodgepodge of items. There were even a few farming implements lying about.

It would be easy to hide the satchel under an assortment of objects available. He would come back tomorrow, at the latest the day after, and deliver to the Oba the plaques he had commissioned his father, the master artisan, to create in honor of the Queen Mother.

But seeing the farm implements, in particular the *hoe,* had given him a better idea. What if by chance someone wandered by and, on a whim, decided to explore the place? What if by some chance he was delayed a day or two—*or more*—in returning? What he must do is *bury* the parcel! The dirt floor was firm and would be easy to deal with, and he was strong. He could get the job done quickly enough and leave the place looking as if no one had stepped foot inside it.

Only the moon and stars would light his way, once he was done. He carried the satchel, containing only the beans now. He had intended to bury the plaques inside it, but to make the parcel less cumbersome, the task less time-consuming, he would have had to dump the beans, which would have been a telltale sign of something having gone on, possibly requiring investigation.

He also took along the hoe. Not to steal it, he would bring it back, of course, but seeing it lying on the floor, even in its inconspicuous spot, had made him nervous. It seemed to give away what he had done, reveal his secret.

As he walked toward the compound's border, he saw, at some distance, four armed men on horseback in the large central area. They were positioned so that each was looking in a different direction. Jomi had never seen such a sight. He wondered if the incident he'd witnessed earlier had prompted this unusual measure of security, for that was surely what it must be. Had these very men been, in fact, part of the melee? He was in one of the horsemen's line of sight, but he did not seem to be paying him any mind.

He walked on.

"What's your business here?"

If the question had merely been called out, Jomi would have turned and made up something innocuous. Maybe they would have believed him, maybe not. But the question had been roared, and so he did not turn. He ran. The satchel bouncing against his hip, the hoe dragging at his side. Even *he* knew it was a ludicrous sight, a ludicrous choice to have made. He must speak to the man on horseback—a good man, doing his duty protecting the Oba!—tell him about his father, the master artisan, and the man would laugh at Jomi's fear and send him on his way.

He stopped dead in his tracks and spun around to begin again.

The man on horseback pulled back on the reins and the horse reared, and the man cried out in horror as the horse came down on the boy with the bag and the hoe, the stupid boy who ran for no reason and in a moment would be with his mother and father in the next world, where he will be asked to explain himself over and over, and they will watch the orphan building move through time, acquiring new uses, new floors, new owners, until it is plundered and renewed.

End Notes

About a year and half ago, I came across an intriguing reference to the Benin Bronzes in a newspaper article. It sparked an idea for an art history mystery. First thing I did was order a copy of Stuart Butler's *Benin: The Bradt Travel Guide*.When it arrived from Amazon two days later, I dug right in. I was reading some fascinating material on Benin's culture and had just embarked on the section entitled "Practical Information," when, on page 38, the following highlighted notice hit me like a pie in the face:

BENIN AND THOSE BRONZES

> I don't like to be the bearer of bad news, but if your chief reason for visiting Benin is to see the homeland of the famous Benin Bronzes then you had better cancel that ticket because you've got the wrong country.

I was humiliated, but not defeated. After all, the notice itself was an indication I was not alone in my ignorance and, as I discovered, like misery, it loves company.I was determined to educate myself on the subject, both for the sake of my potential mystery and, I would like to think *more* so, as a matter of conscience.I read the reviews of books written on the Kingdom of Benin (in modern-day Nigeria!) and, more specifically, on the British "punitive expedition" of 1897, during which thousands of art and artifacts were seized from Benin City, a few in retaliation for an aggressive action that had occurred about a month earlier. Dan Hicks's *The Brutish Museums: The Benin Bronzes, Colonial Violence and Cultural Restitution*, appeared to be the most comprehensive coverage of the event and its surrounding history.

I started my education with the Hicks book, and the sentence of his that most succinctly summed up the event and got my blood boiling was this:

"The sacking of Benin City in February 1897 was an attack on human life, on culture, on belief, on art, and on sovereignty."

Other sources that contributed to my education besides the Hicks book (Pluto Press, 2020) include: *Metropolitan Fetish: African Sculpture and the Imperial French Invention of Primitive Art* by John Warne Monroe (Cornell University, 2019) and *The Art of Benin* by Nigel Barley (The British Museum Press, 2010).

Much gratitude, as ever, to the brilliant and caring triumvirate of Level Best Books: Verena Rose, Shawn Reilly Simmons, and Harriette Sackler. Thanks to Jeanne Thornton for her insightful read. Finally, it's always helpful to bounce ideas off someone you feel comfortable with and whose knowledge of history, geography and the natural world is superior to your own. Lucky for me, my son is just such a person. Thank you, Eric.

About the Author

Claudia Riess, award-winning author of seven novels, is a Vassar graduate who has worked in the editorial departments of *The New Yorker* and Holt, Rinehart and Winston, and has edited several art history monographs.

SOCIAL MEDIA HANDLES:
  http://claudiariessbooks.com
  http://twitter.com/ClaudiaRiess

AUTHOR WEBSITE:
  http://www.facebook.com/ClaudiaRiessBooks

Also by Claudia Riess

The Art History Mystery Series:
  Stolen Light
  False Light
  Knight Light

Semblance of Guilt

Love and Other Hazards

Reclining Nude

CPSIA information can be obtained
at www.ICGtesting.com
Printed in the USA
JSHW021316260622
27359JS00001B/4